"DO NOT YOU TAKE ANOTHER STEP, MY LORD."

Bradford turned back in her direction and saw that she was hurrying toward him. Almost running. She will take a tumble sure, he thought and his legs struck out to meet her before his head so much as debated whether he should. "What is it, Miss Chastain?" he asked, taking her hands into his as they came together. "Has something dire happened?"

"Yes," Eugenia replied, squeezing his hands tightly. "I think something dire has most certainly happened."

"You need only tell me what I can do. I know I am not a very good neighbor, and always cross as crabs, but if there is some emergency . . ."

"I think something dire has happened to you, my lord," whispered Eugenia, staring up into eyes that glittered like blue crystal. "You are pale and your hands tremble even now and your eyes, the lovely light in your eyes has frozen to something hard as ice."

"It is nothing."

"It is something."

"I am generally always as hard and cold as ice, Miss Chastain. You, I think, should know that by this time."

"No, you are not. You only wish to be, and that is not the same as being. Tell me what has happened, my lord."

Zebra Regencies by Judith A. Lansdowne

Amelia's Intrigue
The Bedeviled Duke
Legion's Ladies
Camilla's Fate
A Devilish Dilemma
Balmorrow's Bride
A Season of Virtues
Mutiny At Almack's
Annabella's Diamond
Lord Nightingale's Debut
Lord Nightingale's Love Song

Novellas

"The Valentine Victorious" in *A Valentine Bouquet*
"The Magnifikitten" in *Christmas Kittens*
"The Parson's Mousetrap" in *My Darling Bride*
"Rapunzel" in *Once Upon a Time*
"Rescuing Rosebud" in *Winter Kittens*
"The Emperor's Nightingale" in *Once Upon a Kiss*
"The Hawk Meets His Match" in *Notorious and Noble*
"The Reprobate" in *Mistletoe Kittens*

Lord Nightingale's Love Song

Judith A. Lansdowne

ZEBRA BOOKS
Kensington Publishing Corp.
http://www.zebrabooks.com

To Mrs. Janet Kuczenski
Hi, Aunt Janet. Love You!

ZEBRA BOOKS are published by

Kensington Publishing Corp.
850 Third Avenue
New York, NY 10022

Zebra and the Z logo Reg. U.S. Pat. & TM Off.

First Printing: September, 2000
10 9 8 7 6 5 4 3 2 1

Printed in the United States of America

Preface

Welcome back to the world of Lord Nightingale. *Lord Nightingale's Love Song* is book two of the Nightingale Trilogy. It was preceded by *Lord Nightingale's Debut* and is followed by *Lord Nightingale's Triumph* and *Lord Nightingale's Christmas*. Yes, I know that's four books and not three, but it did begin as a real trilogy and so that word lingers in my brain. For an explanation, see the introduction to book one.

If you haven't read *Lord Nightingale's Debut* you may want to set this book aside until you have. On the other hand, you may not want to set it aside, in which case allow me to provide you with a bit of background. In *Debut*, Lord Nightingale united his singing teacher, Miss Serendipity Bedford, and his new master, Nicholas Chastain, the Earl of Wickenshire. You will get a quick glimpse of that happy couple in chapter two as they depart on a delayed wedding trip. And you will need to know, I expect, that Eugenia is the Earl of Wickenshire's cousin and a close friend of Serendipity, that the dowager Lady Wickenshire is Nicky's mama, that the nefarious Neil Spelling is the earl's cousin on his mama's side, that Delight is Serendipity's little sister, and that despite his attachment to the earl, Lord Nightingale was not invited along on the wedding trip. This leaves him disappointed and longing for something to do.

In *Love Song*, Lord Nightingale and Delight team up to

bring together the physically crippled Miss Eugenia Chastain and the emotionally crippled Edward Finlay, Marquess of Bradford, whose walled-up heart is a far greater handicap than Eugenia's crippled leg. I hope you enjoy their story.

Judith

One

In a gown of white muslin, its bodice and hem embroidered with spring flowers in all the colors of the rainbow, Miss Eugenia Chastain sat on one of the gilded chairs bordering Hathfords' ballroom, perfectly astounded to discover tears forming in her deep brown eyes and an enormous lump rising in her throat. To her left, her Aunt Diana sat engaged in conversation with Lady Hathford and to her right, an empty chair acknowledged the popularity of Miss Bridges, who was even now coming down the line with one of her seemingly endless train of beaux.

What on earth am I doing? Eugenia wondered. Great heavens, I am going to sob in a moment. Of all the extraordinary things! She gave herself a tiny shake and lifted her chin a bit higher, blinking back the threatening tears. I will *not* cry, she told herself angrily. I have not the least reason to do so and I will not so disgrace myself. I have sat here twiddling my thumbs for a good two hours and the ball is almost over. What earthly reason can there be for me to make a perfect spectacle of myself this late in the day?

Still the tears continued to tickle and her throat continued to close. I am going to gasp for air in a moment, Eugenia realized, thoroughly abashed by what she considered to be her own weakness. What a perfect gudgeon I have become! To cry simply because no gentleman pays me attention! I knew perfectly well that I should not take when I came to

Town. Even Papa reminded me not to pin my hopes on the gentlemen of the *ton*. And I agreed that he was quite correct. The only reason I wished to come was to see London itself. And I have done precisely that, and had a splendid time of it, too. What do I care if no gentleman chooses to dance with me? I cannot dance at any rate. I am thankful that not one of them thought to ask me to join him on the floor.

We would be upon the floor, too, Eugenia thought then, with the hint of a smile. Smack down on it, the both of us. What a sight that would be. Aunt Diana would be so very embarrassed. Instead of speaking confidently with Lady Hathford as she is, she would be hiding her face behind her fan and rushing for the door, dragging me along behind her.

Eugenia hoped that the ludicrous vision she conjured of herself and her aunt dashing from the Hathfords' would dispel the ever-increasing sadness that gathered about her, but it did not. The tears still stung persistently at the back of her eyes. The lump in her throat grew larger and larger. Thoroughly abashed by such missishness, she rose and walked, like a sailor negotiating the pitching deck of a man-o'-war, around behind the two rows of gilded chairs and out through the open French doors onto the Hathfords' balcony. "I will not cry," she whispered into the night. "I will not. I have not the least reason to do so. Nothing has occurred that I did not expect from the very moment I agreed to come to L-London." Eugenia's voice faltered and shook with a sob. One delicately gloved hand fisted and went to her mouth. She sobbed again and, desperate to cease such silliness, she bit down on her silk encased knuckles as teardrops tumbled from between her lashes to moisten and cool her flushing cheeks.

"What the deuce?" grumbled a low voice.

Eugenia turned toward the sound, biting down even more

violently on her knuckles as a solid form separated itself from the moonshadows.

"Is there nowhere I can find peace in this place? Every room overflows with peagooses! And now one of them must disturb me even here! Devil it! I knew I should not have come. And I would not have either, if the Old Squire had not forced me into it."

"P-peagooses?" Eugenia's fist lowered as she stared at the tall, broad-shouldered gentleman who had stepped out before her with hands thrust into his breeches pockets, studying her, his lower lip thrust petulantly out, his icy blue eyes gleaming angrily in the moonlight.

"Yes, madam, peagooses like yourself."

It was the oddest thing. Quite as odd as her unbidden tears. Laughter bubbled up inside of Eugenia. "P-peagooses? Are you—are you quite certain?"

"Certain of what?"

"That it is not peageese?" Eugenia giggled.

The gentleman scowled at her, speechless.

"I am s-sorry," Eugenia managed. "You are staring at me as though I am a madwoman. I may be a madwoman. I cannot quite tell. A moment ago I was sobbing for no reason at all and now—it just sounds so very funny, peagooses."

"I am not accustomed to have young ladies laugh at me," growled the gentleman, pacing away from her to the balcony rail and then turning back to glare at her again. *"No one* laughs at me. And you will cease to do so at once or I shall—"

"What will you do?" asked Eugenia, her eyes specking with gold from a moonbeam. "Box my ears?"

"Madam!"

"I am not a madam. I am *Miss* Chastain, from Billows-gate."

"Miss Chastain, then," mumbled the gentleman. "If you are quite done disrupting the small bit of peace I have managed to find this evening, please do take yourself back into the ballroom. I am not in any mood for company."

"Obviously not." Eugenia absolutely knew that she should turn and make her way as speedily as possible back to her Aunt Diana's side, but something about the gentleman who leaned now against the rail and glowered at her caused her to linger. There is something about him, she thought, clasping her hands together to keep them from wandering to pat at her hair or tug at her dress. Her hands were wont to do such things whenever she became nervous or undecided. I have the oddest feeling about him. And he seems so terribly unhappy. Perhaps if I remain a moment or two, I can think of something to cheer him a bit. I have nothing else to do, after all.

"I do not wish to return to the ballroom just yet," Eugenia said then. "I have been crying and people will take note of it."

"Oh, well, as for that." The gentleman freed his hands from his breeches pockets, stood away from the rail and began to search about him for a handkerchief. "I understand that you might not like to call attention to yourself. Here, use this," he offered, thrusting his handkerchief at her. "Wipe the tears from your face and take a deep breath and then walk back into the room with your head high and a smile pinned to your lips. That is how it is done. No one will so much as suspect that you came out here for any reason but to get a breath of air."

"But I do not wish to go back inside at the moment."

"Must I make it more plain, Miss Chastain? Your wishes are not of the least concern to me. This is my balcony. I was here first. I claim it and I intend to hold it against all comers."

Even as she dabbed at the trails of her tears, laughter rippled through Eugenia. "You are laying claim to the Hathfords' balcony? You intend to hold it against all comers?"

"Just so. There will be no secret liaisons on this balcony

tonight, I assure you. No, and I will not allow any rattle-brained peagooses to stand about on it either."

"I am *not* a peagoose!" Eugenia exclaimed, thinking that she ought to be angry with this self-absorbed and most impolite gentleman. But she found that she could not be and smiled widely instead just as her Aunt Diana hurried through the French doors, silk skirts rustling around her.

"My dear, are you all right?" asked the dowager Lady Wickenshire. "I just now noticed that you had gone. You have not got the headache, Eugenia?"

"No, Aunt Diana. I—I just—"

"Gel needed a breath of air. Ought to know better than to be skipping and hopping about on such a warm night," offered the gentleman. "Muttonheaded of Hathford to hold a ball on such a night as this."

Lady Wickenshire's gaze left Eugenia to fall upon the gentleman who leaned again, most inelegantly, against the balcony rail. "Have we been introduced?" she asked in the most frigid of tones while taking possession of Eugenia's arm.

"Highly unlikely, madam."

"And yet you have the audacity to be alone with my niece on a balcony and to make conversation with her?"

"Oh! Oh, no, Aunt Diana. I am not alone with him," protested Eugenia. "That is to say, I did not at all know that he was here when I came out. And he was not in the least expecting me. And as for our having a conversation, why, I have not so much as learned the gentleman's name."

"Yes, and I have not got within four feet of the gel the entire time," drawled the gentleman. "Bit of a letdown, that, eh? Had other hopes? Wishing to marry the gel off to me, no doubt. But it willn't happen."

Willn't? thought Eugenia, forcing down another giggle.

"You, sir, are a presumptuous upstart," declared the dowager countess heartily. "Of all the nerve! To suggest for one moment that I would allow my niece to associate with such a—macaroni—as yourself, sir, much less wish her to marry one!"

"Oh, Aunt Diana, do not call him a macaroni," Eugenia begged, tears of laughter rising to her eyes. She tugged at her aunt's arm to lead her back into the ballroom on the instant.

"I will call him what he is, Eugenia. Just look at him with his high collar and his scarlet waistcoat. I am amazed he does not have jeweled heels upon his dancing slippers. Most certainly a macaroni! A macaroni with the manners of a—goat!"

"Aunt Diana, you ought not! He has not done one thing—"

"Not one thing? Why, he accused us of attempting to entrap him into marriage! As if anyone would wish to marry such a dunderhead. You are very lucky, sir, that my son is nowhere near or he would invite you out to taste some grass for breakfast, let me tell you!" With a toss of her head that set her fuchsia turban to wriggling spastically, Lady Wickenshire turned her back upon the man and accompanied a giggling Eugenia in through the French doors to the Hathfords' ballroom.

Bradford stared after them in something approaching amazement. Not that he *was* amazed. He had ceased to be amazed at anything by the age of seven. But still, the elderly lady had given him back as good as she had got. Better even. And the young lady—Miss Chastain had she said?— limped. Most noticeably.

Devil it! he thought. Had I known the gel was a cripple, I would not have been quite so short with her. Had good reason to come sobbing out into the night most likely. "Not that it is any of my business," he muttered, running his long, lean fingers through his dark curls. "What a ninny-hammer the old lady must be to bring such a one to a ball. As if any gentleman would dance with her. Never go near her, they willn't."

His blue eyes flashed and his hands clenched as he thrust them back into his pockets. "No, I willn't either," he muttered with great determination as the thought came to him. "I consented to be Hathford's houseguest because father said I must. I am attending his wretched ball because father claims it imperative that I do so. But I have been fawned over and toadeaten by everyone in this establishment for a se'nnight and tonight is the very worst. I am not stepping foot back inside that ballroom until every breathing human being is gone from it. If one more eyelash is batted at me or one more fan plied before one more flushing cheek on my account, I shall cascade all over the floor. No matter how tempting it is to give that little gel a bit of happiness and send all those other peagooses to squawking, I willn't go ask Miss Chastain to dance. No, I will not."

"It is all my fault," Lady Wickenshire sighed, slowly ascending the main staircase of Chastain House. "I ought not to have encouraged Nicky. But we are so very fond of you, Eugenia, and Nicky was certain that any number of gentlemen would find your thoughtfulness and your kindness and, oh, all the many good qualities about you, dearest, most appealing." The lady paused upon the stairs to look back at her niece and smiled weakly. "But then, we are romantics at heart, Nicky and I. I ought to have listened to your papa. He told me exactly how it would be. I did never guess, Eugenia, how utterly conceited the members of the *ton* have become over the years. In my day, young people were not such rudesbys as they are today, I can assure you of that."

"I do not mind, Aunt Diana," Eugenia murmured. "Truly, I do not. I expected to be ignored by the gentlemen and I have not been disappointed in my expectations."

Aunt Diana seems so sad, thought Eugenia, and just because what must happen, has happened. She urged her aunt to continue the climb to the second floor, managing the steps herself with a good deal of aplomb. "I have enjoyed seeing London," she said in a most cheerful tone. "Whitehall and the British Museum and Lansdowne House and, oh, just everything! I feel quite special to have had an opportunity to actually stroll through places that I have often read about, and if Nicky's hopes for me did not come to fruition, he was beyond anything kind to sponsor me for a Season. I have truly enjoyed myself."

"Nicky is kind." Lady Wickenshire nodded, smiling softly at the thought of her son. "He has not always been happy but he has always been kind. I had a letter from him yesterday, Eugenia," she added, turning into the second floor corridor. "He and Serendipity plan to travel through Scotland for their wedding trip. Is that not wonderful?"

"Indeed. And it is about time that they set off on a wedding trip. It has been nearly a year since they spoke their vows. Nicky is satisfied that Willowsweep will come about?"

"Indeed. He has hired a virtual army of workmen and William Trent has found him an honest and dependable bailiff. Willowsweep will be up to snuff before winter."

"I should like to see Willowsweep when it is completed."

"And so you shall, Eugenia. But—"

"But what, Aunt Diana?"

"No, I cannot ask it of you. I am a presumptuous old woman to even think that you might."

"Might what? Do tell me. I should be most happy to discover some way to repay you in part for all you have done for me."

"I did nothing. I could not even find you a husband," murmured Lady Wickenshire sorrowfully. "What brainless dolts today's young men are. And gravely spoilt as well!"

Eugenia paused before her chamber door and took the dowager countess into her arms, hugging her gently. "That is certainly not your fault, madam. You did a marvelous job of it with Nicky, you know. He is not in the least brainless or spoilt."

"Well, he could not be. He had so very much to do, Eugenia, to reclaim all that his papa lost. When a boy must take on the responsibilities of a man . . ."

". . . he might well become bitter and envious and dissatisfied with his life," Eugenia interrupted. "But Nicky never did. Because of you, Aunt Diana. Because you raised him with your hand upon his shoulder, guiding him through the most trying of times. And I do not forget how you stepped in to help Papa and me when Mama passed on. Now, tell me what it is that I can do. I should be pleased to be of assistance to you."

The dowager countess nodded. "I fear that I do require your assistance. I am not so young as I was when your mama died."

"I do not understand, aunt."

"It is Delight. Nicky depends on me to watch over her while they are gone and I am not at all certain that I am up to it. She is such a young thing and so full of energy. If there were a governess—but there is not. Nicky and Sera have found no one to fill that position as yet. But if I say that I am not up to overseeing Delight, they will not take their wedding trip."

"Is that all?" exclaimed Eugenia. "Oh, Aunt Diana, I should be pleased to go to Wicken Hall with you and look after Delight. And Papa will not mind in the least if I do not come straight home. Depend upon it, he will be so deep into one treatise or another that he will not even notice. The Season is over and I cannot think of anywhere I would rather spend the summer than with you and Delight. Go and let Mitzie put you to bed and worry no more about it. I shall travel with you to Wicken Hall and remain until Nicky and Sera return, and be happy to do it, too."

* * *

Her nightdress donned, her long brown tresses brushed and braided, Eugenia dismissed her abigail and snuggled comfortably between the sheets. The merest glimmer of moonlight peeked through a tiny space in her draperies and danced about on her ceiling. It made her think of Nicky and the night that she and Sera had gotten locked out and awakened him by tossing pebbles at his window. A slow smile mounted to her lips. Whoever would have imagined that her cousin and her very best friend would fall in love and be married? "Me," she whispered into the night. "I imagined it, but I did not truly believe, because I could not think how they would ever meet each other, much less come to love each other. How odd and wonderful the world can be at times!"

And how dreadful it can be at others, she thought, her smile fading. I shall be relieved above anything to be gone from London. I ought never to have come. It was absurd of me to even begin to hope that there might be one London gentleman in want of a loving and capable wife—just one man willing to overlook my so obvious shortcomings. I am so very stupid! The only gentlemen willing to overlook anything about me are Papa and Nicky.

If only I had not broken this wretched leg or if it had set properly, how different these past few months might have been. I know I am plain, but even so, one of the gentlemen might have liked me. Most certainly one or the other of them would have asked me to dance at the least. I have seen any number of plain young ladies asked to dance.

In the depths of her heart, where she held tightly to her dearest dreams, Eugenia *could* dance and often did. For years, she had waltzed like an angel in the arms of a dark-haired, handsome gentleman, gliding through one grand ballroom after another in a dress of the deepest sapphire silk or the finest pastel muslin, always laughing, always smiling up into his eyes—eyes as clear and blue and gentle as the summer skies. And in the depths of her heart, where her dearest dreams drew breath, that perfectly wonderful gentleman loved her—loved her enough to ask her papa for her hand in marriage. "Anyone may dream," Eugenia murmured into the darkness as she drifted toward sleep. "Surely even such a one as I may dream."

The Marquess of Bradford tramped down the worn path past the Hathfords' privy toward the rear gate that led to Hathford's stables which faced upon Little Portland Street. He kicked at stones as he went, mumbling to himself and not so much as noticing the bright moonlight that glistened along his route. "I have had quite enough," he growled under his breath. "Enough of London. Enough of condescending to be Hathford's guest. Enough of people! I ain't about to stay here another day. Unless Nod cannot go farther," he added, a particularly hard lump forming in his throat. "If Nod cannot go on—" He did not finish the sentence. He did not so much as think of the words that would be required to finish the sentence. He cut himself off short and kicked a stone with such force that it took a sizeable chunk out of one of the bricks which made up the old wall that separated Hathford House from the rear of the stables.

He paused for a moment to stare at the shards of the brick that had scattered in all directions. The truth was, his heart would smash to pieces in just such a way if Nod could not go on. For fifteen years all the love that he possessed he had given into Nod's keeping. Day and night, summer, winter, spring and fall, all of his meager store of love had gone to Nod. He could not bear the thought of losing the animal.

"Pah! I willn't lose him. Not Nod. He is fully recovered from his illness of this past winter. It is merely that he is old now and tires more easily." Bradford began to walk again, scuffing his good shoes through the dust and not caring a bit that Stanley would be obliged to clean them in the morning. With slightly trembling hands, he slipped the latch on the gate and stepped through, pulling it tight behind him.

No light shone in the stables. The last of the guests' carriages had departed a full hour ago. Like as not, Bradford thought, all the hands are asleep by now. He opened the stable door and stepped inside, searched about him for a lantern, found one upon a peg to his right and lit the thing. It took him a good two minutes to do so, and for those two minutes in the darkness, Nod had nickered at him without pause. The other horses had whinnied and stamped and nickered too, of course, all of them sensing his presence. But he knew Nod's nickering too well to mistake it for that of another animal, just as Nod knew his voice and could distinguish it from any other man's.

Holding the lantern high, the marquess made his way down the aisle between the rows of stalls, stopping at none of them until he reached the box stall in the rear, where he opened the door and slipped directly inside, closing himself in with the enormous strawberry roan. "Hey, Nod. Hey, m'lad," he whispered, setting the lantern down on the floorboards and wrapping his arms around the thickly muscled neck, leaning his head gently against the beast. "Missed me, did you? Well, I could not help it, you know. Had to attend Hathford's blasted ball or the Old Squire would have parted my hair with a carving knife. Thought it would never end. Came very close to losing my mind, Nod. Had to retreat to the balcony because my lips hurt so much from forcing them into a pleasant smile. But you do not care about that, do you, m'lad?"

The strawberry roan puffed air through his nostrils in response and then began to nibble at Bradford's curls.

"No, I knew you would not care, you old rapscallion. Nod, cease chewing on me. Are you still determined to make me bald?" Bradford smiled without pretense for the first time that evening. "You are, you old reprobate. Determined upon it. No, do not deny it, even the Old Squire says that you intend to eat every hair on my head and he is seldom wrong. We must both admit that, Nod. Father is very seldom mistaken about anything."

The great horse pulled free of Bradford's hug, shook his head and whinnied softly.

"What? You will not admit it?" The marquess laughed. Nod shook his head and whinnied again.

"Well, but you are braver than I. I think I am a coward, Nod. But that is what comes of having the Duke of Sotherland for a father. I do not so much as possess the courage to refer to him as the Old Squire anywhere within his hearing, and I should. I would feel so very much better about myself if I did."

On that very instant myriad memories sprouted and grew in Bradford's mind like weeds. His smile faded and the budding happiness in his eyes wilted amongst those weeds before it ever came to full bloom. Clutching at the horse, he swung himself atop the roan's back and leaned forward, embracing the beast and resting his head against the silken mane. "You are feeling better, are you not, Nod? You look a deal more rested now. Yes, and you breathe easier as well." Bradford shifted slightly upon the broad back, his long legs dangling.

"The Old Squire was right when he said that we did not stand an icicle's chance in Hades of finding Peter in London. I have searched everywhere and no one has so much as heard of him. It is hopeless, just as Father said."

The horse blew out a bit of breath. The muscles in its shoulders twitched. Other than that it stood as still as if it were painted upon canvas, so careful was it of the gentleman resting nonchalantly on its back.

"I have hired us a house in Kent for the summer, Nod," Bradford whispered sleepily. "It is not a large house, but it has a pasture with a bit of woods bordering so that you can rest under the trees. And you will not need to do anything once we arrive. Nothing but what you wish to do—for three months."

Bradford's eyes were growing heavy and, though he attempted to blink sleep away, it conquered him at the last. The lines of worry that lingered during the hours of his waking smoothed from his brow. Now and again a smile played across his face and he whispered "Peter" or "Nod."

The great roan, who had held his sleeping master just so any number of times since first they had set out together into the world, remained perfectly still, never snorting or stomping or shifting, lest the slight weight on his back—the weight that was his Edward—should slide and crumple to the ground. Hathford's astounded grooms discovered them just so in the morning, the marquess still asleep and the roan beneath him silent and waiting.

Two

Nicholas Chastain, the Earl of Wickenshire, and his new countess waved farewell from their traveling coach for as long as they could see the little group congregated before Wicken Hall.

"I hope Delight will not run Eugenia ragged," Serendipity said as she snuggled comfortably against her husband. "Delight has grown so very bold, you know, since . . ."

Wickenshire looked down at her and grinned. "Since? Since she came under my wretched influence do you mean to say?" His eyes bubbled with laughter and Sera could not help but giggle.

"We have both altered enormously since we came under your wretched influence, Nicholas, but especially Delight."

"She is as sweet and charming as she always was."

"But as brave as she can stare now, Nicholas, and wishing to be friends with everyone she meets. She no longer attempts to hide away because of the birthmark on her cheek."

"No, she is proud of it now."

"Because you told her that it meant she had been kissed by Glorianna. I loved you the moment those words fell from your lips, I think. You have been so kind to her."

"Why would I not be kind to her? She is my little sister-in-law and holds a significant place in my heart—along with Lord Nightingale and Stanley Blithe and Sweetpea, of course. By gawd, Sera, I did never dream to have such a house full of people and pets as I have now."

"You did not?"

"No. If you had not come into my life, tugging them all in with you, I should have gone on forever without the least hope of true happiness."

"Balderdash! Doing it a bit too brown," Serendipity laughed. "Our house is like to become even fuller soon, Nicholas."

"Eugenia intends to take up permanent residence?" asked the earl with the cock of an eyebrow.

"Of course not, but there is someone else coming. Someone who will abide with us for years and years."

"Another pet? Not a pug dog, Sera. Do not tell me that you mean to purchase some yappy little pug dog."

"Oh, you are so very innocent, sir!"

"Me? Innocent?"

"Yes, or so you pretend. Nicholas, have we not been married for ten entire months?"

Wickenshire, a most bemused look upon his face, began to count absurdly upon his fingers.

"Nicholas! Do cease teasing. You know very well what I mean to say to you."

"I beg your pardon, my dear, but I do not. What is it that you mean to say?"

"That I am—that we are—that there will soon be—"

"You seem to be having difficulty in completing a sentence," Wickenshire observed, crossing his eyes at her and sending her into gales of laughter. "Sera, you are not about to inform me that a veritable legion of long-lost relatives intends to descend upon us? Five or six maiden aunts and a mad uncle or two?"

"N-no," managed Serendipity, her laughter ebbing. "You know perfectly well there are no maiden aunts and no uncles. Nicholas, do cease crossing your eyes and staring down your nose at me like that or I shall never get this said."

"I will look out the window while you say it, shall I?"

"No, look at me, but do be serious. Truly, you ought to have guessed at once."

"Guessed what?"

"That I am in a delicate condition, Nicholas."

Wickenshire's jaw dropped. He took his arm from around her, then put it back, then placed both arms around her and tugged her onto his lap where he kissed her thoroughly. Just as suddenly, he ceased to kiss her, set her back on the seat and stuck his head and one shoulder out of the coach window. "John!" he bellowed. "John, stop the coach!"

Laughing, Serendipity tugged at his arm. "Nicholas, for goodness sake, what are you doing? Come back inside."

"John!" he bellowed again. "We are going home!"

"Nicholas, no! Do be still. We are not going home!" Serendipity exclaimed, kneeling upon the seat, putting her arms around him and attempting to pull him back inside the coach. "We are going to Scotland."

As the coach lumbered to a stop, Wickenshire allowed himself to be drawn back inside. "I should think not. How can we possibly go traipsing about Scotland with you in a delicate condition?"

"It is only a phrase, Nicholas. I am not actually delicate. And I do not wish to postpone our wedding trip again. My Bessie and your valet and all of our things set out for Greenwich yesterday and will be waiting there for us."

"Yes, but, Sera, you are going to have a baby!"

"Not at this precise moment, dearest."

"No, but— *Can* you go wandering about Scotland?"

"Nicholas, do you truly think that I would have packed us all up and sent Bessie and Trevor off ahead with all of our things if I did *not* intend to make this journey?"

"I have not the least idea. I have never had a wife in a delicate condition before. A baby!" he exclaimed then, and kissed her heartily upon the lips. "You are the best wife in all the world. I vow that you and the child will want for nothing as long as you live. And I will be a good father, too, Sera."

"Of course you will."

"John!" he bellowed, sticking his head out the coach window once again. "John, we are going to have a baby!"

"Nicholas!" Serendipity blushed as scarlet as the seat covers. "You need not shout it at the top of your lungs."

"Yes, I must," Wickenshire replied over his shoulder. "I cannot help myself."

"John will think we are having it right this very minute!"

"It is all right, John," Wickenshire called up to his coachman, grinning. "We will continue on. We are not having it right this very minute."

The bit of disappointment in her Season that had survived Nicky's caustic comments upon the *ton* and Serendipity's teasing jabs at the dandies, blew quite out of Eugenia's mind on the warm June breeze as she turned back toward the house. The last of her sadness disappeared as quickly as her cousin's traveling coach. She smiled widely at the dowager countess and bid her go inside and rest. With Delight's hand in hers, and Stanley Blithe chasing madly ahead of them while Sweetpea padded daintily along behind, Eugenia made her uniquely rolling way across the drive and into the walled rose garden, which ran the entire length of the west side of Wicken Hall. "Oh, look, Delight! How beautiful the flowers are!"

"Uh-huh. Stanley Blithe, do not *eat* the roses! He is so verimost naughty," Delight sighed, stooping to scoop Sweetpea up into her arms.

"Not at all like Sweetpea?" asked Eugenia.

"Well, Sweetpea is not always very good neither. Sometimes, when Lord Nightingale teases her, she whops him right on the head. An' sometimes she steals yarn an' tangles it 'round all the chair legs. An' once, Genia, she came running as fast as she could an' slippy-slided right across the table in the drawing room an' spilled all the tea things right onto the floor."

"No, did she?"

"Uh-huh. But Nicky only laughed an' gave her what was left of the cream. Nicky says they are not any of them truly naughty, not even Lord Nightingale."

"Well, puppies will be puppies and kittens, kittens," nodded Eugenia. "And heaven knows what sort of nonsense parrots are inclined to get into."

"Lord Nightingale is the very best at nonsense as anyone."

"Awwwk!" came a cry through one of the windows above the garden at just that moment. "Mornin' Genia! Mornin' Genia!"

"Oh! He is saying it!" Delight exclaimed. "That is just what Nicky was attemptin' to get him to say when first you came. Nicky thought it would cheer you up if Lord Nightingale talked right to you. Lady Wickenshire wrote as how you was comin' home with her an' you was not very happy."

Eugenia peered up at the window and giggled. "I did wonder why Nicky kept mumbling to Lord Nightingale all last evening."

"That is precisely why. An' it worked! You are giggling!" exclaimed Delight in triumph. "Nicky is always right 'bout ever'thing!"

Except about my going to London for the Season, Eugenia thought. But then Stanley Blithe came dashing down the cobbled path toward them, startling Sweetpea who leaped from Delight's arms and fled into the rosebushes. Barking gleefully, Stanley Blithe followed and Delight scrambled madly after them crying, "No, no!" And from the window above, Lord Nightingale shouted, "Mornin' Genia. Mornin' Genia. Yo ho ho!" Eugenia's laughter bubbled out into the fine June day and the sad thought of the failed Season disappeared at once.

Bradford stood in the morning room of the house that his father's solicitor had rented for him and stared out at the pasture and the woods beyond. Like the house itself, the pasture was small, but it was emerald green with grass and sprinkled with violets and clover. "At least there is no one about to bother us here," Bradford murmured, raising a cup of coffee to his lips. "Nod will get some rest and I will have a bit of peace for a change. Not that it will take all that long before the Old Squire discovers something obnoxious that requires my attention."

"Pardon, my lord?"

"What? Oh, Stanley, I had not the least idea that you had come in. Just mumbling to myself. How do you find the staff?"

"Proper and discreet, my lord," replied the elderly valet. "Except for the cook."

"Except for the cook?"

"Indeed, my lord. An exceptionally odd person, Mrs. Hornby. But her way with food, I am told, makes up for her oddness. You will decide that for yourself, of course, my lord."

Bradford nodded and returned his gaze to the scene beyond the window.

Thus dismissed, Stanley departed to complete unpacking. "Ought to be unpacking at home," he muttered, unfolding a pair of dove gray breeches and placing them quite properly into the clothes press. "Cannot abide this jouncing about from place to place much longer. My bones will not bear it. I have been following about after the boys since first they began to crawl and—" Stanley ceased to speak when he heard himself mention "the boys." The Duke would have my head did he hear that, he thought. Serve my tongue in melted butter for the second course at Christmas dinner. The boys, indeed. As if Lord Bradford and Lord Peter had never parted ways.

"Though truth be told, 'tweren't the boys what parted ways," he muttered, lifting a pair of dancing slippers from the trunk and placing them on the floor of the armoire. "Had their ways parted for them, they did, an' that's a fact. Broke poor Lord Bradford's heart and likely Lord Peter's as well."

A bitter-sweet vision of two dark-haired boys, their blue eyes aglow as they watched a newborn foal attempt to stand upon its long, wobbly legs, came to the forefront of Stanley's mind. "Look, Stanley," a very young Lord Bradford called in the valet's mind, waving frantically for him to come closer. "He is ours! Father said that we may have him!"

"We are goin' to call him Nod," chimed in Lord Peter, "because his dam is Winkin, you know, and his sire, Blinkin."

"Ah, Lord Peter," Stanley sighed, crushing one of Lord Bradford's morning coats tightly against his chest, "if only you were beside him as you used to be, his lordship would not always be so fratched and furious with the world."

"Are you positive certain that I cannot?" Delight asked, peering up hopefully at Bobby Tripp from deep inside the brim of her poke bonnet.

Wickenshire's groom nodded gravely. "He will nibble ri' through it, miss, an' then off he'll go an' git hisself lost. Too feeble a thing."

"But I maked it with three whole double strands of the very best yarn in all of England."

"Nibble ri' through it," declared Bobby Tripp again. "Yarn ain't nothin' at all to such a one as Lord Nightingale, miss."

"But me an' Stanley Blithe an' Sweetpea are all goin' for a stroll an' Lord Nightingale wishes to come with us. I know he does, Mr. Tripp, because he has muttered at us all through breakfast. We tooked our breakfasts into the summer parlor to eat with him 'cause Nicky has been gone three whole days an' Lord Nightingale misses him, an' we are 'termined to cheer him up!"

"Ah, an' that be exceedin' kind of ye, Miss Delight, but ye kinnot take such a one as Lord Nightingale walkin' upon a string of yarn. Ye must have somethin' stronger. Let me think fer a minit. There ought ta be somethin'." The groom abruptly snapped his fingers in the air. "I have got jus' the thing," he announced, hurrying inside the stable.

Delight, with Stanley Blithe sitting nobly at her right side, Sweetpea rolling happily about in the dust at her left, and the green-winged macaw perched upon her shoulder, listened with some amazement as things inside the stable began to jingle and jangle. Whack! Whack! Whack! and Thump! Thump! Thump! she heard and then a word she knew that she was not at all supposed to hear, and then another whack!

"Yo ho ho!" squawked Lord Nightingale, sticking out his chest and fanning his tail feathers in grand fashion. "Shiver me timbers!"

" 'Ere we go. This be just the thing," declared Bobby Tripp, emerging from the stable with a long strip of braided leather attached to an old brass ring from one of the halters. "We will fit this ring around 'is leg and then he'll be safe. Won't go tweakin' this apart. Safe as 'ouses!"

Lord Nightingale glared at the device. Head cocked to the side, one large amber eye focused upon the dulled brass ring, he mumbled something most inappropriate for Delight's ears. Bobby Tripp grew red with embarrassment.

"What's that mean, Mr. Tripp?" Delight asked.

"N-nothin', miss. Jus' mumblin' nonsense, he be. But you mus' not go sayin' that precise word to no one, Miss

Delight. Be good, now, m'lord, an' don't be a peckin' at me," he added, attempting to attach the bird to the leather. "This jus' be somethin' ta keep ye safe."

It took a good five minutes filled with raucous squawks, a great deal of dashing about and barking from Stanley Blithe, and several pounces, leaps and hisses from Sweetpea, before the parrot was secured and the little party set forth upon their gambol across the fields. Bobby Tripp trailed inconspicuously in their wake, keeping guard over Wickenshire's little sister-in-law, just as he had promised his lordship he would do.

"You do not need to come with us, Mr. Tripp," Delight called back to him as she climbed to the top of a small rise. "I am not a infant anymore. I am almost eight now, an' I have got Stanley Blithe to protect me besides."

Bobby Tripp nodded and kept right on following. She led him over the rise and along an overgrown path that twisted and turned across the next field, and then she ducked into a tiny wood where Tripp knew a small stream bubbled and frothed. He lost sight of her for a moment and came near to having an apoplexy. But then he discovered her again, skipping across the stream by leaping from stone to stone. Bobby Tripp held his breath each time the child tottered as she landed, but he did not call out or prevent her from doing it. "Jus' git a dunkin' does she slip," he told himself quietly. "I be here ta pull 'er out. His lor'ship taught 'er hisself how ta cross upon the stones."

"Stanley Blithe," Delight yelled as the tiny wanderers reached the other side of the stream and the puppy dashed off amongst the underbrush. "Come back at once, sir. We must stick together close an' support one another like mates if we are ever to fine the treasure. Fierce ol' pirates like us cannot bother chasin' about af'er hares!"

"Swab the decks!" cried Lord Nightingale heartily, flapping his wings and setting Delight's bonnet askew. "Batten the hatches! Yo ho ho!"

* * *

Nod ceased to nibble at a flavorful patch of clover and looked up, ears perking toward the sound of heavy paws thumping against the ground and a large body crashing through the underbrush just the other side of the old log fence that marked the boundary of his new pasture. His nostrils flared and he whinnied the slightest bit, pawing at the ground with one heavy hoof as the noise increased. He danced a step or two away from the fence, stopped, danced back toward it again. He had been curious about everything from the very day of his birth. When other horses had chosen to run, Nod had always chosen to stand and see what it was that had made the others run away. This curiosity possessed him now and, head lowered, gaze intent on the little woods, ears at full attention, he waited to see what made such a commotion on the opposite side of the fence.

Nose snuffling, ears flapping, tail wagging, Stanley Blithe galumphed through a tangled stand of blackberry bushes, lost all hope of finding the hare, but then glimpsed Nod and dashed forward. "Rrrrarf. Rrrrarf!" he greeted pleasantly, planting his enormous paws on the second fence rail. Tongue lolling, the large puppy smiled hopefully up at Nod. "Grrrarf!" he said.

The horse, not quite certain what to make of this visitor, took a step forward and whinnied, which Stanley Blithe took as a fine welcome. In joy at having found such a huge new playmate, the puppy dodged away from the fence, dodged back, jumped wildly into the air and then plopped to the ground and rolled exuberantly upon his back.

Sweetpea, stepping daintily forward from behind an elm, glared at Stanley Blithe as though she were the Queen of England and he some uncouth barbarian from the hinterlands, which, of course, he was. Then she leaped to the top fence rail and turned her sultry green eyes on

Nod. "Mrrrr," she purred seductively at the strawberry roan. "Mrrrfurrrrumph."

Both Stanley Blithe's exuberance and Sweetpea's coolly seductive purring urged Nod to take another step closer. And another. And yet, another.

As the horse approached, Stanley Blithe ceased to act like a Bedlamite, sat down properly and stared. Sweetpea stood on her toes, arched her back and stretched, her claws digging easily into the wood of the fence rail.

Nod took another step, extended his neck until the velvety tip of his nose came within Sweetpea's reach and gave her one very cautious lick.

Head cocked to one side, Stanley Blithe determined to have the same greeting as Sweetpea and so he placed his paws firmly on the second rail, whimpered softly and stretched cautiously upward. A snuffling Nod lowered his head and bestowed a wet, quiet lick upon the puppy as well.

"Yo ho ho!" shrieked a voice from out of the woods at that precise moment. "Mornin' Genia!" and Lord Nightingale, leather lead sailing behind him, flew from the cover of the trees directly at Nod. Sheer surprise at such an enthusiastic approach sent Nod dashing away across the pasture. Lord Nightingale soared brazenly after him, circling Nod's head and crying shrilly, "Yo ho! Yo ho ho! Morning, Genia!"

"Nightingale, stop! Stop!" Delight darted from the woods and ran to the fence, climbed over it, tearing her stocking in the process, and jumped down on the other side. "Nightingale, come back! You cannot jus' go flying off on your own. We are pirates an' pirates must stick together like mates! Oh!" Delight gasped, as she abruptly noticed Nod fleeing the macaw, twisting and turning, rearing high into the air, then ducking his great head and kicking his hind legs at the sky. "Oh, what a perfeckly beautiful horse!"

Bobby Tripp, a good ten yards behind the child when Lord Nightingale had sailed away on his own, gasped in horror at the sight that met his eyes as he freed himself from the briars and emerged from the trees. "B'gawd, Miss Delight will be killed!" he gasped. He darted immediately forward, leaped the fence and sprang for Delight just as Lord Nightingale sent Nod to rearing again, the horse's iron-shod hooves slashing at the air.

"No, no, Mr. Tripp!" Delight yelled as the groom's arms came around her to tug her out of harm's way. "I has got to catch Lord Nightingale! Let me go!"

But Bobby Tripp, fearing that any moment the horse would came galloping in their direction, would not let her go. He took her up into his arms instead and prepared to carry her hastily back to the other side of the fence.

"I has got to catch Lord Nightingale!" Delight protested, attempting to free herself from Tripp's grasp. "I has got to catch him! He is bein' naughty an' he is scarin' that horse!"

Stanley Blithe, hearing his little mistress cry out, could not quite comprehend what was happening. Sitting perplexed, he attempted to sort through the matter. It did not look precisely like a game or sound precisely like one either. He at last deduced, to his amazement to be sure, that Mr. Tripp was hurting his mistress. With a frustrated growl, Stanley Blithe backed up six steps, crouched and then sailed clear over the top rail of the fence, knocking an unsuspecting Sweetpea from her perch in the process. In an instant he was scrabbling at Bobby Tripp's arms with his forepaws, whining and barking insistently for Tripp to set the child down. If the man would not, it occurred to Stanley Blithe that he might be forced to bite the groom, but he hoped it would not come to that because it was Bobby Tripp who fed him his dinner and wandered with him about the stables in the early morning.

Sweetpea, with a twitching of her tail, stared angrily at the imbecilic beast who had knocked her to the ground and spit at him. Not at all disturbed by Delight's protests, Stanley Blithe's barking or the hooves that now thundered in her direction, or by the parrot's ceaseless shrieking either, she thought to enter the fray herself, just to teach the puppy a lesson. But the shrill whistle that suddenly split the air caused the cat to turn and spring for the fence rail instead.

Nod, intrigued to discover that the bird circled about him no matter what he did and yet apparently was not bent upon doing him any harm, began to look at the whole thing as a glorious game. He dodged one way and then the other, beginning to enjoy himself immensely and he did not hear the whistle until it was repeated. Even then he was loathe to obey. Still, he had come to that particular whistle for nearly fifteen years and, when it sounded yet again, he turned and headed in the direction of his master who was already sprinting into the pasture with considerable speed.

Amidst Delight's protests, Bobby Tripp's panicked shouting, Stanley Blithe's barking and Nightingale's "Yo ho ho!", Bradford swung himself up onto Nod's back and urged the horse straight toward the tiny battle. Lord Nightingale circled so low over the marquess' head that the leather lead slapped the gentleman across the nose, dangled down the back of his neck and flitted up and down before his eyes. "What the devil!" Bradford bellowed, cuffing at the parrot as he slid from Nod's back directly before Delight and Bobby Tripp. "Release that child, you dastard! Of all the cheeky things I have ever encountered! How dare you attempt to ravage a child—a mere child, sir—right in plain view of my morning room window!"

"R-ravage?" stuttered Bobby Tripp, lowering Delight to the ground a mere second before Bradford's fist cracked into his chin and sent him sprawling.

"For shame on you," Delight cried on the instant. And before Bradford could comprehend why the child should say such a thing to him and not to the man who had attacked her, Delight reached out and pinched the marquess soundly upon the thigh.

"Ow!" Bradford exclaimed, and grabbing Delight's

shoulders with both hands, he gave her a bit of a shake. "What the deuce are you doing, child? I came to help you."

Stanley Blithe, seeing Bobby Tripp replaced in the fray by a perfect stranger, switched his attack to the marquess with increased enthusiasm. He leaped between Delight and Bradford, seized hold of the marquess' lapel and ripped it clean off.

"By gawd!" bellowed the marquess, as the puppy tumbled back to the ground with the lapel dangling from between its teeth. "Are you all mad?" He released Delight, put his hands on his hips and glared at them, Bobby Tripp and Delight and Stanley Blithe as well. Bradford's ears grew red and then his neck and then his face. "Devil take it," he shouted, "if you do not want my help, I ain't about to give it to you! Have I rented a house in the midst of a blasted asylum? Well, you may all go to the devil! I do not care what happens to any of you!"

Nod, shocked by his master's tone, stood motionless and stared at the gentleman. Delight put one tiny hand to her mouth at his choice of words and stared at him as well. Stanley Blithe, the piece of lapel dangling from between his teeth, flopped down on his haunches and blinked in wonder that anyone could shout so very loud, and Bobby Tripp groaned softly and gained one knee. Sweetpea, wishing to be included in the gathering now that all the commotion had apparently ceased, picked her way daintily through the grass until she reached Lord Bradford's feet, where she rubbed against the marquess' gleaming Hessian boots and purred.

Sensing at once that something of great import had happened, Lord Nightingale abandoned the sky to land lightly on Nod's back. He sidled up to perch upon the horse's shoulders and studied Bradford through one large amber eye. Then, in a fit of joyful abandon, he puffed out his chest, ruffled his tail feathers and caused the colorful plumage on his head to stick nearly straight up into the air.

"Knollsmarmer!" he cried happily, and giving a gentle flap
of his wings, he sailed from Nod's back to Lord Bradford's
shoulder where he perched contentedly and set about nibbling at the gentleman's collar.

Three

Jenkins, to his credit, did not so much as cock an eyebrow at the motley crew assembled on the stoop before him. He summarily dismissed a stuttering, flustered Bobby Tripp to the kitchen to have his jaw attended to, ushered Miss Delight—her dress dirty and one stocking torn—into the Great Hall, allowed Stanley Blithe and Sweetpea to scuttle in behind her, then stepped protectively between them and the disheveled, red-faced, angrily glaring gentleman upon whose shoulder Lord Nightingale perched jauntily. "May I be of some assistance to you, sir?" Wickenshire's butler drawled, staring down his nose at Bradford.

"Yes," sputtered the marquess. "Take this blasted fowl off my shoulder and lead me to the master of this house at once."

"Yo ho ho!" Lord Nightingale squawked merrily, shifting from one foot to the other. "Shiver me timbers," he cried and began to nibble at one of Bradford's wayward curls.

"The Earl of Wickenshire is not in residence," Jenkins stated, his tone as chilling as the look in the marquess' eyes.

"Then I will speak with whomever he has left in charge."

"That will be Lady Wickenshire."

"Fine."

"And whom may I say is calling?"

"Whom? Whom?" Bradford fished angrily through his pockets until he managed to locate one slightly crushed card.

"Knollsmarmer," said Lord Nightingale, snatching the card from between the gentleman's fingers.

"Give that back, you wretched excuse for a partridge. You are extremely lucky I have not yet wrung your scrawny neck!" Bradford bellowed, tugging the card from the bird's beak and ripping a corner from it in the process. "Now look what you have made me do!"

Lord Nightingale peered down at the card in Bradford's hand, then straightened himself and chewed thoughtfully on the corner of it that he had kept for his own entertainment. "Knollsmarmer," he said decidedly.

"If I hear that word again, I will punch you in the beak," Bradford declared as he handed what remained of his card to Jenkins. "What the devil does he mean by Knollsmarmer? He has been muttering Knollsmarmer at me since he perched on my shoulder in my pasture. Of all the addle-brained beasts!"

"I have no idea what he means by it, my lord," Jenkins responded, studying the name and the title imprinted upon the calling card. He took one step back, allowed the marquess entrance, and offered his arm to the parrot. "Come with me, my Lord Nightingale. I shall fetch you a pine nut."

"My Lord Nightingale? A pine nut?" muttered Bradford under his breath. "Ye gawds, even the butler is balmy."

Lord Nightingale released the thoroughly masticated corner of Bradford's card, reached out and gave the marquess a most circumspect peck upon the cheek, then ambled over onto Jenkins' coat sleeve.

"I shall ascertain if Lady Wickenshire is in," Jenkins declared with immense dignity and, the green-winged macaw having mounted to his shoulder, Wickenshire's butler turned upon his heel, shooed Delight and the dog and cat before him, and mounted the gracefully curving staircase, leaving the marquess to cool his heels in the Great Hall.

"Devil of a thing," muttered Bradford, brushing in annoyance at the shoulder that Lord Nightingale had vacated. "Batty bird, dastardly dog, balmy butler. Put down my blunt and moved straight into Bedlam. I will have a word with Father's solicitor, I will." His irate glance took in ancient tapestries, suits of armor, maces, spears and swords, as he clasped his hands behind him and began to pace along the length of the Hall, the heels of his Hessians clacking against the stone floor. "Whom may I say is calling, indeed! Ascertain if Lady Wickenshire is in, indeed! I expect I am lucky that some barbarian of a footman did not pour boiling oil down upon me as I approached the threshold!"

"Her ladyship will be pleased to receive you, my lord," Jenkins announced in resonant tones from the foot of the staircase, sans Lord Nightingale. "If you will follow me." And barely waiting for the marquess to so much as turn about, Jenkins spun on his heel and began to mount the stairs. Bradford was hard put to catch him up, but he did so just outside the Blue Saloon which was at the very rear of the first story of the east wing.

The marquess, red-faced and puffing from sprinting up the steps and down the corridor, presented the oddest picture as Jenkins announced him and allowed him to step into the room. His dark curls were in wild disarray. Stanley Blithe still possessed one of his lapels. Lord Nightingale's nibbling had tilted his collar oddly to the right and his once pristine and stiffly starched cravat had wilted completely.

"You!" Lady Wickenshire proclaimed in the most agitated voice before Bradford had straightened from his bow and gotten a good look at the woman's face. "You are Lord Bradford? *The* Lord Bradford who has rented Squire Peabody's house? Well, of all things! I will have you know, sir, that I have confided your previous rudeness to me and my niece to my son. Nicky has assured me that he will call you out if you ever make yourself so very disagreeable to us again. Goodness gracious, look at you! What makes you come calling upon us in such a disreputable state?"

Bradford glared at the woman and, not being asked to take a seat, wandered farther into the room and grasped the back of a chair with such force that his knuckles whitened. "I do beg your pardon, madam, but I thought it best to come in the state into which your band of ruffians put me. A visible demonstration, if you will, of the treatment I have had at their hands and paws and beaks. I have never been so very ill-used in all of my life."

"My band of *ruffians?*"

"Just so. Attacked me on my own land. Chewed me and pecked upon me and—and—pinched me! All because I thought to rescue a child from the hands of a lunatic. Turned out that he was not a lunatic and that she did not require rescuing at all, but how was I to know? Such a ruckus as they raised, anyone might have thought the gel in dire need of assistance. I am not, madam, accustomed to living amongst such madmen and barbarians. I assure you of that. Came to the country for a bit of peace. And I will have it too! I tell you, madam, you had best keep the members of your household off my land, for I cannot say what will happen next time they appear. I will not be bound by civility again. All of the members of your household, madam," he clarified, "including the four-legged ones and the one with wings."

"Oh!" came a little gasp from the doorway just as the dowager was about to reply. "Oh, my goodness! It is much worse than I imagined!"

Bradford turned his head to discover Eugenia standing upon the threshold, her cheeks sweetly blushing, his missing lapel dangling wet and limp from her hand. Silent and imperious, he stretched out his own hand, palm upward, to receive it. Eugenia stepped forward and gave the drool-soaked, tattered cloth into his keeping, blushing even more so as she did so.

"I cannot tell you how s-sorry we are that—that—" Eugenia stuttered as she wavered between embarrassment

and laughter. It was the grumpy-grouch from the balcony
in London! Great heavens, she had not been expecting him.
She had expected, in fact, Squire Peabody. And truly, from
Delight's hurried explanation of the lapel and of what had
gone forward in Squire Peabody's pasture, she had expected
the man to be a sight, but not such a sight as this. It was
most embarrassing and deliciously funny at one and the
same time.

"Damnation, if it ain't the peagoose from Hathford's balcony!" exclaimed Bradford in surprise. "Ought to have
known you would reside here as well. The way my luck
runs today, I will next discover that the villain who attempted to steal my purse on Little Bridge Street last March
is the house steward. Miss Chastain, is it not? I do thank
you, Miss Chastain, for the timely return of my lapel."

"I—I— It was all a most dreadful mistake, my lord,"
managed Eugenia contritely, though a giggle threatened to
emerge right behind her words. "Delight told me what . . .
It was most kind of you to think to save her from. . . . You
must understand, my lord, that she is merely a child and
feared that Lord Nightingale might not come back, and
Bobby Tripp feared that Delight would come to harm, especially when your horse . . ."

"Especially when your bird, you mean, persisted in driving my horse to distraction while your groom, your little
charge and your dog added to Nod's distress by yelling and
screaming and barking and wrestling about in Nod's pasture. Not to mention your cat," he added, rubbing at his
forehead with the knuckles of one hand. "I did not actually
see what the cat did, you know, but I am certain it did
something dastardly—something more than attempt to rub
the shine off my boots. I warn you, Miss Chastain, as I
have just warned Lady Wickenshire. I will not have your
people or your menagerie upon my land again. You will do
me the favor to see that I do not. Good day to you both. I

can very well see myself out," he added as, nose held extraordinarily high, he left the room.

Eugenia put the tip of one finger between her teeth and bit down upon it to keep herself from breaking out into whoops as his boot heels cracked like pistol shots down the hallway.

"I must find suitable carpeting for that corridor," mused the dowager aloud. "I have put it off for much too long."

"You must not go there ever again. Do you understand, dearest?" Eugenia said as she tucked Delight into bed that night. "Lord Bradford does not wish you to visit him and we must respect his wishes."

"We must?"

"Indeed. A gentleman has a right to his peace and quiet. You must promise me, Delight, not to disturb him anymore."

"All right. I promise not to 'sturb him evermore," Delight yawned. She put her arms around Eugenia's neck and kissed her. "We is all happy as grigs that you are stayin' with us, Genia."

"Are you?"

"Uh-huh. Even Lord Nightingale. He is the happiest of all, 'cept me, I can tell."

"How very nice to know. But you must go to sleep now, dearest. You have had a very busy day, I think."

"Uh-huh. Does—do—you like horses, Genia? Lord Bradford has the most beautifulest horse. His name is Nod, an' he is red. Red as strawberries."

Eugenia smiled as Delight lost the battle to remain awake. "I am certain it is not as red as strawberries," she whispered, placing a kiss on the girl's wine-stained cheek. "Sleep well, little pirate."

Pirate, Eugenia thought as she left the chamber and made her way back down the staircase to sit for a time with Lady

Wickenshire. That is Nicky's doing, teaching a girl to play pirates. I do remember when he took me treasure hunting. Oh, my, how many years ago was that?

She turned into the library, took the first volume of *Clarissa* from one of the shelves and continued on to the long drawing room where Lady Wickenshire sat working at her embroidery. "How beautiful, Aunt Diana," she said, stopping to inspect the pillowcase. "Serendipity will be so pleased."

"These linens are not for my daughter-in-law," the dowager replied, selecting a thread of claret to embroider the center of a rose on the pillowcase hem. "These are for my niece."

"For me?"

"Just so. Your mama's are so very old, Eugenia. You will wish to keep them in her memory, of course, but you must have new, serviceable ones once you are married."

A wistful smile touched Eugenia's lips. "I should so like to be married, Aunt Diana. But I do not think that it will happen."

"Nonsense."

"But Aunt Diana, I went to London for the Season just as you and Nicky wished, and I did not take. Not at all."

"Balderdash, any number of gentlemen came to call and enjoyed your conversation immensely."

"No, it was your conversation they enjoyed, Aunt Diana," Eugenia corrected, sitting down upon the sofa and opening her book. "I had little of consequence to say and nothing at all to recommend me."

Lady Wickenshire did not respond, but her eyes sparkled as she set the first stitch in the center of the rose. "You have read *Clarissa* before, I think," she said after a while.

"Oh, any number of times."

"It is a preachy old tome. I much prefer Mr. Fielding."

"Aunt Diana, Mr. Fielding's novels are so very brazen."

"Yes, but they never end tragically. And one is encouraged to laugh at least once on every page."

Eugenia nodded. "And his heroines are not so very stupid."

"You think that Clarissa is stupid?"

"Indeed. And she has not a bit of pluck. I cannot believe that such a wet goose of a woman ever existed."

"Why do you read it then?"

Eugenia blushed. When no answer was immediately forthcoming, Lady Wickenshire looked up from her work and, seeing Eugenia's cheeks pink in the lamplight, she laughed. "Just so, Eugenia. Lovelace! I was intrigued with that villain as a young lady as well. I confess it. Though I cannot think it was at all proper of Mr. Richardson to make him so very evil. He ought to have given the gentleman some redeeming qualities, do not you think?"

"Oh, yes! Lovelace ought to turn about and become a most honorable gentleman in the end. But I expect, since Mr. Richardson meant to warn innocent young ladies against such rascals, he could not have Lovelace abruptly redeem himself."

"Were you in the tale, my dear, instead of Clarissa, the gentleman would not *need* to redeem himself. You would reform Lovelace on the instant."

"I would?"

"Yes, indeed. Even Lovelace could not remain a villain should he become the recipient of your sympathies, my dear. *You* are not stupid, Eugenia. You have more pluck than any young woman I know, and you are not the least bit inclined to withhold your true self from those you love. Lovelace would have been reformed before the second volume had you been the heroine."

Bradford could not get to sleep. He turned up the wick on his bedside lamp, climbed wearily from between the covers, slipped into his robe and began to pace his bedchamber. He ran his fingers through his hair, knocked his nightcap onto the carpeting and never so much as noticed that he had done so. He could not think what it was that kept him awake, but he must discover a way to put whatever it was to rest, because he had not had a good night's sleep since he had first gone to London in the middle of February. "At the moment, I expect it is merely that I am bedded down in a strange house," he muttered. "A strange bed." But he knew that was not the case. The house was quite to his liking and the bed most comfortable.

"Well, I am worried about Nod," he told himself then. "I am always worried about Nod of late. I ought not to be. He is much improved, I think, despite that horrendous incident this afternoon. In fact, if I did not know better, I should have guessed that Nod was enjoying himself prancing about the pasture with that great bird circling over him every step of the way. That cannot be, of course. Any horse must be petrified by such a circumstance, even such a brave old warrior as Nod."

Although, he did not seem at all frightened when that dratted fowl lighted upon his back, the marquess mused. No, not at all, though perhaps he did not realize it had done so. It was not there for any amount of time, actually. Nod seemed more amazed to hear me bellow than to have the bird land on him. Stood like a statue when I began to shout. Well, but, by then he already knew that I would not allow the bird to do him harm. He knows that I will not let anyone or anything harm him. Never. I would die before I let harm come to Nod.

It was the only actual vow that Edward Finlay, Lord Bradford, had ever made in his twenty-two years and his face grew solemn as he recalled it. They had been eight, he and Peter, and Nod barely a yearling when they had gathered together in the shelter of the stables, Peter having swiped the Bible from the chapel for the express purpose of the vow-taking.

"I vow on this Bible and on my honor as a gen'leman never to let harm come to Nod, even if I must die to preven' it," Bradford heard his child-self repeat solemnly after his brother. "I vow it with ever' ounce of me an' I willn't forget, neither. Not never."

"I willn't forget, Peter," he said now, under his breath, pacing to the window and drawing the draperies aside. He looked out into a night filled with stars and moonlight and listened to the intermittent buzz of insects and the soft slappings of moths against the casement windows. "I ain't about to forget you either, Peter," he whispered. "I have not forgot you in all these years and I never will, despite all the Old Squire's rantings and ravings about burying the past. You are out there somewhere and I will find you, old fellow. I will find you and I will bring you home again—yes, and Mama, too, if she will come. Only I cannot think where else to search. I have been in almost every county in England, and to Scotland and Ireland as well. Perhaps you are in France. But if that be the case, I shall be hard-pressed to get any word of you at all until this blasted war has ended. But once the war is over, I shall sail from Dover and discover what I can of you on the continent. You must be somewhere, after all."

Bradford allowed the draperies to fall back across the window and began to pace again, attempting to redirect his thoughts to something less worrisome than the whereabouts of his brother and his mother. He settled at last on a well-rounded little figure in an afternoon dress of pink sprigged muslin. He could see clearly the thick brown hair gathered high upon her head and the deep brown eyes and the most enigmatic look etched across her plain, forthright face as she attempted to apologize to him. "Ought not to have called her a peagoose," he whispered into the night. "I do not truly believe that she is a peagoose. Well, but I cannot unsay the thing now. And besides, if she has any intelligence at all, she will not take it to heart, not when it comes from such a one as I."

Poor girl, he thought. Forced to live in the midst of Bedlam with that old beldam of an aunt, and what do I do but commence to grump at her and warn her to keep herself and the rest of them away from me. What must she think?

A feeling of forlorn fellowship tugged the corners of Bradford's lips upward the merest bit. A cripple—and she in charge of the child, likely. And no one but a crotchety old lady for her to look to for aid and comfort. "Well, I know how she feels, I should think," he told himself. "Not the crippled part, of course, or the looking after the child either, but having no one to look to for aid and comfort except an old grump. I know quite well how that is. I ought not have vented my spleen upon Miss Chastain. It was enough to have given Lady Wickenshire a piece of my mind without ringing a peal over the gel's head."

And then Bradford did an amazing thing. He smiled the most dazzling smile. It was the vision of Miss Chastain standing before him, her cheeks aflame and her eyes dancing, the lapel of his coat dangling soggily from her hand that made him do it.

He is a perfectly dreadful gentleman, Eugenia thought, as she pinned her braids in a circle around her head and set her nightcap upon them. Though I cannot fault him for being so very angry this afternoon. I do not believe I have ever seen a gentleman in quite such a disreputable state. And to be thrust into such a state by a little girl, a dog and a parrot—how perfectly horrid he must have felt. She tied the strings of the nightcap in a bow beneath her chin, rose from the chair before the vanity and wandered into her bedchamber.

"Honestly," she whispered, climbing into her bed, lowering her lamp wick and pulling the covers up to her chin, "I thought he would fall into an apoplexy right where he stood. His face was so very red it looked as though he had dashed all the way up the stairs and down the corridor without once pausing to catch his breath." A particular thought occurred to Eugenia then, and she giggled softly. "No, Jenkins would never think to make any caller run to catch up with him. Not all the way up the staircase and down the east corridor. Well, yes, he might," she allowed, giggling more. "Especially if his lordship returned Delight and the animals to Mr. Jenkins with as much animosity as he displayed to Aunt Diana and myself."

But the gentleman did bring them home safely, she thought. And that was most considerate of him, even if he only did so in order to vent his spleen on Aunt Diana and myself. Had he been Mr. Richardson's Lovelace, he would have slain Bobby Tripp and Stanley Blithe and Sweetpea on the spot, had Lord Nightingale for dinner and sold Delight to some London madam for her brothel.

"I am being completely absurd," Eugenia scolded herself, grinning as she turned on her side, facing away from the bit of light that lingered in the lamp. "Lord Bradford as Mr. Richardson's Lovelace—great heavens, what an idea! Though he is handsome enough to play the role. But he is not at all wicked, merely stubborn and spoilt and quick tempered. And most amusing," she added with a chuckle, "though I doubt he realizes that. Oh, if only he could have seen himself this afternoon. Only the look on Aunt Diana's face was more amusing."

What a shame, she thought then, tossing about to find a more comfortable position, that Nicky and Sera and Aunt Diana should have a new neighbor and he turn out to be Lord Bradford, who has the very worst temper of anyone in the whole world, and does not give a fig for anyone's opinion of him.

"Of course!" she exclaimed abruptly, sitting up in the

bed and striking the mattress with one fist. "Of all things! That is precisely why Aunt Diana petitioned me to accompany her to Wicken Hall. It had nothing at all to do with Delight. Why that old schemer! She *knew* that an unattached gentleman had rented Squire Peabody's house. Likely Nicky and Sera wrote to tell her so. And wrote with matchmaking in their minds, I will lay odds upon it. It was all piffle about Aunt Diana not being able to look after Delight alone. A plot to bring me here in hopes that the neighbor and I would find each other desirable and—and—come together."

Eugenia could not help herself. She pictured Lord Bradford standing behind the chair, his face red, his knuckles white, his hair looking quite as if it had not seen a comb since the Thames had frozen over, and one lapel completely gone from his coat. She fell back on the bed and laughed until tears came to her eyes.

"And worse than his appearance and his scathing tongue, he has turned out to be the very gentleman from the Hathford's balcony!" Eugenia swiped at the tears of laughter with the backs of her hands, took a very deep breath and then rolled over and buried her face in the pillow in an attempt to muffle her lingering giggles. It would not do at all for Aunt Diana to hear her and come to see what was going on. How could she explain it?

"Well, but I expect that Aunt Diana's hopes have been completely dashed now," she giggled into the pillow. "How wretched for her to discover that *he* is the new neighbor."

It would have been much nicer, Eugenia thought, as her giggles subsided and she began to ease toward sleep. It would have been so much nicer had the squire rented his house to a family with children. Some boys and girls for Delight to play with. Or he might have rented it to an elderly lady with a young companion. Both Aunt Diana and I should have had new friends then. Friends are so much easier to make in the country than in London. But I expect it cannot be helped. The grumpy-grouch is quite installed at

Peabody House, I expect, and will not leave until his lease has expired. We must just do our best to avoid him, that is all. I shall warn Bobby Tripp the very first thing in the morning that Delight is not to go anywhere near the place.

Eugenia was just beginning to doze off when Lord Nightingale shrieked raucously and caused her to sit straight up in the bed again. "Oh, for heaven's sake!" she gasped, one hand going to her heart. "And he is half a house away! How did I ever grow so accustomed to his noise as to sleep right through it last year when I stayed with Nicky at Willowsweep?"

"Villain! Villain!" squawked Nightingale. "Avast ye villain! Mornin' Nightingale! Mornin' Genia! Arrwwk!"

Eugenia lay back down, laughing again, and pulled the pillow up around her ears. Nightingale would cease his ruckus in a moment and settle down and go to sleep. It was only his protest at having Jenkins drop the cover over his cage and nothing more. She would wait patiently with the pillow wrapped 'round her head until she was certain that there would not be another squawk or screech or complaint out of him.

"And then I will go directly to sleep," she murmured, her voice echoing in her ears. "And I will not give Lord Nightingale or Lord Bradford another thought. They are both of them quite eccentric. Thinking of either one of them is not at all conducive to a good night's rest."

Four

Mr. Neil Spelling set his fork aside and gazed across the table at Mr. Arnsworth. "I cannot believe that I did not think of it at once, Arnsworth," he declared, his dark eyes aglow with enthusiasm. "I only pray that it is not too late. But no, it cannot be too late. If she were engaged, we should have read of it in the papers."

Mr. Arnsworth, having finished the last drop of his port, set the crystal wineglass gently upon the table and then folded his hands in his lap and sat back in his chair.

"Let me pour you a bit more, Gilly," Spelling urged.

"No, thank you. I do not care overly much for spirits. It does not matter, Spelling, if your cousin is engaged to be married or not. She will not like me."

"Not like you? Of course she will like you, Arnsworth. Eugenia likes everyone." Spelling did have the good grace to lower his eyes as this veritable whopper came spurting from between his lips, but otherwise there was nothing at all to indicate to Arnsworth that his new friend might be lying.

Well, it is near to the truth, Spelling thought to himself as he watched a certain anticipation grow in the eyes of the gentleman across from him. Eugenia does like *almost* everyone. She is just not terribly fond of me. "I shall send a note around to Wickenshire House and inform her that I intend to come and pay my respects, shall I?" he said.

"Then you and I will pay her a call and I will introduce you to the gel."

Mr. Arnsworth nodded appreciatively. "I would be exceedingly obliged to you for it."

"Well, as to that, my dear fellow, no obligation involved. None at all." Unless you actually marry the gel, Spelling added in silence. In that case, a bit of the ready might not come amiss. Bah! I am being greedy. I will marry the lad off to Eugenia thereby winning the blasted wager with Carey and no word of it will reach Uncle Ezra's ears. I will be able to breathe easily again. That ought to be enough for me.

"You do not think that Miss Chastain will be put off by my—circumstances?" asked Arnsworth quietly.

"Put off? By your circumstances? Oh, your lineage, do you mean, Arnsworth? I should think not. Eugenia ain't at all uppish. Accepts a fellow for what he is. Nothing more, nothing less."

"Well then, I *should* like to make her acquaintance."

"And so you shall. Do have another glass of this port, Arnsworth. Nothing to fear in two glasses of wine, I assure you. Must learn to loosen up and enjoy life, dear fellow. Not be such a stickler when it comes to the bottle. Sets you apart from the rest of us, you know. Betrays your lineage to the aristocrats at once. Terribly nouveau riche, Arnsworth, all this frowning at a man's getting a bit merry after dinner."

Arnsworth watched with some dread as Spelling poured him another glass of wine, but he took the glass up and sipped at it, because if there was anything in the world that Gilly Arnsworth did not desire, it was to be considered one of the nouveau riche, though that was exactly what he was.

"At any rate," Spelling continued happily, "I shall send a note around to my Aunt Diana the first thing in the morning. You will like Eugenia. I am certain of it." Spelling was so very pleased with himself at having lit upon this splendid solution to his dilemma and so very pleased, as well, with the anticipation that he read in Arnsworth's eyes, that he could barely keep from rubbing his hands together in glee.

What a match! Spelling thought. Gilly Arnsworth and Eugenia! Not only will it bring a bundle of ready cash into the family—and that in the hands of a gentleman who will feel himself indebted to me for the rest of his life—but it will flat out win the wager and I shall have the deed to Tivally Grange back in my possession weeks before Uncle Ezra's next delivery arrives from Ireland. Perfect! Perfect!

"I say, Gilly," Spelling offered with the greatest of good-will, "might you like to pop in at Drury Lane tonight? We shall sit in my box and gaze about at the ladies, eh? Perhaps Eugenia will be there and I can point her out to you."

"What is the play—at Drury Lane?"

"There, that is just the thing you ought not do, Gilly."

"What? Ask what play we go to see?"

"Precisely. We are not going to see the play. We are going to see the audience."

"But—"

"No, Arnsworth, do not protest. No one of any conse-quence actually goes to a theater to see the play. You must accustom yourself to that. If you actually sit there and pay attention to the actors strutting and spouting upon the stage, everyone will suspect immediately that you come from among the lower classes."

Mr. Arnsworth's cherubic face colored up all the way to his scalp. He grew so very pink that one might see the glow right up through the fine strands of his white-blond hair. "I am not lower class," he protested quietly.

"Yes, you are, Arnsworth. Your father manufactures fur-niture and your grandfather kept a shop."

"Even so, I am not one of the Great Unwashed."

"Well, but I did not say that, Gilly. Only that you are not of the upper class. Do not let it bother you. You have enough money to buy most of the nobility and the gentry, I should say."

"Yes, but they still do not wish to know me. I told Mama how it would be, but she will have it that I . . ."

"I wish to know you, Arnsworth, and I am the cousin of an earl and the grandson of an earl and the great-grandson of—well, never mind," Spelling interrupted. "And Eugenia will wish to know you as well. You may count on it."

It came as a rather severe shock to Spelling the following day when his footman returned from Wickenshire House with the disagreeable news that his aunt and cousin had departed to Wicken Hall and were not expected to return to Town. It might well have sent him into the dismals. But Neil Spelling was not a man to abandon his hopes easily and so it did not.

"To Wicken Hall, eh?" he muttered as his valet helped him to don his morning coat. "A bit sticky that."

"Sir?" queried his valet, thinking he had misheard.

"Nothing, Carson. Nothing at all. Speaking to myself. Carson, the Season is over and company is dwindling in Town."

"Yes, sir. Indeed it is."

"Yes, and I find myself longing for some country air. We shall make a trip into the country soon and pay a visit to my cousin, I think."

"Into the country, sir? Your cousin, sir? You do not mean to go to Willowsweep?"

"No, no, not to Willowsweep. The way you turn pale when you mention that name, Carson, anyone would think that you had been there with me."

"Yes, sir. I mean, no, sir. I mean—"

"Never mind, Carson. You have not the least idea what occurred at Willowsweep and I do not wish to hear you mention the place again."

The valet, his neck growing quite scarlet, clamped his lips tightly together and instructed himself never to mention

Willowsweep again, though he did wonder precisely what had happened there. The state of his master's clothes upon his return from the place had convinced the valet that it had been something dire. And the fact that Viscount Upton, who had been a frequent visitor to Spelling House that year, had cut off all association with Mr. Spelling immediately upon their return to Town, had confirmed him in his belief.

Shooting his cuffs into place, Spelling spun about on his heel and strolled from the dressing room. "I shall require my black coat tonight, Carson," he called over his shoulder. "The one by Weston. I do hope you have got the spots completely off it. I cannot go jaunting about Town looking like a veritable rag peddler, you know."

"I have got every single spot off it, Mr. Spelling."

"Good. Good. And you might set about preparing my country clothes, Carson. We shall depart on Wednesday, I think. That will give my letter time enough to reach Wicken Hall." And leave no time at all for Aunt Diana to write back refusing to have me, he thought, studying his reflection in the looking glass at the end of the corridor. "Yes, Wednesday. Perfect." Whereupon, Spelling descended the staircase to the first floor, stepped along the corridor and into his study and took pen and paper from the drawer of his writing table. It took him only five minutes to decide what he would write to his Aunt Diana and he managed to get it all down with but one ink blot on the page. "That will do it," he murmured, folding the page in half and fishing a wafer from his drawer. "I have expressed a desire to help Eugenia find a husband and am bringing a likely candidate with me. Aunt Diana will welcome me with open arms and think me reformed, too."

Well, and I am reformed, he thought cheerily as he stepped back into the corridor and deposited the letter upon the table to be posted in the morning. I have not done anything despicable since I attempted to steal Lord Nightingale, set Willowsweep afire and threatened to turn Nicky over to the excisemen. I have been a veritable saint since then.

Delight made her way cautiously to the fence, gazing about her every three steps to see if anyone was near. She had managed to sneak away from Lady Wickenshire, Eugenia, Mr. Tripp, Stanley Blithe, Sweetpea and Lord Nightingale all at one time and her heart pounded with the sheer excitement of such success. "Shhhh," she told the enormous strawberry roan as she climbed up on the lowest of the fence rails, her bonnet dangling down her back from the strings still knotted around her neck. "We must be most quiet or someone will hear us an' chase me away."

Nod watched the child from across the pasture, his ears pricking to catch her whispered words.

"Come here, Nod," she said softly, holding out one hand toward him while the other clung to the rail. "I have brought you a present. Come an' see."

The horse took a hesitant step forward, whinnied, gave an energetic shake of his head, and eyed the outstretched hand. Then he snorted and pawed at the ground with indecision.

"You are the most prettiest horse in all the world," whispered Delight, her eyes wide and her voice filled with awe as she watched the gelding arch his neck and prance about. "You are even more prettier than Nicky's Grace."

Nod nickered as if in agreement and, having made up his mind in favor of satisfying his curiosity, he trotted quite regally in Delight's direction.

"Good boy, Nod. Come an' see what I have brought you. Gracie likes them the very best of anything."

Nod advanced on the tiny palm, sniffed the object that lay upon it and then gobbled the sugar cube straight down.

The feel of his wide lips and the dainty touch of his enormous teeth on her hand made Delight giggle.

He looked at her and puffed air through his nostrils.

"I have gots three more," Delight informed him grandly. "I gotted them from the sideboard. Not one person in the whole house saw me, not even Mr. Jenkins. I could not let anyone see, you know, or they would have asked why I did not eat them right then and there an' I should have had to make up a verimost whopper. You may have two more, Nod, and I shall have one." Whereupon, Delight fished the remaining sugar cubes from her dress pocket, popped one into her mouth and placed the others in her palm. Nod took them without the least hesitation and then stuck his nose through the rails and poked Delight here and there, searching for more.

Delight laughed and climbed up onto the second rail so that she could put her arms around the horse's neck, although they would not go all the way around no matter how she tried.

Nod, who had been hugged just so by persons quite as tiny as this one many years ago, stood very still while Delight whispered to him and twisted her fingers into his red-gold mane. She was a veritable stranger, this child, but she had plied him with sugar cubes and, if he was in luck, she might do so again. With his hopes high and memories of two most generous little boys flitting through his senses, the great horse concentrated on supporting Delight as she leaned trustingly against him, her small walking shoes balanced precariously upon the fence rail.

Lord Bradford allowed a low whistle to escape him. "If Nod takes so much as a step back, the child will fall and break her neck," he muttered, a piece of buttered toast in his hand as he stood staring out the morning room window. He was dressed for riding in a russet morning coat, buff breeches, and top boots. His intention had been to rise early, break his fast and then take Nod for a slow gambol about the countryside. The case clock in the vestibule had been striking seven when he had descended the stairs and strolled into the morning room to find his breakfast awaiting him just as he had requested. And then he had gazed out the window and discovered the child already clinging to the fence, attempting to call Nod to her.

His first inclination had been to storm out into the pasture and frighten the girl off, but he had chosen instead to watch and see what Nod would do. Now he set his partially eaten toast back on the sideboard, strolled into the corridor and made his way toward the kitchen door, his spurs jangling with every step.

"Good morning, my lord. Is there something . . . ?"

Bradford cut the Peabody butler off with a shake of his head and continued on, startling a little maid into a quick curtsy and sending the pot boy scurrying like a frightened mouse into the kitchen ahead of him to hide behind Cook's skirts. Never had Squire Peabody found cause to come within sight of his kitchen. Squire Peabody, his staff was positive, did not even know his way to the kitchen.

"Mooornin', looor'ship," greeted the cook in a voice that brought Bradford's determined stride to an abrupt halt.

"You are the cook?" he asked, cocking an eyebrow at the little pot boy who peeked out from behind her.

"I do behehe," replied the woman who was as round as she was high and possessed of one of the longest faces Bradford had ever encountered. "I behehe Mrs. Hooornbehehehe, looor'ship."

Laughter swept over Bradford like a storm out of the north. If a mare could speak, he thought wildly, it would sound just like that. It was all he could do to keep from breaking into whoops upon the spot.

"Behehe there somethin' I kin dooo fer yehehe, m'looor'?"

"N-no," managed Bradford, his face crinkling up despite his efforts. "N-nothing. Merely, ah, t-taking a shortcut through the kitchen door."

"Ahhh," nodded the cook. "Just soooo. Come, Williehehehe, do not behe hidin'," she added, reaching behind her with one hand and tugging the pot boy out. "Say moooornin' ta his looorship."

The tyke, no more than six, was thoroughly discomposed and attempted to scuttle back into hiding. His little feet scurried against the stone floor, but Mrs. Hornby held the rest of him in the air with a meaty-handed grasp on the collar of his coat. Coming quickly to the conclusion that he was getting nowhere, Willie's little feet ceased to scurry and he hung limply from Mrs. Hornby's hand. He ducked his head as best he could and tugged a forelock at the marquess.

Bradford, knowing he was positively going to burst into whoops, nodded curtly at the child and stepped quickly through the kitchen door as Mrs. Hornby, apparently determined to convince him that she actually *was* a mare made human, actually snorted her approval of his condescension behind him.

Bradford dashed as far as the end of the kitchen garden before he halted and doubled over with laughter. Tears rolled from his eyes. He had not laughed so hard since—he could not remember when he had laughed so hard. Fighting, at last, for composure, he straightened, tugged his handkerchief from his pocket and wiped away the tears. "Come, Williehehe," he whinnied in quiet imitation of the cook and that set him off again, though not so thoroughly as at first.

Enough, he scolded himself. Remember where you are bound. You will not make the least impression upon the child if you are laughing with every word. Schooling his face into as near a scowl as he could manage, Bradford set out toward the pasture.

Nod, hearing the jangling of his lordship's spurs and

catching his scent on the breeze, snorted and shook his head. But then he ceased all movement because Delight gave a tiny cry as she almost fell from the rail. "Good boy, Nod," Bradford whispered to himself, increasing his pace. "Stay right where you are, old fellow. Do not come to me. Not just at this moment."

The marquess did not run, only let his long legs take their longest strides. When at last he reached Delight, he came to her from behind and put a sustaining hand around her waist first thing so that she would not fall, then he placed one booted foot on the lowest of the rails and murmured in her ear, "Be careful that you do not fall, m'dear." She turned her head at once to smile at him.

"I has gived Nod some sugar cubes."

"Have you? How very kind."

"Nod is the verimost beautifulest horse in the whole world."

"Yes, I think so as well. But you ought not to be here. Your name is Delight, is it not?"

"Uh-huh."

"You ought not to be here, Delight. Did not Lady Wickenshire or Miss Chastain tell you not to come?"

"Genia did. She said as how me an' Mr. Tripp an' Stanley Blithe an' Lord Nightingale was much too noisy yes'erday an' disturbed your peace, so I sneaked away without them. I am bein' verimost quiet. I am not 'sturbin' your peace now, am I?"

Bradford, who remembered well the logic of his own eight-year-old mind saw the legitimacy of this tack. He and Peter might well have seen the problem in the same way and done likewise. He smiled. Then he thought how odd it was that he had smiled and laughed any number of times in the past few days. He warned himself that he stood in danger of becoming a jovial sort of gentleman and that made him smile more. "You are not afraid of Nod?" he asked.

"Uh-uh. Are you?"

"Me? No. I have known Nod from the very day he was born, my dear. Of course, he was not so very large then."

Nod, recognizing the repetition of his name, knew himself to be the topic of conversation. He snorted, poked Bradford's chest with his nose and nibbled at one of the big brass buttons on his master's coat.

"He is eatin' your button," giggled Delight.

"Yes, because he hears that we admire him and thinks he may take any sort of advantage of us. Especially me." Bradford gave the horse's nose a pat and shoved him away. Nod shoved back and nibbled at the button again. "You are the stubbornest animal in all the world and the most spoilt," Bradford declared. "No, Nod, you may not eat my button. I need it. Now cease and desist."

"That is what Nicky always says to Lord Nightingale an' Stanley Blithe, an' Sweetpea too," giggled Delight. "Seize and desists, you scounderals! Perhaps Nod will leave your button alone if you call him you scounderals! It works for Nicky."

"Who is Nicky?"

"He is my dedicated knight, an' I am his fairy princess."

"Oh?" Bradford chuckled.

"I am special, you know. Nicky tole me. I have been kissed by the Queen of the Faeries. She is called Glorianna. An' when she kisses a infant they have always gots a mark upon their face like mine an' it will not go away no matter how hard you scrub. An' Nicky says that's a good thing, too, because if it goed away, no one would know that you had been kissed by Glorianna—not even Glorianna herself!"

Bradford nodded. "Quite so. But kissed by the Queen of the Faeries or not, m'dear, you ought not to have given your keepers the slip and come traipsing over here all on your own. You are much too young to be gallivanting about the countryside without someone to keep watch over you."

"I am eight whole years old."

"Even so. And I did not invite you to come, you know."

"But I am bein'. 'ceptional good and 'straordinary quiet, too."

"That is not the point, Delight. The point is that you were not invited to come and visit. The polite thing to do is to wait until you are invited."

"Was you thinking to invite me today?"

"No."

"Tomorrow?"

"Well, no."

"That is just what I thought to myself this very morning when I waked up," declared Delight most seriously. "I thought that you were not never goin' to invite me 'cause we maked you so verimost angry yes'erday. An' that was not my fault, but you would not know it until I showed you how excellent I can be when I am by myself. An' I am bein' 'ceptional excellent."

Bradford opened his mouth to respond and then closed it again without saying a word.

Mr. Gilly Arnsworth wandered aimlessly along Bond Street at the unfashionable hour of nine o'clock on Monday morning, his hands unceremoniously stuffed into the pockets of his dove gray breeches, his head lowered and his gleaming Hessians, instead of cracking against the paving stones with energy and enthusiasm, barely dragging along with a scuff here and a scuff there. He had given the entire thing a great deal of thought ever since Spelling had informed him that the ladies were from Town. He had pondered it most seriously and he had not the least hope that the ladies would invite him to accompany Spelling to Wicken Hall as Spelling had assured him they would.

Not that Spelling was not a good chap. Gilly was exceedingly pleased that Neil Spelling had seen fit to take him up—especially since no one else appeared inclined to do so. There was something about Spelling and the way he spoke and the things he said that tended to raise Gilly's hopes. But then they would go crashing down again when he was left to contemplate things on his own. And when they came crashing down again, everything seemed twice as bad as before.

"The *ton* is filled with fortune hunters," Arnsworth mumbled to himself. "Everyone says as much. And some of them must be ladies. Why can I not get just one respectable but impoverished lady to hunt for my fortune?"

Gilly looked up to study himself in one of the shop windows. What he saw only sank him deeper into the dismals. His clothes were fine and fashionable and tailored to perfection, but the man inside the clothes was short and a bit rotund with straight, almost white hair, cheeks like a chipmunk's once it had stuffed food into them, and eyes the color of elm bark. "And even that is not the worst of it," Arnsworth sighed disconsolately. "My papa is a manufacturer and my grandpapa kept a shop."

The *ton* would have nothing at all to do with him. He might possess enough gold guineas to sink the *HMS Valiant*—he *did* possess enough gold guineas to sink the *HMS Valiant*—but even so he could not garner one invitation to a place where the *ton* frolicked. The gentlemen would not have him in their clubs and the ladies would not have him in their drawing rooms. What on earth made Spelling think that the dowager Lady Wickenshire and Miss Chastain would have him to stay at Wicken Hall?

"And why does Spelling have anything at all to do with me?" Gilly wondered aloud, weary of studying his all too familiar countenance in the shop window and scuffing sluggishly along again up Bond Street. "He is rich as Croesus and comes from a noble family and belongs to any number of clubs. And yet ever since we met at the Three Sevens, he has gone out of his way to further our acquaintance and he seems determined to introduce me to this cousin of his, too. I cannot think why."

Well, she will not have me, Gilly thought then, crossing the street to avoid a group of loungers who would undoubtedly comment raucously on his height or his girth or his pale hair—or stick a cane out into his path just when he least expected it and send him sprawling, which had already happened twice since he had come to London to attempt to fulfill his mama's dreams and marry into a family of ancient and honorable lineage.

I told Mama that it would never happen, no matter how I dress or how much money I have and I was correct, he mused. They see me immediately for what I am. And they will not have me. Wait and see. Miss Chastain will not wish to make my acquaintance either. Her answer will come to Spelling and not be at all what he expects. Likely she will tell him to come ahead but to leave me behind. And then he will attempt to let me down gently.

The very thought of needing to be let down gently produced a subtle hesitation in the beating of Gilly's heart. In his pockets, his hands began to shake the merest bit. Not only was it humiliating to need to be let down gently, but the mere thought of it genuinely filled Gilly with grief.

"I am as good as any of them," he whispered to a crack in a paving stone. "I am educated and honorable and rich. I cannot help it if my family cannot trace their ancestors back to William the Conqueror. No, and it is not my fault that my money smells of the shop either."

Five

"Lord Bradford is not inorbitantly fond of children," Delight explained seriously as Eugenia attempted to brush the tangles from the child's pale ringlets. "That is precisely what he tole me, Eugenia. But he is a very nice gentleman all the same an' I like him. He gived me a ride home on Nod."

"Yes, I saw you sitting up before him in the saddle when he came up the drive. But you promised me that you would not go onto the gentleman's land again, Delight, and you broke your promise."

"Uh-uh. I only promised as how I would not 'sturb him ever again, Genia. An' I did not. I was verimost quiet. I lef' Lord Nightingale an' Stanley Blithe an' Sweetpea an' Mr. Tripp at home on purpose so as they would not be making a reg'lar rumgumption like they did yes'erday."

"A rumgumption?" asked Eugenia, all hope of appearing stern lost at that moment, her lips curving upward into a wide smile.

"Uh-huh. 'Specially Lord Nightingale an' Mr. Tripp. They was the biggest rumgumptioners of all. It were not Stanley Blithe's fault that he did not know zactly what to do zactly. Stanley Blithe is not the most intelligentest dog in the world, you know. Nicky says so all the time."

"I do not think there is such a thing as a rumgumption or rumgumptioners, dearest. I think what you mean to say is that they were making a ruckus."

"Precisely. They were all of them making a reg'lar ruckus. And Lord Nightingale an' Mr. Tripp was the biggest ruckusers of all an' so they could not come with me today."

"You ought not to have gone either. You were not invited."

"That is jus' what Lord Bradford said. But he would not never have invited me. He 'mitted that right out. An' I had to go, Genia. I did, 'cause I have falled right down into love."

Eugenia, in the midst of fashioning a ringlet around her finger stopped on the spot and sought Delight's reflection in the looking glass. "Love? Delight, do you mean to tell me that you fancy you are in love with Lord Bradford?"

Delight giggled. "I am much too little to fall down into love with a gen'leman! I have falled down into love with Nod!"

"Oh. With Nod. That is Lord Bradford's horse."

"Zactly. Nod is the most beautifulest horse in all the world. It is Lord Nightingale who has falled right down into love with Lord Bradford."

Eugenia laughed aloud at that thought. "Oh, my goodness, no! What makes you think so?"

" 'Cause all the way home yes'erday, Lord Nightingale sitted on Lord Bradford's shoulder an' whispered Knollsmarmer in his ear an' kissed his cheek like he does with Nicky, an' he did not once bite him neither."

"Perhaps Lord Nightingale was merely exhausted from all the flying about he did, and he did not have enough energy left to bite Lord Bradford."

"Uh-uh. I am positive. Lord Nightingale has falled down into love, jus' like me. Lord Bradford says as how, since my affections are enraged, I may visit Nod again, Genia."

"I do not believe it."

"Yes," declared Delight, springing up from the vanity bench and dancing about the chamber with an excited little hip-hop, her ringlets bobbing. "I may visit Nod again. I may visit Nod again," she sang in a gleeful voice. "I may, I may, I may visit Nod again—but I may not go there alone," she added, her song coming to an end. "Lord Bradford says as I mus' bring someone big with me. So I am going to bring you, Genia. Nod will like you very much."

"I do not think so," Eugenia grinned. "I am not fond of horses and Nod will know."

"How?"

"Because you will introduce us quite properly, and I will sneeze right at him. You know that horses make me sneeze, darling, most violently."

"Nod willn't make you."

"He *willn't?*" That word immediately called to mind Lord Bradford sulking upon the Hathfords' balcony and a giggle tickled at Eugenia's insides. "Willn't is a most unusual word, Delight. What you mean to say is will not.' "

"Lord Bradford says 'willn't.' He said it to me right out loud, plain as patches. 'Will you let me ride Nod all by myself?' I askeded him. An' 'No, I willn't,' he said right back."

"Yes, I know that Lord Bradford says willn't. But it is not proper and he sounds like a nine-year-old whenever he uses it."

"I am merely eight!" giggled Delight, spinning about in a circle, "an' already I have got a word for nine!"

It did occur to Eugenia as, laughing, she took Delight's hands into her own and danced awkwardly around the little chamber, that Lord Bradford's use of willn't was, in fact, a charming eccentricity that made him a deal less intimidating than he attempted to appear. And he was kind enough to bring Delight home on his strawberry roan, she thought, which he must have known would prove a tremendous treat for her. And he watched her safely into the house just as a gentleman ought. Then he rode away again without one angry word to anyone. He is not the ogre he pretends to be, I am certain of it. And he may say willn't whenever he wishes without one word of criticism from me, just because he has proved to be so unexpectedly kind.

From all appearances, the gentleman had not so much as rung a tiny peal over Delight's head for trespassing on his property again. She had been just as cheery as sunshine when she had come galumphing into the morning room pretending to be Nod and whinnying and jumping as though she were pawing at the air. There had not been so much as the trail of one tear down Delight's cheek. Perhaps Lord Bradford is not inordinately fond of children, Eugenia thought, but he is careful of their feelings, I think, or he would have returned a sobbing child into our arms instead of such a jolly, exuberant one.

"I am thinking, Stanley, to pay a visit to the public room of the Red Rose Inn in Wicken this evening," Bradford announced as he entered his chambers to discover his valet carefully stowing a stack of freshly laundered neckcloths away in the chest of drawers. "I thought, perhaps, you might like to accompany me."

"Me, my lord? Accompany you to a public house? You cannot possibly mean that you wish me to join you in a drink there?"

"No, I expect I cannot, eh? Even though I have no friends at all with whom to share a drink or two?"

"No, indeed, my lord. You cannot intend such a thing."

"Stupid of me to think of it."

"Yes, my lord. I mean, no, my lord. You are not stupid."

"Yes, I am. Sometimes I think I'm the stupidest, most impossible human being ever put on earth."

"You, my lord?"

"Me, Stanley. If I were not so stupid and so impossible, I would have *some* friends *some*where. But no, everyone fears to approach me, unless they are bent on toadeating me because of father. You are the only one who does not tremble or grovel when I'm about. I wish you were just another gentleman and not my valet; then I should have a chum with whom to lark around. At any rate, I intend to eat at the Red Rose, Stanley, so you may tell Mrs. Hornby that I shall not require dinner. I shall spend the afternoon looking about the village and the evening in the public room. And I may go just as I am, eh? No reason for formal dress in the country, is there, Stanley? A man may make do if he is merely lounging around a tiny village of an afternoon."

The village of Wicken, which they had driven through on their way to Peabody House, was not quite so tiny as his lordship imagined it to be, Stanley knew. His lordship had, in fact, nodded off in the coach before they had reached the place and had come awake only as they were leaving it. "You will be surprised at the size of Wicken, I think," Stanley replied. "And you are quite like to meet a gentleman traveler or two at the inn, my lord, because it sits on the coaching road to Dover. Someone will be pleased to share your table and a drink or two." And then he recalled the letter and the package that Mr. Waggoner had given into his care. "There is something has come for you, my lord," he added quietly, crossing to the cricket table before the window and returning with package and letter in his hands.

"Damnation," muttered Bradford, recognizing at once the hand that had franked the missive. "What is it m'father has thought up for me to do now? That will be all, Stanley," he added, wandering from the dressing room into his bedchamber. He flopped down into the wing chair beside his window, balanced the package upon the chair arm and slit the wafer with his thumbnail. Then he stared at the bold, broad strokes in horror. "I cannot possibly," he whispered. "Why the devil should I? Does he mean to break my heart completely by forcing me to meet this woman face to face? Well, I willn't do it. Not in a million years."

* * *

Eugenia clung to the side of the gig with one hand and to Delight with the other as Lady Wickenshire urged the mare through the gate and out onto the road at a spritely canter. "Is it not excellent weather, girls?"

"Y-yes, Aunt Diana," Eugenia answered, attempting to keep her teeth from clacking together as they bounced into and out of a particularly deep rut.

Squeezed securely between the ladies on a seat meant to hold only two, Delight giggled and Lord Nightingale, balanced on the topmost back of the seat, squawked and jiggled from one foot to the other, talons clinging tightly.

"I do not think, Aunt, that this gig was made to go at such a pace," Eugenia ventured nervously.

"I expect not," Lady Wickenshire replied, "but I cannot help myself and neither can Raggedy. Only see how full of vigor she is. Why, she has been waiting for an outing almost as long as I have. She does so love to be between the traces."

Eugenia smiled, but she did not let go her hold on Delight or the side of the gig. "Are you certain, Delight, that you have tied Lord Nightingale's leathers securely?" she asked. "We do not want to lose him. Nicky would never forgive us were he to fly away and never return."

"I tied them in a doubled knot," the child responded with pride. "It is the very firstest doubled knot I have ever tied all by myself. I did it excellent."

"Of course you did," said Lady Wickenshire encouragingly. "Eugenia, do cease to worry about every little thing. We have come out to enjoy ourselves, dearest. We will not go very far. Not in this old thing. But I have not driven since we departed for London and I do so love to tool along the high road with Raggedy. It reminds me of when I was young."

"It does?"

"Indeed. This gig and the old traveling coach were the only vehicles that Nicky and I managed to save after your

Uncle Evelyn died. And we kept a young mare, very much like Raggedy, to pull it. Oh, but we had some marvelous times, Nicky and I."

"To hear Nicky tell, all he did was work, Aunt Diana."

"Yes, I know. And he did work very hard, but we had good times, too. I taught Nicky to drive in this little gig."

The fact that her Cousin Nicky had learned to drive at the age of thirteen and that he was now approaching thirty-three did give Eugenia pause. "Goodness gracious, this vehicle is twenty years old at the very least, Aunt Diana. Are you certain it will not fall all to pieces beneath us?"

"If it has not fallen to pieces in twenty years, I doubt it will pick this very afternoon to do so. Oh, Eugenia, do cease your fretting. Nothing untoward is going to happen. I have been handling the reins since I was a girl of twelve."

"Yes, but you are not a girl of twelve any longer, Aunt, and this gig is as old as I."

"Awwk!" shrieked Lord Nightingale, flapping his wings and dancing about on the seat back. "Dead ahead! Dead ahead!"

"What is dead ahead, you silly bird?" laughed Lady Wickenshire, slowing Raggedy to a brisk trot. "I am so very pleased that Nicky managed to keep that bird, are you not, Eugenia? Only think how sadly your Cousin Neil would have treated the old fellow had he taken up the guardianship. I have not the least doubt that by this time Nightingale would have given up his ghost if he had been left in Neil's care."

"Who is Cousin Neil?" asked Delight.

"Mr. Spelling," Eugenia informed her. "You remember him, dearest. He came to visit us with Lord Upton while Sera was teaching Lord Nightingale to sing."

"I almost do not remember him."

"How lucky for you, darling," laughed Lady Wickenshire. "I wish that I did not almost remember him."

"Aunt Diana!" Eugenia giggled. "He is your nephew!"

"Well, he is such a bounder, Eugenia. I was much afraid that he would make an appearance at one of the entertainments in London just to set your teeth on edge. Come to think of it, I am surprised that he did not do precisely that. I wonder he should deprive himself of such an opportunity to tease you, my dear."

"Perhaps he has learned his lesson. He did, after all, refuse to join in Lord Upton's scheme against Nicky. Perhaps Neil has turned over a new leaf, Aunt."

"An' what was under it?" asked Delight.

"Under what, dearest?"

"Under the new leaf."

Eugenia was just about to explain to Delight that Neil did not turn over an actual leaf when a horse and rider appeared before them on the road. "Do be careful, Aunt Diana," she said instead. "There is someone ahead."

"I see him, Eugenia. There is certainly enough room to pass him without incident. Do not fret so, child."

Lord Nightingale, focusing one amber eye on the horse and rider before them, mumbled and began to pick at the knot in his leathers that held him securely to the seat back.

"I do hope there is nothing wrong," murmured Lady Wickenshire. "The gentleman rides so slowly. I have never known a gentleman not to take advantage of a quiet road and a beautiful day to let his mount have its head and ride full-out just for the joy of it. Even Nicky is prone to do it."

"Perhaps he is an elderly gentleman," Eugenia offered.

"Even so. Unless the gentleman is on his last legs—or a parson—he is most unusual. Even your Uncle Ezra would be going at a gallop, Eugenia, and he is nearing sixty-five."

"Yes, but Uncle Ezra is mad as a hatter."

"Not when it comes to riding. Perhaps it is Reverend Butterberry, do you think? Though he is dressing more fashionably these days, if it is."

Eugenia squinted slightly at the figure before them.

"That cannot be Reverend Butterberry, Aunt. That gentleman has shoulders under his coat."

"Reverend Butterberry gots no shoulders," Delight giggled, with one tiny hand pressed to her lips, and Eugenia and Lady Wickenshire giggled right along with her.

Lord Nightingale paid the gaggle of ladies not the least attention and continued to nibble at the knot in his leathers, his thick, heavy bill working industriously. "Knollsmarmer," he muttered to himself. "Knollsmarmer."

Lord Bradford, hearing a vehicle approach behind him, reined Nod to the very side of the road. He did not so much as glance over his shoulder to see who it might be. He knew no one in Kent. He only hoped the driver would have the good sense to pass him at a sensible pace so as not to send Nod into a dither and cover both him and his mount in a layer of dust.

"Do not be straining at the bit, Nod, my boy," he murmured, giving the roan's neck a loving pat. "We are not in the least hurry, you and I. This is to be a leisurely expedition."

Nod neighed sedately and gave a shake of his head as the vehicle pulled out to give them the go-by. And then man and horse heard a raucous screeching and the beating of huge wings. In a moment, Lord Nightingale hovered above them. "What the devil!" shouted Bradford, dropping the reins and slapping upward with both hands as the parrot dove straight at him. "Get away, you fiend! Cease and desist! You will give Nod an apoplexy."

Nod, recognizing Lord Nightingale at once and anticipating a jolly frollick, whinnied and danced and reared in welcome, which sent Bradford to grasping for the saddle bow with one hand while he continued to bat at the bird with the other. Lord Nightingale was overjoyed with such an enthusiastic reception. He fluttered and climbed and dove and swerved. At one point he flapped so very close to Bradford's head that one of his wings knocked the marquess' splendid beaver right off his curls and into the road.

"Oh, my heavens!" exclaimed Eugenia, as the gig slowed to a halt. "Surely the poor gentleman is going to take a tumble! Aunt Diana, his horse is going to throw him straight into the ditch! Lord Nightingale, come back this very minute, do you hear me! Come back at once, sir!"

But Nightingale paid her not the least bit of attention. And Nod, feeling more energetic than he had in months and vastly entertained by the parrot's shrieking and flapping, leaped the ditch, dashed up the small hill beside it, soared over a low hedgerow and ran full tilt off into the meadow beyond with Bradford clinging, one-handed, to the saddle bow while waving the other hand angrily at Nightingale, who flew around and around them, his leather lead floating gaily on the breeze.

"Gracious heavens," whispered Lady Wickenshire, staring after them. "We must do something, Eugenia. The horse has gone mad. The gentleman will be killed and it will all be Lord Nightingale's fault."

"It is not a horse an' a gen'leman," offered Delight, still giggling behind her hand. "It is Nod an' Lord Bradford. They are only jus' playin'. They are sooo funny!"

"Oh my goodness! It *is* Lord Bradford!" Eugenia exclaimed. "Aunt Diana, I had best go after them. Perhaps I can catch hold of Nightingale's leathers and bring the chase to a halt."

"Go after them? Eugenia, you cannot. How will you even begin to get through that hedgerow? It is so dense that a hedgehog could not penetrate it, and you certainly cannot step over it, not dressed as you are." Lady Wickenshire had been about to add that even if she did somehow make her way into the meadow, Eugenia could not possibly have run fast enough to catch Lord Nightingale up, but she thought better of it on the instant. "I know," she said instead. "Whistle, Eugenia."

"Whistle? What good will that do?"

"Perhaps Lord Nightingale will hear you and return. I have heard Nicky whistle at Stanley Blithe to get him to come."

Eugenia doubted the efficacy of this plan, Lord Nightingale being a parrot and not a dog, but she would rather do something than nothing and so she placed two fingers in her mouth and blew heartily. The shrillness of the sound pierced everyone's ears. Delight covered hers and laughed. Lady Wickenshire flinched and held tightly to Raggedy's reins, and Nod, frollicking about the meadow, came to such an abrupt standstill that Lord Bradford, still batting at the parrot and not paying the least attention to his horse, joined Lord Nightingale in the sky for a moment as they both soared directly over Nod's head.

"Oh, my heavens, the man will have broken his neck," Lady Wickenshire observed. "Is he moving, Eugenia? Can you see?"

"He is not dead, Aunt Diana. He is struggling to rise this very minute."

Bradford stumbled, a bit off balance, to his knees and then to his feet. He brushed distractedly at his coat and breeches, rubbed his hand along the back of his neck and cursed under his breath. But his mind was fixed upon Nod and he looked around him quickly to discover the great horse gazing repentantly at him from a few feet away, huge brown eyes filled with contrition while Lord Nightingale perched jauntily, just where Bradford ought to have been perched himself, on the saddle.

"No, do not look at me with such contrite eyes, Nod," Bradford declared, advancing on the horse. "You are not the least bit penitent, I think. You were having the time of your life with that bird, were you not? Frollicking about like a yearling. Prancing and rearing. And at your age, too."

"Knollsmarmer!" cried Lord Nightingale happily as the gentleman gave Nod's nose a pat. "Knollsmarmer!" With a single flap of his wings, the macaw glided from Nod's back directly onto Lord Bradford's shoulder.

The marquess had a good mind to land the wretched fowl a facer and his right hand formed into a fist to do it, too, but then he recollected himself. Land a parrot a facer? he thought. A parrot? Am I out of my mind? Besides, it is not as though he intended to see me tossed. I expect he thought only to play with Nod just as Nod thought to play with him.

"Yo ho ho! Knollsmarmer!" Nightingale squawked happily, shifting about on the broad shoulder and nibbling at Bradford's collar, which had gone most horribly askew.

"Yo ho ho, Knollsmarmer, indeed," muttered the marquess, stroking the parrot's breast feathers with one long finger. "Attempting to cajole me into good humor, are you?"

Nod nickered and nodded his head enthusiastically as Nightingale tugged at one of Bradford's curls.

"Both of you are attempting it? To turn me up sweet? I warn you, it cannot be done, m'lads," Bradford murmured, a smile playing about his lips.

Nod poked him in the stomach and began to munch at one of the brass buttons of his morning coat.

"Hey theremister—I—sawHiramkissyer—sister," Nightingale sang huskily in Bradford's ear.

Bradford struggled to keep a straight face.

"Down intheshadeof the ooooold oooooak treeee."

The marquess, who knew that entire song—and not the drawing room version of it, either—began to chuckle. "You would not dare continue," he whispered to Nightingale as Nod poked and prodded at his button which lay in the precise spot where Bradford was extremely ticklish.

"Hey there misterit were notmewhat kissed'er," Nightingale sang joyously as the marquess squirmed beneath Nod's pokings. Bradford gasped and chuckled and gasped again, until at last, in surrender, he threw his arms around Nod's neck, buried his face in the horse's mane and burst into whoops.

"What is he doing now, Eugenia?"

Eugenia stared into the meadow. "I do believe Lord Bradford *has* injured himself," she replied most seriously. "He has put his arm around his horse's neck and buried his face in the mane and his shoulders are shaking as though he is having a fit of some kind. Oh, for goodness sake, our Nightingale is stomping all over the poor gentleman! I do believe he is biting at his ears!"

"Uh-uh," Delight denied heartily. "Lord Nightingale willn't bite his ears, Genia. Lord Nightingale is falled down into love with Lord Bradford. He would not never bite his ears."

Apparently this was the case, for at that moment the marquess straightened, swiped at his eyes with the back of a gloved hand and climbed into the saddle without once attempting to divest himself of the parrot.

His back straight, his shoulders still trembling the merest bit, his hair sticking out from his head at the most improbable angles and his clothes grass-stained and disheveled, Bradford turned Nod's head toward the hedgerow, urged him into a gallop and they sailed over the thing with ease, Lord Nightingale clinging to his perch on Bradford's shoulder with both feet and a beak firmly implanted in the gentleman's wayward neckcloth.

No sooner had the marquess brought Nod to a halt beside the gig than Delight peered up at him from around Eugenia. "I did not make one screech nor nothin'," she said. "I didn't not tie Lord Nightingale's knot correckly, but I did not do none of the ruckusing. Honest. I behaved perfeckly excellent!"

"You did, did you?" asked Bradford, attempting to keep a stern voice though Eugenia could see perfectly well, as he gazed at Delight, that his cool blue eyes had warmed considerably and were bubbling with laughter.

"It was Genia who whistled," Delight offered then, clasping her little hands together most properly in her lap. "I din't whistle. You are not ter'ble angry, are you? You willn't say I must not see Nod never again?"

The marquess shook his head. "No, m'dear, I willn't say that. Good afternoon, Miss Chastain, Lady Wickenshire," he added, bowing as best he could from the saddle with a parrot clinging determinedly to his shoulder. "We meet again."

"Indeed," replied Lady Wickenshire. "You are not injured?"

"No, no, merely bruised a bit."

"Lord Bradford, you are the verimost dreadful mess I have ever seen since Nicky foughted our fire," Delight observed then, bouncing a bit on the seat. "Your hair is all flying ever which way an' your neckcloth is comed undone, an' your coat is lopsidedy, an' you has lost your hat."

"Is that so?" Bradford replied, attempting to brush some of his curls back into place with one hand. "And your Nicky was as much a mess as I, eh? Well, I expect the wretched parrot had something to do with it then."

Eugenia giggled. The giggles made her blush and the blush made her plain face positively glow in the sunlight.

"What did I say, Miss Chastain, that proves so humorous?"

"He d-did," giggled Eugenia.

"He did? Who? Did what?"

"L-Lord Nightingale. Had something to d-do with it. He s-started the fire."

"Knollsmarmer," declared Lord Nightingale, for all the world as if he were proud of that fact, and he gave one of Bradford's newly straightened curls a tug. "Yo ho ho! Knollsmarmer!"

Six

"Delight, take Lord Nightingale back to his cage, child. He has had quite enough flitting about for one afternoon," the dowager Lady Wickenshire said, doffing her hat and pelisse and handing them into Jenkins' care. "Eugenia, dearest, do not worry your head about it. The gentleman will simply return to his house, change his clothing and go on about his business. He did not appear to be the least bit distressed over the incident."

"No, he did not, Aunt Diana," Eugenia replied, handing her hat to Jenkins as well. "That is precisely what worries me. You know how crotchety he is, and yet he did not rant or rave at us at all. Not one insulting word fell from between his lips."

"Thank goodness for that."

"But, Aunt Diana, he was attacked by a parrot and jolted about and thrown from his horse. He ought to have been livid. And rightly so. I have been considering it all the way home and I cannot help but think that perhaps he was seriously injured and would not admit as much to us. Really, we ought to have accompanied him to Peabody House to assure ourselves that he arrived home safely."

The dowager countess smiled. "Do you think that he hit his head and jarred his brains loose, Eugenia, and that is why he acted with such unaccustomed decorum toward us?"

"No, not at all, but—"

"Well, if he did not jar his brains loose, then he is perfectly capable of finding his way home all by himself, my dear. He would have been highly insulted had we so much as intimated that he required our help for any reason—unless he were upon the verge of death, of course."

"He would have been insulted did we offer our assistance?"

"Indeed. Gentlemen are like that. Even Nicky. They cannot bear to admit that they require a lady's aid in anything that is not purely earth-shattering. Pride, you know."

"Well, it is purely stupid pride."

"Indeed, but you will not convince the gentlemen of that. What is this, Jenkins?"

"It arrived in the post, my lady, just after you left."

"Oh?" Lady Wickenshire peered at the letter she had picked up from the silver tray on the trestle table at the entrance to the Great Hall. "It is not from Nicky. It is not even franked." She turned the letter over in her hands and then turned it back again. "I do hope nothing has gone wrong with your papa at Billowsgate, Eugenia. Come up to the summer parlor with me, dearest. Jenkins, we will have tea," she said distractedly, mounting the curving staircase that led to the first floor, staring all the while at the letter in her hand.

"You ought to slit the wafer, Aunt Diana, and read the thing," Eugenia said, as she settled on the green silk sofa beside the dowager. "All this pondering cannot be good for you. I am certain it is not from Papa. He would have addressed it to me, I think, rather than to you."

"Yes, yes, he would, would he not? He has always done so before. And if it is not from your papa or from Nicky—Oh, I do hope nothing has happened to Ezra. He is the most trying of all brothers, but I could not bear it if something happened to him. Fetch me my little silver knife, dearest. I left it in my box of threads, I believe."

Eugenia did just that and then settled beside her aunt, curious to know what the letter contained. "I do not recognize the writing," she said, peering at the note over Lady Wickenshire's shoulder.

"Oh, my dear," murmured Lady Wickenshire, studying the lines. "Oh, my goodness."

"What is it, Aunt?"

"It is from your cousin Neil. He intends to pay us a visit."

"Neil? Come here? But Nicky expressly forbade him to ever darken your doorway again."

"No, no, he did not say that precisely. He refused to have Neil at Willowsweep. But this is not Willowsweep, and Neil means to arrive this very day!"

"Well, of all the nerve!" Eugenia exclaimed. "He does not even give you the opportunity to reply and forbid him to come."

"I expect he does not because he fears I may do just that," sighed the dowager. "And he brings a guest with him."

"A guest?"

"Indeed. Though it is not that dreadful Lord Upton. We may give thanks for that. It is a Mr. Arnsworth. Oh dear!"

"Oh dear what, Aunt?" queried Eugenia, moving a deal closer to her aunt and attempting to read the scraggly black lines that crisscrossed the page.

"Nothing. Nothing," murmured the dowager, folding the letter and setting it aside before Eugenia could make head or tail of it. "It is merely that the gentleman he brings is unknown to me, but I am certain that he is a fine young man."

Eugenia's eyes widened in disbelief. "You are? A fine young man? Why would a fine young man have anything to do with Neil?"

"Well, well, perhaps Neil is no longer a scoundrel."

"Neil has been a scoundrel since we were children!"

"Yes, but he came very close to having his head handed to him upon a platter at Willowsweep. Perhaps that was enough to reform the boy. I must think it was enough. The prospect of standing in your Uncle Ezra's bad graces, you know, is a most frightening thing. I am certain it gave Neil considerable pause."

"But a horse does not change its spots," Eugenia declared.

"I think that is a tiger and its stripes, dearest. We must take Neil and his gentleman friend in regardless, I think."

"Can they not abide at the inn?"

"At the Red Rose? No, I think not. They had best come here as Neil proposes."

"But why, Aunt? The inn is a perfectly respectable place. And it is not as though Nicky is here to entertain them."

"We are family, Eugenia. If Neil wishes to visit us, then we must welcome him—and his friend."

Lady Wickenshire chose to ignore the disbelief in her niece's eyes and welcomed the interruption of their conversation by the arrival of the tea things. She sent for Delight to join them and was even happy to have Stanley Blithe come galumphing into the room to beg for cakes. And as much as she feared another incident with Sweetpea and the tea tray, she encouraged the cat to come sit with them as well.

Neil wishes to introduce Eugenia to a very rich gentleman who is in the market for a wife, the dowager mused, glancing at a suspicious Eugenia and then glancing quickly away again. Certainly I cannot turn the gentleman away simply because he is accompanied by my nephew. No, most certainly I cannot. Eugenia wishes to marry just like any other young lady, and perhaps this Mr. Arnsworth is the perfect gentleman for her.

No matter how nefarious Neil is, I cannot think for a moment that he would play me false upon such a serious matter as this, Lady Wickenshire told herself in silence. Though why he should—but there, what does it matter if all works out between my girl and Mr. Arnsworth? But to advise me of their arrival on such short notice! Thank goodness we need not expect them until after dinner. I must tell Jenkins to prepare chambers for them at once.

Gilly Arnsworth peered about him, his eyes tearing as he trudged into the public room at the Red Rose Inn through three separate layers of tobacco smoke floating like long, lean clouds in the air. His nose twitched at the pungent aroma of boiled beef and cabbage, and his stomach lurched at the thought of eating the stuff. He despised cabbage, and boiled beef did not so much as resemble the stuffed partridge he had been dreaming about the whole day long. "But if we are expected," he said, following Spelling to the only empty table available in the dimly lit room and taking a chair, "I cannot think why we do not continue on."

Spelling sat down, pushed the chair back from the table and stretched out his long legs with a sigh. "Ordinarily, I would continue on, Arnsworth, but I do think it would be best to arrive at Wicken Hall having already dined."

"Why?"

Because Aunt Diana is likely to season my meat with hemlock for not providing her time to write back and tell me to go straight to Hades, Spelling thought, but he grinned at Arnsworth and gave a slight shake of his head. "You do not wish to have your first meeting with my Cousin Eugenia across the dinner table, Arnsworth. Especially not when we have been driving for almost an entire day. I am near to starvation and you must be as well. You will be so interested in eating your dinner, old fellow, that you will forget to say a word to the gel and she will think you an uncivilized boor."

"I am not a barbarian, Spelling. I can eat and speak at one and the same time," Mr. Arnsworth replied sullenly.

"Of course you can. But do you not think it would be more auspicious to make Eugenia's acquaintance in the splendor of the long drawing room with all of the lamps alight and the family settled cosily together, well-fed and feeling fine? You might even stand beside her at the pianoforte and turn the pages for the gel as she plays, if she will play for us this evening."

Arnsworth could not help but think this a poor excuse for being forced to dine at a coaching inn and choke down boiled beef and cabbage, but he could not for the life of him think of any other reason that Spelling could have to insist on their dawdling about in the village of Wicken when their destination lay a mere five miles to the south. "You are certain that Lady Wickenshire invited me?" he asked quietly. "I mean, I know you said—"

"Of course m'aunt invited you. Be damned nervy of me to drive up to her door and saddle her with a guest she don't want."

"Y-yes," nodded Arnsworth uneasily. "That is not what you intend to do, is it, Spelling? That is not why we—"

"No, no, we are waiting for an hour or two and dining here for precisely the reason I gave you, old fellow. And you will thank me for thinking so very far ahead, too. You will feel a good deal easier meeting Eugenia for the very first time after dinner. I know. I have been through these things myself."

"Oh, well, if you have experience in the matter."

"Endless experience, Arnsworth. Been invited to dinner by any number of mamas hoping I would court their gels. Take my word. Dinner is not an auspicious way to begin."

Bradford, tired of roaming about Wicken, having viewed the shops, the village green, the ducking pond and the church that dated from near the fourteenth century, strolled up the High Street in the direction of the Red Rose Inn. Freshly scrubbed after his mishap and sporting a claret coat, dove gray breeches and a gray waistcoat with pearl buttons, his tall, lean, broad-shouldered form drew any number of glances along the way, including the glance of one particular young woman—a pretty girl of near twenty years with glossy black hair and eyes as changeable as seawater. She stood near the window of the draper's shop and gazed out at him, her lips parted in wonder.

"Mary, what *are* you staring at?" asked her mother, who stood before a counter of ribands and threads. "Come, girl, and help me to choose which ribands you will have to match your dress."

"Mama," Mary replied, turning slightly away from the window. "Mama, you must come and see before he disappears!"

"See whom?"

"Peter, Mama! It is Peter strolling up the street or my eyes fail me. Only come and see how splendidly he is dressed. He must have made a veritable fortune in India to return in such style!"

Mrs. Butterberry, who was the wife of the Reverend Butterberry and the mother of six daughters, the eldest of whom was Mary, dropped the cherry riband she was holding and the swatch of cloth she had been matching it to and hurried to the window. "Goodness gracious," she whispered softly. "He does *look* like Mr. Winthrop. Mary, we must go home at once and inform your father. That gentleman did never go to India, I am certain of it, and if he has returned to Wicken in such fine fashion, he has done something horrible to accomplish it!"

Unaware of the irregular pounding that his appearance had produced in two stout female hearts, Bradford continued on his way, his boots clacking along the walk with a steady rhythm in the direction of the inn. He paused for a moment at the edge of the stable yard, thinking to pop into the stable to check on Nod. This he did, and satisfied that his horse was safe and well cared for, he made his way across a broad expanse of dirt and dust and onto the front porch of the main establishment.

Neville Dothan's heart almost came to a standstill when he stepped out from beneath the staircase and caught sight of the gentleman poised upon his threshold. The hands he had casually folded across his bulging belly beneath his white apron began to tremble of their own accord and the healthy pink of his cheeks faded to a ghostly white. And then the gentleman stepped toward him and bowed stiffly.

"You are the proprietor of this establishment?" Bradford queried, feeling quite pleased with his excursion about the village and therefore inclined to be polite to its occupants.

"Ye know I be," Dothan replied on a gasp.

"Well, yes, I assumed you were. And your name is?"

"D-Dothan," stuttered the proprietor, eyeing Bradford as though the marquess were short a sheet.

"Yes. Well, Mr. Dothan, I have come to enjoy a bit of dinner and a drink or two in your public room. I assumed it would be—within sight—but unfortunately, it eludes me."

As the marquess stepped closer, Neville Dothan took a deep breath, and then the color crept back into his cheeks, his hands ceased to tremble and he all but sighed in relief. Whoever this gentleman was, he was not Mr. Winthrop. No thin white line parted this gentleman's left eyebrow and trailed down his cheek to his chin. None. Spitting image of Winthrop, he might be, but he was not the actual man.

"It be there, upon yer left, lordship," Dothan offered, convinced by the set of Bradford's shoulders and the tone of his voice that he was Quality. "Right through that door there. We do a amazin' amount a coachin' business 'ere at the Red Rose, an' we din't think it proper to force the ladies to be traipsin' through the public room to reach the private parlors, an' so we moved the public room aside an' made this little vestibule instead, lordship."

Bradford nodded. He now knew more about the Red Rose Inn than he had ever wished to know and could not think of one thing to say in reply to it. "Boiled beef and cabbage," he said at last, the aroma so strong that he felt certain it would permeate his coat and he would smell like the stuff everywhere he wore the thing from this day forward.

"An' pease puddin'," nodded Dothan. "If ye will find yerself a seat at one of the tables, lordship, I shall be pleased to have my Molly fix ye up a tidy bit of it. Yer sure ye wish ta dine in the public room? I have got a private parlor—"

"No, no, the public room will be fine. Make myself a new acquaintance or two, perhaps. I will have a tankard of ale, Dothan, before my dinner arrives, eh?"

Bradford turned on his heel and strolled toward the public room before the proprietor had time to so much as nod his head. *Ought to have introduced myself to the man, I expect,* the marquess thought as he stepped across the threshold and peered into the smoke. *Ah well, they will all of them know who I am before the week is out. Peabody's servants will come drinking here, no doubt, and my name will be bandied about for an entire evening. Now where the devil am I going to find a place to sit? Never seen a public room so crowded so early in the evening.*

Spelling looked up from his dinner, recognized Bradford at once, and choked. He coughed and stood and coughed and coughed again. Arnsworth leaped from his chair and began to thump Spelling heartily between the shoulder blades. Every head in the public room turned in their direction, including Bradford's.

"It is the boiled beef," Arnsworth muttered and continued thumping. "Danged stuff will not go down one's throat without a fellow swallows a gob of butter first to grease the way. Never favored boiled beef." He thumped again and the beef at last dislodged. Spelling spit it out and gulped for air while the other patrons sent up a cheer and went back to their own dinners.

"Spelling, what the devil are you doing in Kent?" growled Bradford as he strolled up to the table and hooked back one of the empty chairs with the toe of his boot. "Ruralizing, are you? Hiding out from someone?"

"Hiding out?" asked Mr. Arnsworth nervously, returning to his own seat. "Why should you think Spelling to be hiding out?"

"Because he has a propensity for making enemies—some most unfortunate enemies," Bradford responded. "Myself among them—though we have settled that little misunderstanding between us, have we not, Spelling? Just so. Always amazes me whenever I see Spelling that he is still alive."

"No, no, do not grow pale, Arnsworth," Spelling sputtered. "It is merely Bradford's little joke."

"It is?" asked Bradford with a significant cock of an eyebrow. "Imagine that. Grown a sense of humor, have I?"

"Bradford, may I present Mr. Gilly Arnsworth," Spelling pressed on despite the urge to land the marquess a facer. "Gilly, Lord Bradford. Marquess of Bradford," he added in a low whisper for Arnsworth's ears alone.

"Mr. Arnsworth," Bradford nodded civilly. "You do not mind if I join you, eh?"

"I should be pleased, your lordship," Gilly managed, his eyes grown large. Marquess? Had Spelling said the man was a marquess? The palms of Gilly's hands began to perspire and he was forced to wipe them on his breeches before he could be certain that they would be dry enough to enable him to pick up his fork without it slipping away and sliding to the floor.

Eugenia tucked Delight into bed, turned down the lamp and placed a gentle kiss upon the child's brow. "Sleep, now," she whispered. "You have had a very busy day."

"Yes, an' so has you an' Lady Wickenshire an' Lord Bradford too. An' Lord Nightingale an' Nod."

"Never mind, dearest. I do not require an entire list. Now close your eyes, you rascal, and go to sleep."

"My eyes do not want to close."

"No?"

"Uh-uh. They is 'termined to remain open."

"They are?"

"Oh, yes. They is waitin' to see Mr. Spelling an' the other gentleman."

"They will see them in the morning," grinned Eugenia, "and not a moment sooner."

"Do you think Nod is sleeping, Genia?"

"Yes, indeed I do. Sleeping all safe and sound in his stable and dreaming of oats and hay."

"No," giggled Delight. "Dreamin' of sugar cubes an' Lord Nightingale an' friskerin' about the meadow. Do you think Stanley Blithe is sleepin' too?"

"I know that Stanley Blithe is sleeping. He is right over there on your window seat and he is snoring. Cannot you hear him? Listen."

"Do you think Sweetpea is sleepin'?"

"I think," whispered Eugenia, "that you are trying very hard to stay awake until Mr. Spelling and his friend arrive, and I am not going to help you do it. No, and even if you manage it, I am not going to invite you down to say hello. Give it up, you pixie, and close your eyes. If you do, the morning will come quick as the twitch of a bunny's nose and you will meet both of the gentlemen the very moment they come downstairs. And I shall introduce you to them quite properly too, so that you may show them how well you have learned to curtsy. You will like that."

"Uh-huh," murmured Delight, her eyelids beginning to flutter. "I will cur'sy excellent, an' they will bow."

"Just so."

"An' I will be so very growed up that they will think I am almost nine."

Eugenia grinned and bestowed another kiss upon the child. "Good night now, dearest," she whispered, rising from the edge of the bed, turning the lamp completely out and making her way to the door of the chamber. Really, she knew perfectly well how Delight felt. She had never liked to give in to sleep herself.

But one begins to long for sleep as one grows older, she thought, leaving the door open a smidgen behind her so that Stanley Blithe might leave the room if he wished and Sweetpea might enter should the whim come over her. Right this moment, I wish that I were young enough to be sent to my bed at this hour and not expected to remain in the drawing room to welcome Neil and his Mr. Arnsworth. I cannot imagine why Neil should think himself welcome here. No, or why Aunt Diana will have him after all he put us through last year at Willowsweep.

Eugenia made her way slowly down the east staircase and along the corridor to the drawing room, wishing every step of the way that she might develop a headache and thus excuse herself from awaiting the gentlemen's arrival. Alas, it was not to be. She felt perfectly well and continued to feel so all the way into the room. She smiled at Lady Wickenshire, sat down in the largest and deepest of the wing chairs and took the second volume of *Clarissa* into her hands. She lost herself in Mr. Richardson's story for what she imagined to be the longest time. When at last she glanced away from the printed words, the clock on the mantel put the hour at ten. "Perhaps something has happened, Aunt Diana," she said, "and Neil is not coming after all."

"Do you think? No, he said it would be after dinner."

"But it is a good deal past dinner and almost into tea."

"Yes, I expect it is. Oh, there they are now. I hear them coming along the corridor. I really must find some decent carpeting, Eugenia, for these corridors. I know Nicky does not give a fig about the clatter, but it is most annoying. And it is not as if we cannot afford to do something about it now."

"Mr. Spelling and Mr. Arnsworth, my lady," Jenkins announced, ushering the gentlemen into the room.

"I do apologize, Aunt Diana, for the lateness of the hour and the state of our dress," declared Spelling rather loudly, stepping past the butler and going directly to bow over his aunt's outstretched hand. "We stopped to dine at the Red Rose and who but Lord Bradford should wander in. I was that surprised, let me tell you! Ah, Eugenia, how wonderful to see you again," he added, crossing to her and strategically missing the back of her hand with his lips. "Ladies, may I present to you my friend, Mr. Gilly Arnsworth. Arnsworth, my aunt, Lady Wickenshire, and my beloved cousin, Eugenia."

Eugenia came near to bursting into whoops to hear the words *beloved* and *cousin* fall from between Neil's lips in one and the same breath. Good heavens, is he foxed? she wondered. No, he would not dare be foxed. Not tonight. Not when just arriving before Aunt Diana. And then she set all thought of Neil aside as Mr. Arnsworth came to bow stiffly before her.

"I am most pleased to make your acquaintance, Miss Chastain," Gilly said. "Your cousin has told me a great deal about you."

"He has?" asked Eugenia. "Why on earth would he do that?"

"Eugenia," hissed Lady Wickenshire.

"Oh, I am so sorry. I did not—"

"Do be seated, Neil, Mr. Arnsworth," the dowager interrupted. "Are you one of the Newcastle Arnsworths?"

"No, your ladyship. I have never been to Newcastle. I am from Bath," Gilly replied, sitting down most uncomfortably upon the very edge of a ladder-back chair, his hands clasped tightly together and his wrists resting on his knees.

I wish I had not come, he thought, his neckcloth threatening to strangle him. I really wish I had not come. His hands began to twitch and he was forced to clasp them even more tightly together. I really, really wish I really had not come.

Eugenia was most aware of the stiff back and the straight shoulders and the trembling hands. The fact that Mr. Arnsworth was a friend of Neil's notwithstanding, her heart went out to him. Why, the poor gentleman is frightened to death of us, she thought. I cannot think why, but he is as nervous as I was when I attended my first drawing room, and he is growing pale.

"From Bath?" asked the dowager countess politely, attempting to put Mr. Arnsworth at his ease. "I had no idea that there were Arnsworths living in Bath, but I have been out of Society for a good many years and have lost track of almost everyone. It must be most pleasant to reside in Bath the year 'round. We did not have the pleasure of making your acquaintance in London, Mr. Arnsworth. Did you not come up to London for the Season?"

"Yes, ma'am, but I was not invited to many places."

"A quiet, stable gentleman, Gilly is," Spelling interrupted. "Not one of your bucks or dandies, always gallivanting about the Town. Fond of home and hearth and all that rot, ain't you, Arnsworth? Make Eugenia a perfect husband."

Mr. Arnsworth turned so very pale that Eugenia thought he would pitch straight off his chair and face down onto the floor in a dead faint. "Neil, what a thing to say! You *are* foxed!" she exclaimed. "Do not pay him the least bit of attention, Mr. Arnsworth. Were Neil sober, he would never think to say such a thing and so very boldly, too."

"I admit I am chirping merry," nodded Spelling, grinning widely. "Gilly ain't, mind you. Are you, Gilly? No. Of course you ain't. But it is all Bradford's fault. Joined us for dinner, he did. What the devil is Bradford doing here? At any rate, forced to let him join us. No other place for him to sit. Ought to enlarge that public room, Dothan ought, but he never will. Called for a tankard, Bradford did, and then another and another. I thought to keep up with him. Matter of pride. Did, too. But it made me a bit merry, eh?"

"You did not participate, Mr. Arnsworth, in this little drinking bout?" Lady Wickenshire inquired quietly.

"No, your ladyship. I—do not care much for ale."

"Nothing better than ale on a warm night in the country," declared Spelling. "Of course, drinking it with Bradford makes it taste a bit bitter going down. Dependable fellow, Bradford. Never disappoints. Whenever we meet, I always expect him to be haughty and cross as crows, with a tongue like a viper, and he never fails to meet my expectations."

Seven

The Reverend Mr. Butterberry paced the floor of his study, his bedroom slippers whispering across the worn carpet, his robe flapping with every step. Peter Winthrop! But no, it could not be. That young man would never have the audacity to show his face in Wicken again. Not for as long as he lived—if he were still alive. "If ever a lad was born for the gibbet," Mr. Butterberry mumbled. "Likely hanged the boy in London before the last snow came."

"Henry, do come to bed," whispered Mrs. Butterberry, peeping in at the door. "You will wake the children with all your muttering and pacing about."

"In a bit, my dear. In a bit."

"You are worried about Mr. Winthrop, are you not?" asked Mrs. Butterberry quietly, stepping into the study and pulling the door closed behind her.

"Are you certain it was Winthrop you saw, m'dear? You could not have been mistaken?"

"That is just the thing, Henry. He did look a good deal like Mr. Winthrop, but then again, the shadows were lengthening and I did not see his face so very clearly. I should not depend upon its being him. He was dressed far too fine. I cannot think that Mr. Winthrop could ever afford such elegant clothes. And this gentleman walked in a most distinguished manner."

"Walked in a distinguished manner? What on earth does that mean, Emily?"

"It means that he did not bounce or scuff along as some young men are like to do. And he did not swagger—which Mr. Winthrop always did. You know he did, Henry. You were accustomed to remark upon it every time he entered this house."

"So you do not think it was Winthrop?"

"No. The more I ponder it, the more I think not. Though he did look a bit like."

"Yet our Mary is positive that it was he."

"Only because she—has a very good imagination."

"That is not what you were going to say, Emily."

"No, but I do not wish to set you even more on edge, Henry. You will get no sleep at all."

"What were you going to say?"

Mrs. Butterberry studied her husband's face in the lamplight, gave a shake of her head and smiled the oddest smile. "I was going to say that Mary is positive that the gentleman was Mr. Winthrop because in her heart she wished for him to be Mr. Winthrop and returned from India rich as Croesus."

"Oh, no! Not still!"

"I am afraid so, Henry. He was the only gentleman, you know, in whom our Mary ever showed the least interest."

"Yes, and so we allowed him to run tame about this house. And he took the greatest advantage of us and stole all the monies that the Ladies' Aid Society had collected and my grandfather's amber stickpin as well."

"That is what you believe, Henry."

"That is what the entire village believes.

"Well, yes, everyone but our Mary."

"The child's head is stuffed with feathers."

"No, it is not," sighed Mrs. Butterberry. "I know that you will never understand it, my dear, but our Mary's head is not stuffed with feathers at all. It is stuffed with dreams."

* * *

His hands tucked into his breeches pockets, Bradford strolled along the High Road with Nod keeping step complacently behind him. Above them myriad stars filled the night sky like diamonds carelessly strewn across black velvet. "What a glorious night," Bradford whispered. "Nod, m'lad, what a perfectly glorious night it is. Listen, old fellow, to the chorus singing all about us and feel how soft and gentle is the kiss of the breeze. I was correct to come to Kent, even though I doubted it at first. I am feeling beyond anything splendid."

Nod nickered in reply.

"Yes, I knew you would think I was correct as well. And you have not even downed six tankards of ale to give you a more pleasant perspective on the situation. I cannot think, Nod, when I have felt more at ease with myself." As if to prove the point, Bradford began to whistle. He whistled for the longest time as he wandered beneath the glittering cloak of the night sky, and then he began to hum. When the hum became words, Nod began to prance a bit behind him. Bradford turned and laughed. "Yes, exactly so. Dance for me, Nod. Hey there, mister, I saaaw Hiram kiss your sister, down in the shade of the ooold oak treeeee. Hey there, mister, it waaas not I who kissed her. I was just awaaaatching, sir. It was not meeeee!"

Nod tossed his head and picked up his great hooves with quaint delicacy and pranced merrily about, turning in tight circles left and right and left again, nickering and whinnying in time with his master's song. Bradford, his eyes aglow with good humor and his baritone accompanied by the gentle burring of crickets and the soft hooting of owls, attempted to *contradanse* with the beast, his boots skimming lightly over the surface of the road as he stepped and skipped and turned. "All for loooove and love for allll. May all men riiise before they faaallll. How can we not heed Cupid's caaalll when country girls surround us aaalll and Hiram's kissed your sister?"

Laughing as he reached the end of the chorus, Bradford bowed gracefully to Nod who, as he had been taught to do years before, made a leg in return with great aplomb. "Excellent, m'lad. Excellent. You are, as always, the best dancing partner I have ever had," chuckled Bradford, and then he swung himself up into the saddle, leaned forward and gave the horse an enthusiastic hug. "I hate to say it, Nod, but I think we must go home at last. Stanley will be waiting for us, you know. Most likely pacing the floor by this time, wondering if we have been eaten by wolves." He sat up straight again and urged Nod forward along the road in a slow trot, which was interrupted from time to time by a sudden whim upon the strawberry roan's part to stop and prance in a circle before continuing on. Each time he did, the marquess laughed aloud and the very sound of it set Nod's heart to dancing right along with his hooves.

They would have gotten safely home within an hour's time, even with all their frolicking about, if the sound of sobbing had not wafted to them upon the breeze. "What the devil is that?" Bradford murmured. "Nod? Do you hear?"

Nod whinnied and pricked his ears.

"Just so, Nod. From somewhere within that stand of trees." Bradford dismounted and made his way cautiously across the ditch beside the road, up the embankment and into a small woods, Nod tagging along behind him. "Hello," the marquess called out as he entered beneath the canopy of leaves that blocked out the stars and deepened the darkness considerably. "I say, is anyone here?"

"P-Peter," gasped a small voice. "Oh, Peter, you *have* come! You have not forgotten me!" And then Bradford heard a rustling of ground cover and the snapping of twigs and a veritable wraith of a young woman dashed headlong from among the trees and threw herself into his arms. Flinging her arms about his neck, she tugged him downward into a long, lingering kiss. Nonplussed, but chirping merry and then some, Bradford kissed the damsel back. But then he came to his senses and pulled away to stare down into a most piquant face draped in shadows.

"Did you call me Peter?" he asked, his hands holding tightly to the young woman's shoulders.

Mary Butterberry's hand went to stroke his cheek. "Of course I called you Peter. That is your name, silly."

"No, no it ain't, but it is my brother's name."

Eugenia woke with a start and could not think what had awakened her. She lay very still in her bed and listened to the creakings and settlings of the Hall and wondered if perhaps it was nearing six and Mr. Jenkins had uncovered Lord Nightingale and set the bird to squawking. "Oh, it cannot be six already," she whispered after a moment. "I feel as though I have barely slept at all." She listened again. No, Nightingale was not squawking. He always made such a racket in the morning. Certainly he had never ceased at one raucous cry before.

Turning up her lamp the merest bit, Eugenia climbed from the bed and padded to the window to draw the draperies aside. The night spread out before her, ablaze with stars. "Well, it is certainly not morning," she told herself with a smile. "And there are no sounds about except the usual settlings of an ancient house. I expect it was something I dreamed, though I cannot remember now what it was." With the draperies open wide, she settled upon the window seat, tucking her legs up under her and resting her elbows on the sill. What a perfectly splendid sky, she thought, gazing up at the stars. I do not remember the last time I saw such a perfectly splendid sky. One could barely see the sky in London. Certainly the stars never sparkled so brightly or seemed so alive. She smiled again and the smile lingered softly upon her lips.

Such a night as this, she thought, was made for lovers.

And she imagined her Cousin Nicky and Serendipity wandering out under this very same sky somewhere in Scotland. Hand in hand, they would be. Or Nicky would have his arm about Sera's waist. Or Sera would have her arm tucked comfortably into the crook of Nicky's arm. Eugenia sighed. "If only—" she whispered and then ceased to think the thought at all. What good to make my heart ache by picturing myself in such a setting, she thought, when such a thing can never be. I must get over all this girlish nonsense and face the truth of the matter. I am not the sort of young woman with whom a gentleman falls in love. I am not even pretty. And I limp. And all the things that Nicky ever said to me about the mysteries of love and how Cupid comes on silent wings tossing his arrows about with abandon and striking the most unlikely hearts, he only said to give me the strength to go on hoping. And to cheer me. He did never intend to imply that I would truly find romance, only that if the wind blew in the right direction, and the sun tilted just so and faeries arose from the rose garden, I might stand the chance of it. That was all.

"And I do stand the chance of it," she murmured. "I do. But it is a very slim chance at best. I have not seen the sun tilt or faeries arise from the rose garden yet, but I may." Oh, I am such a fool! she thought then. I do never learn my lessons. First, I will have love, and then not, and then I will again. What is wrong with me? Why can I not simply accept the state in life that has been doled out to me and make the very best of it? I ought to go home this very moment and begin to keep the house for Papa, because that is all I am good for and I will likely be doing precisely that for years and years to come. Especially since Aunt Diana's last hope—the unattached gentleman who rented Squire Peabody's house for the summer—has turned out to be Lord Bradford. "Why did he turn out to be Lord Bradford?" she asked of the stars. "Why could Aunt Diana's

new neighbor not have turned out to be someone less handsome and—and—less elegant?"

Although, he does never look so very elegant once Delight and the pets have had their ways with him, she mused,
a smile rising to shine in her eyes. Still, Lord Bradford is
quite beyond my touch. He might have any young woman
in all of England simply by crooking his finger in her direction. Why could Aunt Diana's new neighbor not have
turned out to be someone like—"Mr. Arnsworth!" she exclaimed hoarsely. "A gentleman like Mr. Arnsworth might
be brought to give me a second glance!"

Mr. Arnsworth? Eugenia paused and considered. Did not
Neil cause that gentleman to glow red all the way to the
roots of his hair by mentioning what a fine husband he
would make me? Yes, he most certainly did. And I thought
Neil merely jesting. Perhaps he was not jesting. Perhaps—
"But why would Neil think to look about him for a gentleman to marry me?" she whispered. "Why would he think
to do such a thing as that?"

"You look so amazingly alike," Miss Butterberry whispered, turning about in the saddle to stare up into Bradford's
eyes.

"Turn back around, Miss Butterberry, or we will both
fall," the marquess warned. "I am not so steady as I ought
to be and I am not accustomed to having young women up
before me. And I think Nod is foxed," he added.

"You are the one is foxed, my lord," Mary offered.

"Yes, well, I think Nod has been eating some fermented
oats as well, the way he has been prancing about all evening. You are certain you can climb back inside your window with no one the wiser, eh, m'dear?"

"Oh, yes. I can pull it right open and slip inside. Clara
will have left it unlatched for me."

"Good, good, then you must pretend that you never left,

eh? Your father would have an apoplexy to think that you had run off alone into the night."

"But I had to run off. I thought surely that you were Peter, and Peter would expect me to meet him at the Conqueror's Tree. It is where we always met to speak in private. I have five sisters. There is no privacy at my house. Peter did not steal the monies from the Ladies' Aid Society, my lord. I am certain of it. No, and he did not steal Grandpapa's amber stickpin either. I do not care that the entire village thinks he did. He did not."

"No, of course he did not," murmured Bradford. "Why would the son of the Duke of Sotherland steal from a parson? It makes not the least sense."

"The D-Duke—of Sotherland?"

"Did not Peter tell you that he was—"

"No. Never a word."

"Well, perhaps he did not wish to frighten you off. He told you he was bound for India, eh, Miss Butterberry?"

"Yes, to make his fortune. He promised to return and marry me as soon as he was rich."

Bradford fell into a ponderous silence as Nod carried the two of them competently back in the direction of Wicken. Most certainly the Peter Winthrop of whom Miss Butterberry spoke was his twin brother. Miss Butterberry had thought them one and the same until she had noticed the absence of some sort of a scar across his cheek. When had Peter acquired a scar? Why had he taken his mother's maiden name for his own? How had he come to be living in such a place as the Village of Wicken, giving out that he was the son of a carpenter? And where the devil has he left Mama? Bradford wondered. If he came here alone and set up his digs at some tiny boarding house, and never once had a visitor or anything delivered by the post as Miss Butterberry says, what the devil did he do with Mama?

* * *

Mr. Arnsworth literally leaped from his bed the following morning, his heart stuttering and his ears tingling and his hands trembling in fear. "Oh, my lord," he gasped. "Oh, my lord, what was that? Someone is being murdered right here in this very house!" And then he happened to gaze at the brass knob on his chamber door and saw it turn slowly, steadily, without the least sound. Mr. Arnsworth panicked and dove under his bed.

"Arnsworth?" Spelling stared at the disheveled pile of sheets and pillows and the quilt lying upon the floor. "Arnsworth, are you here?"

"Sp-Spelling? Oh, thank gawd it is you!" Mr. Arnsworth exclaimed, crawling out from beneath the ancient four-poster, his nightshirt up about his thighs. "There is a murderer in the house, Spelling! Did you not hear that screech echoing through the corridors? Someone has been hacked to death or something else quite as ghastly. When I saw the knob turn—and so silently—I thought—I thought—the murderer had come for me as well. But perhaps it is not too late," he added, tossing his nightcap on to an ottoman and rushing about in search of his breeches. "Ah, here they are. Perhaps we may yet save whoever—oh, my gawd! Do you hear that? Another one! He has felled another one!"

Spelling could not help himself. He burst into laughter.

"What? Spelling, my gawd, man, pull yourself together. There is a veritable slaughter going on. If we cannot save the poor blokes he has already killed, we must at the very least save Miss Chastain and Lady Wickenshire!"

"I—I—it—" Spelling attempted, but his laughter would not let him get two entire words out together. He raised one hand into the air to signal Arnsworth to wait for a moment, turned himself to the wall and pounded on it with his fists so very hard that one of the paintings tilted to the left.

Mr. Arnsworth, with one leg in his breeches and one not, stared at his friend, completely bewildered.

"It is not a murderer," Spelling managed in a great gush

as he turned around to face Arnsworth again. "It is Lord Nightingale being uncovered." And then he had to turn away again as his laughter once more bubbled out of control.

"L-Lord Nightingale? Being uncovered?" Gilly searched his mind for some meaning. He had heard that name before. Lord Nightingale. But when and who— "Do you mean to say it is that parrot, Spelling? A bird makes that horrid screeching?"

Spelling turned away from the wall and nodded, his eyes brimming with tears.

"What are they doing to it?" gasped Gilly. "It sounds as though they are roasting it alive."

"No, no, he always s-sounds that way," Spelling managed. Then he inhaled deeply, wiped at his eyes and banned the laughter from overcoming him again. "It is worse in this barn of a house because of all the stone. It echoes everywhere. You will grow accustomed, Arnsworth. First thing in the morning and last thing at night. You did not hear him last night?"

"N-no."

"Well, you were sleeping soundly then, I expect. I heard the beast, let me tell you. At any rate, I came to see if he had waked you and to explain so that you would not— panic—but I did not wish to wake you if he had not and so I attempted just to peek in without knocking."

"It does not belong to Miss Chastain, does it?" Gilly asked, loosing his hold upon his breeches and letting them fall to the floor. "I mean, she does not actually own the thing?"

"Never fear, Arnsworth. If you wish to marry the gel you need not marry that bird into the bargain. Nightingale belongs to Nicky. I am going to dress. I shall come and fetch you when I've done. You will never find the morning room else and will die of starvation wandering about the corridors. This is the most inconvenient old pile of stones ever stacked one upon the other."

* * *

Eugenia, dressed in a gay garden dress of cherry-striped muslin, stood waiting impatiently near the window of the summer parlor. "Are they never coming down, Aunt Diana?" she queried.

"You know how gentlemen are, dearest."

"No, I do not. I only know how Papa is and Nicky."

"Oh, well, gentlemen do not generally rise quite so early as we do here at Wicken Hall. When they have been traveling, they generally do not appear until very close to noon, if then. It takes them some time, Eugenia, to be shaved and to tie their neckcloths just so and to select precisely the right morning coat. And they spend hours before the looking glass coaxing their hair into just the proper look."

"Coaxing their hair into—Aunt Diana, surely you jest. They hack their hair off the moment they are out of short coats. What have they left of it to coax into anything?"

"You would be surprised, my dear. At any rate, I did hear them in the morning room as I came by. They are eating at this very moment and I have left word with Jenkins to send them to us here. What do you think of Mr. Arnsworth, Eugenia? I found him a rather pleasant young man, though he does not seem to have a great deal to say for himself."

"He was tired from his journey, Aunt Diana, and a stranger in a strange house. One could not expect him to be garrulous."

"Very true," nodded the dowager. "You did not take him into sudden dislike, did you, Eugenia?"

"Take him into—my goodness, no. How could I?"

"Well, he did come with Neil."

"Aunt Diana, for shame."

"Yes, I know."

"You, yourself, said that it was likely that Neil had turned over a new leaf."

"Yes, I know."

"And besides, I do not think it at all likely that Mr. Arnsworth is anything at all like Neil's other friends. At least, not like any of them that I have had the misfortune to meet. Mr. Arnsworth seems a very nice sort of gentleman."

"But not very handsome," murmured Lady Wickenshire, watching Eugenia out of the corner of her eye.

"Not every gentleman can be handsome, Aunt."

"Quite true. Handsome is as handsome does, and a young woman ought to peer under a gentleman's exterior." Lady Wickenshire colored up the moment she said the words. "That is to say," the dowager continued, taking a hand-painted plate from its stand upon the mantel and nonchalantly fanning her face with it. "It is not always what one sees that counts when one looks at a gentleman."

"Just so," Eugenia nodded, attempting not to giggle at the thought of peering under Mr. Answorth's exterior. "A kind heart is worth a thousand handsome faces."

"Yes, exactly!"

"I cannot think what is keeping them so very long. They have had enough time to eat a five course dinner."

"You are so anxious to have their companionship, Eugenia?"

"Yes. No. Yes. It is—I cannot wait to see what will happen when Lord Nightingale discovers Neil's presence." Eugenia glanced up to the top of the chandelier.

Lady Wickenshire followed her gaze and giggled girlishly. "What on earth is he doing up there? Nightingale, come down at once you silly bird."

"Yo ho ho," the macaw replied and pecked thoughtfully at the nearest candlewick. "Arrrrffff. Mrrrrr. Yo ho."

Arrrrffff. Mrrrr. Yo ho? mused Mr. Arnsworth as Spelling escorted him down the corridor. They keep a dog, a cat and a pirate in their summer parlor? He smiled to himself at the thought. Must be the parrot, I expect. I wonder if it will look at all like the stuffed one?

"Devil it, they are in with the wretched fowl," mumbled Spelling. "Be very careful, Arnsworth. One never knows what Lord Nightingale will do. Do not, above all things, let him come close to your finger. Snap it right off."

"He will?" asked Gilly, his eyebrows rising.

"Right off," nodded Spelling. "Not to be trusted, that bird. Ah, here you are Aunt Diana, Eugenia," he said, ushering Arnsworth into the room.

"Villain!" squawked Lord Nightingale, standing straight up and ruffling his feathers. "Villain! Bite! Villain!" and seizing the closest candle by the wick, Nightingale tugged it from its holder and sent it crashing down to the floor, where it bounced across the carpet and came to rest at Neil's feet.

Eugenia laughed. She could not help herself. Her brown eyes glowed and her cheeks flushed and her lips parted in the most delightful way. Mr. Arnsworth ceased to look at the parrot and the candle and looked at her instead, and his heart leaped the tiniest bit. She is pretty when she laughs, he thought. And then another candle came crashing to the floor and the sound of flapping wings took his attention from Eugenia.

"Look out! Arnsworth, back away!" Spelling cried, ducking behind the closest piece of furniture, which happened to be the sofa. "The fiend is after us!"

"No, Mr. Arnsworth," Eugenia giggled, stepping forward and taking Gilly's arm just as he was preparing to duck behind something himself. "The fiend is after Neil. They have known each other for years and years. Since Neil was a child."

"And they have never gotten on," sighed Lady Wickenshire with a shake of her head. "I cannot think why they do not, they are both of them scoundrels in their own way."

"I protest, Aunt Diana," muttered Neil, peeking up from behind the sofa to discover Nightingale perched on the back of the wing chair across the way. The bird positively glaring at him. "I may well be a scoundrel, but Nightingale is the devil incarnate."

"Awwwk! Villain! Bite!" cried Nightingale raucously.

"No, you will not," declared Eugenia. "You are being a rascal and well you know it, too. Come, Mr. Arnsworth, and meet the ruler of my cousin's household." She led Gilly across to the wing chair, her hand holding firmly to his arm. "This is our Lord Nightingale. My lord, may I present Mr. Arnsworth."

"He is magnificent," breathed Arnsworth staring at the crimson bird with its white-and-red-striped face and its green- and turquoise-tipped wings. "I have never seen any bird at all to rival him. Not even the stuffed one at the fair."

"The stuffed one?" asked Eugenia. "At the fair?"

"It was the only parrot I ever saw up until now," explained Mr. Arnsworth, "and I did wonder if they all looked alike. They do not, let me tell you."

"Hello," said Nightingale peering up at Mr. Arnsworth with rapt attention. "Mornin' Genia. Hello."

"If you hold out your arm, he may come to you," Eugenia smiled, thoroughly enjoying the awe in Mr. Arnsworth's eyes.

"Do you think?"

"No, do not, Arnsworth. He will come to you, walk up your arm and take a chunk right out of your ear," warned Spelling, having come out from behind the sofa to stand beside his aunt.

"I do not think that he will," offered the dowager. "He is a good deal more sociable since he has come to live with us, Neil. Delight is forever playing with him and dressing him up and taking him out for walks. You would not believe what the old curmudgeon puts up with these days."

Gilly held up his arm and bent it at the elbow, holding his breath for fear his breathing might frighten the bird.

"Say, Come, Nightingale," Eugenia whispered in his ear.

"Come, Nightingale," repeated Gilly, and with one flap

of his wings, the macaw left the wing chair behind and landed upon Mr. Arnsworth's arm. As Gilly watched him, fascinated, he sidled slowly upward, one taloned foot then the next until he reached Gilly's shoulder. Arnsworth closed his eyes and bit his lip in preparation for a bite on his ear, but it did not come. "Avast, me hearty," the parrot said instead and reached down to nibble on Gilly's collar. "Mornin' Nightingale. Mornin' Genia."

"What do you think, Aunt?" Neil whispered into Lady Wickenshire's ear. "Arnsworth is not a paragon, but see how they stand together and beam at that wretched bird."

"I wonder," murmured the dowager, hope rising in her heart. "I do wonder if you have not at last done something right, Neil."

Eight

The marquess' valet was not at all certain what ought to be done. He swiped his fingers through his graying hair, fidgeted with his waistcoat buttons, ran one finger around the inside of his collar and sighed. He shuffled across to the window, opened the draperies and stared out into the afternoon sunshine, jiggling the chain of his pocket watch. At last, Stanley clasped his hands behind his back and began to rock in place—from heel to toe to heel to toe to heel to toe.

Bradford, tiny rays of sunlight creeping over him, warming his face and sneaking between his eyelashes, turned over in the bed and struggled to keep his eyes from opening, but he lost the battle. "What the deuce are you doing, Stanley?" he growled at his valet's back, blinking blearily at the man from the depths of the bedclothes. "Cease with your rocking, you are giving me the mal de mer. What time is it? I fancy I have slept straight through my breakfast, eh?"

"And through your luncheon, my lord," announced Stanley, ceasing to rock and turning to face his lordship.

"Ah. And you were rocking because you thought that I intended to sleep through my dinner as well and feared that I might die of starvation?"

"No, my lord."

"Why then?"

"No reason, my lord."

"Mr. Stanley," grumbled Bradford, struggling to a sitting

position amidst the tangle of bedclothes, "I have known you my entire life, and in twenty-two years, sir, you have never rocked for no reason. Out with it!"

"I did not wish to wake you, my lord, but Mr. Waggoner—you do remember Mr. Waggoner, he is the butler— he informs me that there is a young person at the kitchen door asking for you."

"A young person?"

"A young *female* person, my lord."

"Oh, is that all? Anyone would think, from your rocking, that you had gotten news the sky was falling. Just tell him, Stanley, to send the gel out to the pasture. Oh, but send word to one of the grooms to accompany her, eh?"

"Send the girl out to the pasture, my lord?" Stanley's eyes widened considerably at the thought.

"Yes, just so. She has come to see Nod, and I will not forbid her. She is in love with the old fellow, Stanley, and brings him sugar cubes and tells him how beautiful he is. And he will encourage the gel, you know. He takes the cubes from her hand and allows her to hug him. He is that fond of her. She has not got that great lummox of a puppy with her, has she?"

"N-no, my lord. Mr. Waggoner did not mention a puppy, but she is apparently accompanied by another young woman, my lord, who has chosen to wait in the stable yard."

"Another young woman? Well, that will be Miss Chastain, I expect. We will not need to send one of the grooms then. Miss Chastain is perfectly capable of seeing to the gel's safety. Simply say that they are both welcome to go out to the pasture, and say that I will join them when I have got dressed. And then come back and help me get dressed, eh, Stanley? I have got the most vile ache behind my eyes. Drank a deal too much last evening. I cannot trust my own hand with a razor in it, I think. And there is something I wish to discuss with you, Stanley. Something quite important."

Mr. Stanley nodded and strode toward the door. He paused midway and glanced back at the marquess, opened his mouth to speak, but then thought better of it and continued out into the corridor. Send them to the pasture? he thought. Can he possibly still be in his cups, after sleeping all this time?

Mr. Waggoner, who was enjoying a cup of tea in the kitchen with Mrs. Hornby, and who had invited both young women to join them while they awaited the marquess' response, stared blankly at Stanley as the valet entered and announced that his lordship had suggested that the visitors go out to the pasture where he intended to join them shortly.

"Go out to the paaasture?" queried Mrs. Hornby, in amazement. "Whyyyy would Miss Butterrrrberrrry and Miss Claaaara wish to go out to the paaaasture?"

Spelling gazed down into the rose garden through one of the casements in the summer parlor and shook his head in disbelief.

"What is it, Neil?" Lady Wickenshire queried, setting her embroidery aside for a moment. "You appear thoroughly amazed."

"They are out there walking along and talking as pleasantly as you please, Aunt Diana."

"Are they? How very nice. And Delight and the pets accompany them, do they not? I do not wish Eugenia and Mr. Arnsworth to be strolling through the garden alone, Neil. If so, we must join them at once."

"They are surrounded, Aunt. That great beast of a puppy is chasing the cat in and out amongst the bushes, Delight clings to Eugenia's hand and that wretched bird is perched upon Arnsworth's shoulder."

"How delightful. I do not know what possessed you to bring that young man here, Neil, but I do thank you for it. He seems remarkably kind."

"Yes, he is. Gilly is a bit of clunch, but he is kind."

"A clunch? Oh, Neil, no. He merely lacks confidence in himself. But Eugenia will provide him with that. I do believe she conceived a sympathy for him from the very first. And he has engaged her feelings even more deeply today by his enchantment with Lord Nightingale and the pets, and his eagerness to form a friendship with Delight."

"As I said, a perfect clunch," replied Neil. "I knew how it would be. He is caught up with Eugenia and he will fancy himself in love with her in another hour. Tomorrow, he will quite likely be thinking out what he must say to ask for her hand."

Lady Wickenshire laughed the most charming laugh. "You are too confident, Neil. No gentleman forms an attachment so rapidly as that. But Eugenia's limp does not put him off, and that is a very good sign. It was kind of you to think to bring them to each other's attention."

Mr. Spelling turned from the window and shrugged his shoulders. "All for love," he mumbled. "A gentleman does what he can for the females in his family, eh?"

Lady Wickenshire's jaw came near to dropping at this reply, but she did not allow it to do so. Truth to tell, she had conceived the idea that something quite beyond Eugenia's happiness had prompted her nephew to escort Mr. Arnsworth to Wicken Hall. She still thought as much, but she also thought that to inquire into Mr. Spelling's motives when things looked so very promising for her niece would be a most inappropriate thing to do. After all, she mused, what do Neil's motives matter? If his ends are served at one and the same time that Eugenia's happiness is secured, where is the harm in that?

"We are going to Lord Bradford's!" exclaimed a tiny voice from the corridor, and in an instant Delight came dashing excitedly into the room followed by a merrily barking Stanley Blithe. "Genia an' Mr. Arnsworth is taking us! All of us! An' they are goin' to make certain that Stanley

Blithe an' Sweetpea an' Lord Nightingale do not make no ruckus. We will all of us be allowed to play with Nod without 'sturbin' Lord Bradford at all! Mr. Arnsworth says as how he cannot see why it cannot be done!" And having so stated, the little girl hopped happily from flower to flower across the carpeting, bounced up beside Lady Wickenshire upon the sofa and gave that lady a smacking kiss on the cheek. "I am so verimost overjoyed!"

"Yes, I can see that you are," laughed the dowager, returning Delight's kiss with one of her own. "I do hope Lord Bradford will feel likewise."

"Oh, he will! He likes us. He is just not inorbitantly fond of all our ruckusing. An' Genia an' Mr. Arnsworth intends to devote themselves to 'liminatin' that."

"We propose to attempt eliminating that," declared Eugenia, entering the room on Mr. Arnsworth's arm. "Mr. Arnsworth assures me it is possible. He has three dogs of his own at home and all of them as uniquely bred as Stanley Blithe, Aunt Diana."

"Three? And all of them mongrels? How very democratic of you, Mr. Arnsworth," Lady Wickenshire observed. "You do not truly intend to take Lord Nightingale with you?"

"Oh, yes, ma'am," nodded Mr. Arnsworth, rubbing one finger along the bird's breast. "From what I have been told, he is excessively fond of Lord Bradford. It would be cruel not to take him, especially since he has a sturdy lead to keep him safe and seems most accepting of it. Do you care to join us, Spelling, for a bit of a walk?"

"No, thank you," Mr. Spelling responded. "I have not the least desire to stroll all the way to Peabody's in the company of that miserable fowl."

"Villain!" Lord Nightingale responded heartily from Mr. Arnsworth's shoulder.

"Just so, Nightingale," Spelling muttered. "Precisely what you are. A villain."

"Take Bobby Tripp with you, Eugenia," Lady Wickenshire said, smiling widely.

"You do not think that we have chaperons enough, Aunt?"

"Delight and the pets do nicely for our own rose garden, my dear, but it is most improper to be strolling about the countryside without someone of a more advanced age to support you. One never knows."

Eugenia watched Mr. Arnsworth's ears tinge slowly red at her aunt's words, and she gave his arm a bolstering pat. "It is not that Aunt Diana does not trust you, Mr. Arnsworth," she said. "It is merely a matter of what the neighbors may say."

Although it was precisely because she did not yet trust Mr. Arnsworth completely—he had come with Neil, after all—Lady Wickenshire nevertheless chose not to contradict her niece.

". . . and the gel told me that Peter has gone off to India to make his fortune," Bradford completed his story. "Ouch! Damnation, Stanley, if I had wanted to be cut, I would have shaved myself!"

"I am sorry, my lord," murmured Stanley, hurriedly pressing a corner of the towel against Bradford's chin. "I am merely—the news made me—it is most extraordinary, you must admit. We have been searching for news of Lord Peter and her ladyship for ever so long, and to discover quite by accident, as you have done that—India? He has gone to India to make his fortune?"

"That is what he told the gel."

"Well, the rascal lied to her, by gawd!"

"Stanley!"

"I beg your pardon, my lord. But he did. He must have done. Why would Lord Peter traipse off to India to make himself a fortune when he need only send a letter to your papa's solicitor to come by anything he requires."

"I have no idea."

"I expect it was merely a bouncer to take leave of the young woman without breaking her heart."

"Unless the Old Squire has been feeding me a Canterbury tale for all these years and he did not make the provisions for Mama and Peter that he assured me he had. No, even Papa would not tell such a whopper as that, do you think?"

Stanley offered the marquess a damp towel to wipe his face and turned away to clean the razor. It had never before occurred to him that for all of the duke's faults, he would actually lie to his lordship about such an important matter as the welfare of his mother and brother. "You ought not call him the Old Squire," Stanley mumbled, wiping the razor clean with a towel.

"I cannot help myself. He has always acted precisely like some little squire mad for power and never like a duke. *Do* you think he has been lying to me, Stanley?"

"No," the valet said after another moment's thought. "I do not. He is a formidable gentleman, your papa, a veritable despot, and as unforgiving a man as was ever born, but he is not a liar."

"So I think as well," Bradford agreed, slipping into his shirt. "So either Peter lied to the girl, or he is twitching against Papa's hold on him and thinks to make his own fortune as a form of revolt. But either way, he would never have thought to steal money from a church, or wander off with a parson's amber stickpin in his pocket."

"What!"

"Oh, I did not mention that part. Miss Butterberry says that her father and everyone else in the village suspect Peter of having stolen money and an amber stickpin before he disappeared."

"Miss B-Butterberry?"

"Yes, Stanley. Are you growing hard of hearing? Miss

Butterberry. That is the young woman's name—the one who fancies she is in love with Peter and told me the tale."

"Miss Butterberry," sighed Stanley, lifting a stack of neckcloths from Lord Bradford's drawer.

"Yes, Miss Butterberry. You *are* growing hard of hearing!"

"No, no, I am not," Stanley protested. "It is merely—"

"What?" the marquess asked as he took a neckcloth from the stack in Stanley's hands and prepared to tie it.

"The young person who called for you at the kitchen door, my lord. It was a Miss B-Butterberry."

"Oh, my gawd! Stanley, do not tell me that you sent Miss Butterberry out to the pasture!"

"You distinctly said, my lord—"

"You did! Damnation, she must think me dicked in the nob."

"But you said, my lord, that you knew who she was and—"

"I assumed it to be Delight, the child from Wicken Hall, and that her companion would be Miss Chastain. I never gave Miss Butterberry a thought." Bradford tied his neckcloth into a knot resembling nothing more than a knot and turned from the looking glass. "My coat, Stanley. I cannot leave Miss Butterberry and her companion standing alone in a pasture. What a thing to do!"

In a matter of moments Bradford was charging down the back stairwell, dashing along the corridor and slamming out through the kitchen door with barely a nod to Mrs. Hornby as he passed her by. "Weeeellll, ain't weee in a hurryyyy," she observed, ceasing to roll her bread dough and staring after him. "Off to speeeak with the paarson's gels, no doubt."

They walked slowly across the fields talking and laughing and enjoying every bit of the warm summer afternoon.

Mr. Arnsworth took the time to throw sticks for Stanley Blithe to retrieve and to dangle vines in the air for Sweetpea to leap at. He ran after Delight in an extemporaneous game of tag, from which he returned to Eugenia's side, puffing the least bit, with a wide smile upon his cherubic face. "I have grown a bit stout for that game," he said, offering her his arm to lean on once again. "Is Lord Nightingale growing heavy? Let me take him back on my shoulder."

"Yes, I should be grateful for that," Eugenia replied. "It is not that he weighs so very much, but that his talons prick through the muslin of my dress."

"I ought to have thought of that. I am so very sorry."

"No, you need not apologize. I am pleased to have you play with Delight. I am no good at all when it comes to games like tag, you know."

"Does your—limb—bother you, Miss Chastain? Perhaps we ought not walk so very far. We may easily turn back, if you wish to do so."

"And have Delight and all of these creatures protest? I think not. Besides, my limb rarely hurts at all, Mr. Arnsworth, unless the weather is very damp or cold. You do not mind that—that—you must walk so slowly?"

"Slowly? Never. Why look at all the time it gives me to play with Delight and her pets."

"Yes, but—"

Mr. Arnsworth, transferring Lord Nightingale back to his own shoulder, stopped a moment and stared deep into Eugenia's eyes. "There are much worse things in the world, Miss Chastain," he said, "than to walk slowly across a meadow with a pleasant companion in the midst of summer sunshine."

Eugenia blushed. She could not help herself, for he had spoken in such a sincere tone and his eyes—his eyes spoke even more sincerely.

"I am obliged that you stroll anywhere with me at all,"

he added, gazing off across the field and setting forward once again. "I did not expect such condescension upon your part—and to a perfect stranger."

"Oh, no! It is not condescension. That is a truly despicable word, Mr. Arnsworth. It implies that one thinks oneself so very high and others so very low."

"Do you think so? In my world it is not at all a despicable word. In my world, to be condescended to by such as you is an occurrence devoutly to be wished and, if achieved, to be cherished forever in one's memory."

What? Eugenia wondered. What does he say? Whatever can he mean by that? She thought to ask him, but just then Delight came running up to show them both the most intriguing bug that she and Sweetpea had caught, and Mr. Arnsworth, who was obviously fond of bugs, became quite distracted by the thing.

Eugenia smiled as her two towheaded companions studied what she thought, from a much more distant vantage point, to be a mere cricket. It does not matter, after all, what he meant by *his world,* she told herself. I will ask him one day, but not today. Today, I shall just enjoy getting to know the gentleman and hope to set him at his ease, which we do seem to be doing quite nicely, the lot of us. She smiled contentedly as both Sweetpea and Stanley Blithe added their noses to the bug investigation.

When at last the little captive was set free, the party continued on, going by way of the woods, across the little stream, which demanded some assistance from Mr. Arnsworth on Eugenia's part, for hopping from one stone to another was not a thing she could do with confidence. He held her hand and guided her, catching her at one point when she tipped, laughing, to the side, and saving her from a wetting.

She is the most splendid young lady, Mr. Arnsworth thought, laughing with her as they reached the shore and then continued on through Squire Peabody's woods. I do

not mind at all that she limps. How absurd of Spelling not
to tell me straight out that she did. As if it would make any
difference at all when she is so kind and gentle. And how
could he think her shy? She is not at all shy. No, not one
bit. That is my failing. Though I do not feel the least bit
so any longer. It is Miss Chastain chases the shyness from
me. But what will she think, he wondered then, gazing
down at her, when she learns that I am not a gentleman at
all? At least, not a born gentleman. Will her attitude toward
me alter? I must tell her the whole terrible truth, after all,
sooner or later.

Mr. Arnsworth opened his mouth to broach the subject,
because he thought sooner would be best. He could not bear
to actually fall in love with Miss Chastain and then be
forced from her by the unalterable horror of his parentage.
He opened his mouth, but before so much as one syllable
slipped out, a light voice hailed them.

"Eugenia! It is true! You have come to Wicken Hall for
the summer! Oh, I am so pleased!" And in a moment, two
young ladies were rushing toward them.

"Mary, Clara, what a wonderful surprise!" exclaimed
Eugenia, suddenly enveloped in hugs from the Butterberry
sisters. "Oh, how you both have grown! And how marvelous you look, Mary, in that dress! And Clara, how beautiful
you have become! Mr. Arnsworth, do come and let me present Mary and Clara to you. They are the parson's daughters. We have not seen each other in three whole years, I
think."

"An' present them to me, too!" cried Delight, tugging
upon Eugenia's skirt. "I am Delight," she announced to the
two young ladies. "An' this is Stanley Blithe," she added
as the puppy came bounding up. "An' that is Sweetpea,"
she pointed at the cat as it sat down on a stump and haugh-
tily studied the newcomers. "An' Lord Nightingale is right
there on Mr. Arnsworth's shoulder. We all of us belong to
Nicky."

Mr. Arnsworth winked at Delight and then turned. His elm-bark-colored eyes met, on the instant, a pair of the most gorgeous blue ones. Mr. Arnsworth was so taken aback at the glow in those marvelous orbs that he nearly gasped aloud.

"This is Miss Butterberry," Eugenia said, squeezing Mary's hand as they both attempted not to giggle at the sudden jolt in Mr. Arnsworth's breathing. "And the young lady you are just now staring at is Miss Clara Butterberry."

"Oh. Oh! Oh, your servant!" stuttered Mr. Arnsworth, barely able to take his eyes from Miss Clara in order to include Mary in his awkward bobbing bow.

"Whatever are you doing here?" asked Eugenia, strolling toward the pasture fence with Mary's hand in hers and leaving Mr. Arnsworth to trail behind with Delight and Clara and Bobby Tripp far back in their wake. "Do not tell me that your papa has sent the two of you here alone to make the new neighbor's acquaintance, because I shan't believe that, Mary."

"No, Papa has not the least idea that we have come. Have you met him yet, Eugenia?"

"Indeed. He came to visit us shortly after we arrived. Mary, do you mean to say that you have come here without permission?"

"Yes. Well, I had to come, Eugenia. I shall likely never get such another opportunity to escape in this direction as came to me today and I have something that I must deliver, you see. Something quite important, I think."

"Something that you must deliver to Lord Bradford?"

"Just so. It is the oddest thing, Eugenia. Clara and I intended merely to stop for a moment so that I might give this—particular letter—into Lord Bradford's hands. We did not at all intend to remain. But then, he sent word down to the kitchen that Clara and I should await his presence in this pasture. He said that he would join us here when he was quite ready to do so. Can you imagine? Await him in a pasture? Well, Clara has been giggling madly about it ever since. She thinks the gentleman's cupboard is filled with chipped china. I did not think so when first we met, but—"

Eugenia burst into gales of laughter. "He s-sent you here to this pasture? He s-said that he would come when he w-was ready? Oh, oh, how very much like Lord Bradford that does sound! Sometimes he is s-so f-funny!"

Bradford was but half the distance to the pasture when he saw a number of figures emerge from the cover of the little woods. He squinted his eyes to see if he could make out who the people could be, but they were yet much too far away to be identifiable. Then he heard a young lady cry out and saw the ladies he assumed to be the Butter-berry sisters hurry forward to meet the newcomers. Oh, no, he thought. Now word will get 'round the entire village of Wicken that I sent them to await me in a pasture and every person in the place will think I am dicked in the nob! I have got to get to them and explain Stanley's mistake before they decide to wait no longer and stroll away with the story of my insanity bubbling upon their lips! And he increased his somewhat presentable jog into a dead run.

Nod, who had wandered to the far side of the fence in hopes of more sugar cubes the very moment that Delight's voice had reached his ears, looked up and over his shoulder the instant he heard the rapid pounding of boots against the ground. He blinked his great brown eyes once, twice. He turned around and shook his head and pawed at the ground. He stared again at the most unusual sight and then trotted off toward his running master. Never had he seen Lord Bradford travel at such a pace, and when the gentleman actually leaped the fence rail and came down still running, Nod was thoroughly impressed. So impressed, in fact, that he trotted along right beside Bradford, prancing about a bit in an effort to slow his pace enough to match Bradford's own.

Stanley Blithe, too, heard the pounding of boots and the snapping of stray twigs among the grass, and equally enthralled with the running gentleman, he squiggled beneath the lowest fence rail and ran to greet him, leaping about the marquess when he came close enough and barking enthusiastically.

"Get down, you great clunch of a puppy," grumbled Bradford, necessarily slowing his pace so as not to step on Stanley Blithe's feet. "Nod, go away. You are both doing nothing but drawing attention to me. Off with the both of you!" he shouted, coming to a complete halt and waving his arms at them.

Eugenia looked up to see him and her hand went immediately to cover her smile. His hair was windblown, his neckcloth flapping wildly outside his coat, and Stanley Blithe was tugging at his sleeve while Nod nickered and attempted to nibble on his ear. "Knollsmarmer!" Lord Nightingale squawked from Mr. Arnsworth's shoulder, and then he was flapping his beautiful wings against the sky and Mr. Arnsworth was running below him, holding tightly to the leathers and crying for the parrot to halt. But Lord Nightingale paid not the least attention. "Knollsmarmer!" he cried again and continued his flight.

Mr. Arnsworth did not so much as see it coming. He was so concerned to keep hold of the leathers and so preoccupied, staring up into the sky, shouting at Lord Nightingale to settle again upon his shoulder, that he ran smack into the pasture fence at top speed, hitting the bottom rail with his shin, the middle rail with his stomach and the top rail with his nose all at one and the same time. "Ommph!" was the only sound that Eugenia and the others—including Bobby Tripp, who was rushing, himself, in pursuit of

Arnsworth—heard as the leathers slipped from Mr. Arnsworth's hand and that gentleman melted right into the ground.

Nine

Mr. Arnsworth lay upon the Peabodys' ancient fainting couch, a piece of sticking plaster on his nose, a wet towel on his brow and a silver knife pressed to the back of his neck, while Mary and Clara Butterberry and Mr. Stanley hovered around him. Eugenia had been inclined to hover around him as well, especially when a muttering marquess had thrown the poor man over his shoulder like a sack of potatoes and stomped off with him to the house without the least concern that Mr. Arnsworth might be a bit uncomfortable with his head bobbing about against the marquess' back, but she had since changed her mind.

"Well, how else am I to get him to the house?" Bradford had grumbled angrily, when Eugenia had mentioned Mr. Arnsworth's awkward and likely painful position to him. "He ain't about to walk there on his own, Miss Chastain."

"Bobby Tripp can help you to carry him," she had responded, quite sensibly, she thought, since Bobby Tripp was right there and most willing to relieve the Marquess of some of Mr. Arnsworth's weight, but Lord Bradford had merely shaken his head in exasperation and stomped onward.

Now that she came to think of it, ensconced as she was in one of the Peabodys' wing chairs and studying Lord Bradford intently, she thought that the marquess was a most stubborn man, and that he must be a good deal stronger than he appeared. Mr. Arnsworth is certainly not a featherweight, she thought, and yet Lord Bradford did not have the least trouble in carrying him so very far. I expect Bobby Tripp would have had to set the gentleman down a considerable number of times, were he only carrying a half of him. Although— "Why you did not place Mr. Arnsworth on Nod's back and carry him to the house, I cannot conceive," she murmured. "He would have been a deal more comfortable along the way."

"Nod is not a pack animal," muttered Bradford in return. "And your Mr. Arnsworth is no worse off now than he was when he was lying upon the ground. So I jiggled his head a bit. Of what conceivable consequence can that be, Miss Chastain? He has regained his senses already, has he not?"

"Almost," Eugenia conceded.

"Completely."

"No, not completely. He is greatly confused about where he is and how he got here."

"Balderdash! He knows exactly where he is and how he got here. He is merely enjoying the great outflow of concern for him that gushes from two peagooses who do not have the sense to let him be. And to that point, why in heaven's name are *you* not fluttering about him like a bee about a blossom? He traveled all the way from London simply to make your acquaintance, my dear Miss Chastain, and there you sit, ignoring the man."

Eugenia stared at Bradford in disbelief. Mr. Arnsworth has traveled all the way from London to make *my* acquaintance? she thought. Where did he get such a ridiculous idea as that? Does he not realize that the gentleman is a friend of Neil's and has accompanied Neil to Wicken Hall? That they have likely come to—to—well, I cannot think why they have come, she thought abruptly. I only suppose that Neil has some reason, but now that I think on it, what reason could there be?

"What? No one told you as much?" Bradford queried. He could not think why else she would stare at him with such a look upon her face, and a very real pang of sympathy for her touched his heart. "I apologize, Miss Chastain. I thought you knew. I would not have made mention of it else."

"What was it made you think—"

"Spelling told me as much last evening. We dined together—the three of us—at the Red Rose Inn. He said that Arnsworth was most anxious to make your acquaintance and had come to Wicken precisely for that purpose. He made it quite clear that Arnsworth was in search of a wife and that you— Well, Arnsworth did not gainsay him, Miss Chastain."

Eugenia could not think of a word to say. Her lips parted the tiniest bit and her forehead collapsed into a thoughtful frown. Her eyes lowered. Her fingers smoothed the creases in her dress. And just as she raised her gaze again to Bradford's, a most rotund woman entered the room leading a sobbing Delight by the hand. Eugenia made to rise, to go to the child, but had only moved the slightest bit when Delight released Mrs. Hornby's hand and dashed straight to Lord Bradford. Without the least hesitation, she climbed up into the astounded marquess' lap, threw her arms around his neck and buried her wet little face in his neckcloth.

"Shehehe was sooo mightily upseeet, looorship," Mrs. Hornby neighed at her startled employer. "Not nothing I could saaaay would cheer her. Shehehe would onlyyy saaaay as how shehehe wished to speeeak with you."

"Fine, Mrs. Hornby," the marquess managed, attempting to decide just how to place his arms around the now wailing child. "You may go."

Mrs. Hornby bestowed a most sympathetic look upon Delight and raised her hand the slightest bit in Eugenia's direction as if signaling her to remain in her chair. Then she fairly galloped from the room.

Lord Bradford took a deep breath, smiled weakly in Eugenia's direction and then leaned his chin on Delight's silken little head. "Delight," he whispered, "why are you crying so? Your friend Mr. Arnsworth will be all right."

The child clung to him more tightly and continued to sob.

"Delight, I promise you that Mr. Arnsworth will be fine. He has just hit his nose a bit and—and—well, he knocked himself out, you see, on the fence rail. But he is much better now."

"I is n-not cryin' about Mr. Arnsworth," sobbed Delight into his neckcloth.

"Oh. Well, what are you being such a peagoose about?" he asked loudly enough for Eugenia to understand every word.

"Do not call her a peagoose," Eugenia protested and she rose from her chair and went to kneel beside Lord Bradford and Delight, rubbing the child's back with one hand. "Of all the dunderheaded things to say. She is a little girl and she is frightened. Calling her a peagoose will only make her cry all the more."

"Oh."

"Do you know nothing at all about children?"

"I know they are annoying," Bradford responded, but his fingers went to smooth Delight's ringlets from her face and place them delicately behind one tiny ear just the same. "Hush," he murmured. "Eugenia thinks you are frightened, but you are not, are you? You are the bravest little gel I have ever met. Such a ruckus as we have just had did not truly frighten you."

"That is jus' it!" sobbed Delight, sitting up straight and staring up at him, her eyes shining with tears, her nose runny and her face red and sticky with saltwater.

"What is 'just it?' "

"They was all ruckusing again!" sobbed Delight heartily. "I tole them an' tole them how you didn't not want your peace 'sturbed an' Genia an' Mr. Arnsworth promised as how it wasn't not gonna be, an' now they has!"

"Oh."

"An' now you willn't not let me ever come an' see you an' Nod ever again!" Delight wailed and buried her face back in his neckcloth.

Eugenia glanced up to see a most unholy light flicker and catch in Lord Bradford's cool blue eyes, a light that warmed them considerably.

"That is not necessarily so, my dear," he murmured, blowing in Delight's ear, "that I willn't let you come and see Nod and me ever again."

"It is n-not?"

"No. You did not cause the ruckus after all."

"N-no, I din't!" sobbed Delight, wiggling about in his lap to stare up at him again, one fist twisting itself into her curls while the other swiped at her runny nose. "I knowed you did not want no ruckuses an' I warned ever'one, even Stanley Blithe an' Lord N-Nightingale."

"I am quite certain that you did," nodded Bradford.

"Yes. An' we was all bein' verimost good until Mr. Arnsworth went an' throwed himself against the fence an' made Genia an' them other ladies screech an' holler."

"Precisely. Exactly so," nodded Bradford, a smile playing about his lips. "It is all Mr. Arnsworth's fault."

Eugenia's hand flew to cover her mouth. She came near to choking on a giggle. Of all the things that this peculiar gentleman might have said, she had not been at all prepared to hear him lay blame for the entire episode on the unfortunate Mr. Arnsworth.

"Here, scoot over a bit, m'dear," Bradford urged the child, glancing for a moment at Eugenia, his eyes shimmering with laughter. "Let me see can I snag my handkerchief from my pocket, eh? There, that's got it. Now," he added, dabbing at Delight's tears and wiping her nose, "enough of this Cheltenham tragedy. I am not going to forbid you to come and visit Nod. Such a thing never entered my mind."

"It did not?"

"No, but I am thinking gravely about forbidding Mr. Arnsworth to do so."

When he had at last gotten Arnsworth and Eugenia and Delight comfortably settled into Squire Peabody's old carriage, Lord Bradford plucked Sweetpea from the dust of the drive and handed her into Delight's keeping. "And you must promise me to hold tight to this miscreant's string, Miss Chastain," he declared, taking Lord Nightingale from a very nervous Stanley and depositing him in Eugenia's lap.

"Knollsmarmer," the parrot commented, stomping about upon the muslin of her dress until he found a fair purchase on her knee and settled there.

"Yes, Knollsmarmer indeed. He has nibbled at every vegetable and piece of fruit in my kitchen, you know, Miss Chastain, so I now have a considerable investment in that bird. Do not let him fly away from you."

"No. No, I will not, my lord."

"Arrrffff!" exclaimed Stanley Blithe, tethered directly beside Mr. Stanley by one of the marquess' neckcloths tied firmly about his neck.

"No, sir, you are much too large and wiggly to ride inside the carriage with Arnsworth when he is not feeling quite the thing," Bradford responded directly to the puppy. "And Jake and Mr. Tripp will not have you up top with them, so you must wait until I can walk you home myself. Which will be in a matter of moments," he added with a laughing glance at Eugenia, "because of all the things I do not wish to hear snuffling about my house, Miss Chastain, this gudgeon is number one upon the list. Now, everyone set?" he asked, raising the steps and closing the coach door. "Off with you then, Mr. Tripp," he ordered, stepping clear of the vehicle. "And see Mr. Arnsworth gets safely inside."

"Aye, m'lor'," replied Bobby Tripp. "Git 'em all home

safe an' soundlike and then I be bringing yer coach right
back." He gave the two ancient coach horses the office to
start and in an instant the old vehicle was moving down
the drive toward the road.

Eugenia peered back out the window and was surprised
to see the marquess standing and waving at them. She
waved back with considerable enthusiasm. "He is not so
cross as he was used to be when first he came," she mused
once the carriage took the turn in the drive and the marquess
was lost to her sight.

"I thought him most considerate and thoughtful," Mr.
Arnsworth responded nasally.

"Yes, indeed, but I cannot think why."

Bradford watched the carriage until the turn and then
spun about on his heel and strolled toward the house, taking
Stanley Blithe's hastily arranged lead from Mr. Stanley and
tugging the puppy right along with him. "Now," he said to
Mr. Stanley who followed behind a step or two, "where
have you put the Butterberry sisters, Stanley?"

"Mr. Waggoner has put them in the front parlor, my lord,
and provided them with tea and cakes."

"Did you hear that, you lummox of a puppy? Tea and
cakes. I cannot believe we have any cakes left after the
foray you made into our stores."

"You know, my lord?" asked Stanley in surprise.

"Know what?"

"About—that the puppy—how he—"

"Oh, yes, know all about it. Caught hold of the little pot
boy flying by me in the corridor and he spilled the beans.
'The monsker 'as done broked away from Mr. Waggoner
an' eated ever'thin', 'is what he told me. At first I thought
he was talking about the dratted feather duster, of course,
but then I remembered this fellow and knew he must be
the one."

"The parrot did nibble on all of the vegetables and the fruit that Mrs. Hornby had set out for dinner," sighed Stanley. "Apparently, neither Mr. Waggoner nor Mrs. Hornby actually knew what a macaw might eat and so they offered it everything in which it appeared to develop an interest. Shall I take the dog, my lord?" the valet added as they entered the house.

"Take the dog?"

"Yes, my lord."

"Why, Stanley? Do you want the beast?"

"No, my lord, but the Misses Butterberry await you in the front parlor and—"

"And they have one another for chaperons," the marquess pointed out.

"Yes, of course. No one thinks the least thing of the parson's daughters coming to visit you, my lord. At least, it is not done, but I have warned the staff not to let word of it slip out or you will have their heads."

"Very good, Stanley. Nicely done. And I will have this beast beside me every moment that I remain in the parlor with the notorious Butterberry sisters. Stanley Blithe will be my personal chaperon, so even if word does slip out, we can all say how adequately and ferociously our morals were guarded, eh?"

Bradford, though he laughed a bit at his own choice of a chaperon, was perfectly serious about not being put into a compromising position with Miss Mary Butterberry. She is not a bit better than she is forced to be, he thought to himself as he approached the parlor. She has obviously made it a practice to sneak away of an evening to meet my brother beneath that old tree. Yes, and she must have kissed Peter a few times, too. She knew full well how to kiss me, that is certain. Well, I am not about to be called to the altar for allowing her to come calling upon me. I will make quite certain of that. I do not care that her sister remains with us, Stanley Blithe will be tethered at my side for the entire interview.

"Now," he said, standing as far from the Butterberry sisters as the room allowed, "what is it that I may do for you, Miss Butterberry? I have explained about the—pasture— have I not? Yes, I have. Well then, tell me why I am so privileged as to have you upon my doorstep this afternoon."

Mary Butterberry looked up at him, her flashing eyes filled with wonder. "You are so like him," she said.

"Yes, well, we are twins, Peter and I."

"Even your voices are like."

"That is generally the case with twins, Miss Butterberry."

"And you are just of a height, too," added Miss Clara Butterberry. "No wonder Mary thought that Mr. Winthrop had returned when first she caught sight of you."

"No wonder," nodded Bradford, wondering just what these two were doing in his parlor.

"We need not be overly careful of what we say, my lord," Miss Butterberry advised then. "Clara knows all."

"Clara knows all?" What the devil is there to know? Bradford mused.

"Yes, I do," replied that young woman. "I even know that Mary went to meet you last night beneath The Conqueror's Tree. It was I who returned after Mama and Papa had gone to bed and unlatched the window again so that she could get back in."

"Just so," agreed Mary Butterberry. "Clara has been a perfect saint about everything. I could never have had a moment alone with Peter without her assistance."

"I begin to think that you would have been a deal better off if you had not managed a moment alone with my brother, Miss Butterberry."

"No! Why?"

"Because he compromised you and, instead of doing the honorable thing and marrying you, he spun you some Canterbury tale about India and abandoned you to your own resources."

"He did not!" Mary exclaimed, setting down her teacup upon the table with considerable force. "He did not compromise me or abandon me! How can you think such a thing of your own brother?"

"I have not set eyes on my brother since we were eight, Miss Butterberry. I have no idea what sort of gentleman he has turned out to be, or what his thoughts and foibles regarding young ladies are, but I begin to suspect that he is not quite the thing, you know."

"You have not seen him since you were eight?"

"No. Nor have I the least idea where he is or where he has been—except, of course, that I now know that he has been in the village of Wicken."

"How dreadful!" exclaimed Miss Clara, her glorious blue eyes growing wide and soulful. "Give it to him at once, Mary. You must. I have never heard of anything so tragic as twin brothers separated and kept forever apart."

"Well, we are not exactly kept forever apart," mumbled Bradford. "I mean to say, Miss Clara, that I have been hunting for Peter for the past four years. And I will find him, too, and then we shall be together again, you see."

"Oh, Mary, you must give it to him," urged Clara. "Cannot you see? He is just the person Peter meant to have it. 'Give it to the gentleman whose shadow I am,' he said, 'if ever you should chance to meet him.' Most certainly he meant his brother."

"I expect so," admitted Miss Butterberry. "That is precisely what I thought this morning. But I have a good mind not to give it to you," she added with a scowl. "Such a thing, to doubt your own brother's honor."

"What? Give me what?"

"This," she replied, tugging a piece of vellum sealed with a wafer from her reticule, and holding it out to him.

Bradford stepped across the carpeting at once to fetch it

from her. Still holding to his neckcloth with one hand, keeping Stanley Blithe contentedly by his side, he slit the wafer with his thumbnail and shook the vellum open. In complete silence, he stood before the young ladies and read what was written upon it from beginning to end. "When did he write this?" he asked then, his eyes filled with sadness. "Were you with him, Miss Butterberry, when he wrote it? Do you know what it contains?"

Mary shook her head from side to side. "I think," she said in a very small voice, "that he wrote it long before he came to Wicken. I think it is a letter he has written many times and left at many places. He told me it was not the only missive of its kind, and it looks very old. But he would not tell me what it said. He told me I must give it to the gentleman whose shadow he was, if ever I should lay eyes upon the man. I thought he had gone mad when he said that. As if he were not a man himself—but only the shadow of someone else! I truly feared that he had lost his mind." Mary took her gaze from Bradford, whose face was growing steadily more pale, and she studied the flower pattern upon the carpeting instead.

"Peter gave it to me the night after the church money and Grandpapa's stickpin disappeared," she murmured. "He said he must leave Wicken at once because everyone thought him the thief and they would hang him as soon as look at him. He said that he would get passage to India and make his fortune and come back for me. He was so very upset that the entire village should be crying out for his blood!"

"No one ever liked Mr. Winthrop except Mary," Clara offered in way of explanation. "Everyone was forever plaguing him about one thing or another, and so, when the money was stolen, who better could they find to lay the theft upon? No one knew, after all, that he was the son of a duke. He most certainly did not look the part."

"You told her?" asked Bradford with the cock of an eyebrow.

"I told Clara that you are the son of a duke," Mary replied with some asperity. "Do you think my sister such a featherbrain as not to realize that if Peter is your twin, then he is the son of a duke as well?"

"But he claimed to be the son of a carpenter when he was here," added Clara softly. "And he did a good deal of work on the church. The pews and things, you know. Still, he was very distant in his dealings with people and they did none of them ever trust him or conceive a fondness for him—except for Mary, of course, and—and—me."

"You conceived a fondness for my brother, Miss Clara?"

"Yes, but merely as a friend. I am not in love with him. It is Mary who is in love with him, and he with Mary. I saw how happy he made Mary and it was because of that, that I came to be fond of him whether anyone else liked him or not."

Just as the sun began to set, Eugenia saw him coming across the park with Stanley Blithe frisking around his legs. He is very late, she thought for the twelfth time that hour. He did not set out just after we departed as he proposed to do. She rose from the window seat in the Gold Saloon and made her rolling way out into the corridor and down the staircase to the front entrance. "His lordship is coming at last, Jenkins," she informed the butler. "I shall just step out to meet him and relieve of him Stanley Blithe."

"I shall step out with you, miss," Jenkins replied.

"No, you need not."

"I shall be glad of a bit of fresh air, miss. I shall merely stand outside the door and breathe and nothing more."

Eugenia grinned. "Nicky has given you word that I must not be alone with a gentleman ever, has he not?"

"Yes, miss."

"Oh, what a monster of propriety he is! Very well, Jenkins. Step outside with me and breathe if you must. But I warn you that I am going to walk across the drive and into the park to meet the gentleman."

Jenkins nodded. "And I will remind you, Miss Eugenia, that my eyes will be open while I am breathing, and so you ought to advise Lord Bradford."

"Balderdash! As if the gentleman had the least interest in me. You know he does not, Jenkins. He is a marquess and I am a plain miss with one leg shorter than the other."

Eugenia watched Bradford as he walked slowly toward her. With the sun setting all pink and red and purple behind him, he seemed but a vision of a man. A sad vision of a sad man, Eugenia thought, as she crossed the drive, her gaze fastened upon him. What can have happened between the time I left him and now?

Stanley Blithe barked and lunged against the neckcloth, causing Bradford to look up from the grass at his feet. He saw Eugenia walking toward him with her oddly rolling gait. The flames of the sunset shimmered in her face and set her hair afire with reds and golds as warm and inviting as would be the summer night to come. She looked to him like an angel feathering out to meet him at the gates of heaven, and for a moment he thought to himself that perhaps he might learn to believe in heaven if such beings as Eugenia promised to be there.

"I am mad," he whispered then, and Stanley Blithe cocked a crooked ear in his direction. "The more I think of it, the more lunatic I grow, and there is no place to hide myself away. I must lose my mind in front of all the world it seems."

"Rrrrrarf!" Stanley Blithe replied and took the middle of the length of neckcloth into his teeth, tugging the marquess insistently in Eugenia's direction.

Bradford came near to tripping over his own feet as the puppy leaped and tugged and scrambled forward, and so he halted and freed Stanley Blithe from the tether. "You will not get lost now, you great beast," he murmured. "You are safely home. Go to her then. Go!"

Stanley Blithe did so with the greatest enthusiasm, dashing across the green and leaping up at Eugenia, coming very close to knocking her to the ground.

"Down, Stanley Blithe. Down, sir," she ordered, never taking her gaze from the marquess.

"So, you have the rest of your menagerie back safely, Miss Chastain," Bradford said loudly enough for his voice to cover the space between them. "Good evening to you then." He raised his hand to her in a small wave and turned about for home.

"Do not you take another step, my lord," Eugenia called back. "Wait right where you are."

Bradford turned back in her direction and saw that she was hurrying toward him. Almost running. She will take a tumble sure, he thought, and his legs struck out to meet her before his head so much as debated whether he should. "What is it, Miss Chastain?" he asked, taking her hands into his as they came together. "Has something dire happened?"

"Yes," Eugenia replied, squeezing his hands tightly. "I think something dire has most certainly happened."

"You need only tell me what I can do. I know I am not a very good neighbor, and always cross as crabs, but if there is some emergency—it is not Mr. Arnsworth? He has not taken a turn for the worse? I was certain that the drive back would do him no harm. Never mind. Only tell me what you require of me. Have you no one to ride for a physician? I shall take one of the Hall's horses then and—"

"No, no, Mr. Arnsworth is fine, my lord."

"He is? Then what? Not your little Delight? Nothing has happened to the child?"

"No, Delight is fine as well, and all the rest of us."

"But you said that something dire had happened."

"I think it has," whispered Eugenia, staring up into eyes that glittered like blue crystal. "I think something dire has happened to you, my lord. You are pale and your hands tremble even now, and your eyes, the lovely light in your eyes has frozen to something hard as ice."

"It is nothing."

"It is something."

"I am generally always as hard and cold as ice, Miss Chastain. You, I think, should know that by this time."

"No, you are not. You only wish to be, and that is not the same as being. Tell me what has happened, my lord."

"I should like to," Bradford whispered hoarsely, staring down at her and feeling his heart fill with such a dreadful ache that he thought it would explode upon the very next beat. "Every moment of silence seems to make it grow more and more painful. I should like to tell someone."

"Then let it be me," urged Eugenia softly, freeing his hands and tucking her arm into the crook of his elbow instead. "Lend me your support back to the Hall, my lord, and tell me what has overwhelmed you so along the way. We are friends, you know, and friends are bound to support each other in every way they can."

"Are we friends?" asked Bradford, his aching heart thumping oddly against his ribs. "Are you certain you wish it to be so?"

"Most certain, my lord," Eugenia replied, giving his arm a reassuring hug. "In fact, I can think of nothing I wish more."

Ten

"Bradford would not come in with you, eh?" asked Neil, meeting Eugenia on the staircase. "Most likely a good thing, m'dear. Definitely not the type of gentleman for you."

"Be quiet, Neil. You know nothing about it."

"Yes, yes I do. You are of an age to be married, m'dear, and you wish to be married, too. And Bradford is not at all a likely candidate. Foul-tempered, stubborn, stiff-rumped. What is this? Tears? Eugenia, you are not fool enough to have fallen in love with that—that—"

"No!" Eugenia exclaimed, shaking off her cousin's hand as he attempted to take her arm. "I have not fallen in love with Lord Bradford or anyone else, Neil. And I am not crying. I have merely got something in my eye. Do go away. You are as annoying as a gnat these days, always hovering about me every way I turn." And with an angry swipe at her tears, she shoved Mr. Spelling aside and hurried up the staircase as best she could.

A gnat? Hovering about her? I have been keeping strategically out of the gel's way since we came, Mr. Spelling thought in amazement. What the devil has Bradford done to turn her into a veritable harpy in a matter of ten minutes? "Jenkins," he called, continuing down the stairs. "What the deuce did Bradford want?"

Mr. Jenkins, who had given Stanley Blithe into the head footman's care and had just started off through the Great

Hall toward the kitchens, came to an abrupt halt. "I beg your pardon, Mr. Spelling?"

"I said, Jenkins, what the deuce did Lord Bradford want?"

"He merely returned Stanley Blithe to us, sir."

"And for that reason he felt compelled to stand upon our doorstep for a full ten minutes conversing with my cousin?"

"I expect he was merely being sociable, Mr. Spelling," murmured Jenkins, his eyebrows sternly indicating that he did not care to continue the discussion. He did not, in fact, care to discuss so much as what day of the week it was with this cousin of the Earl of Wickenshire. He had never liked the gentleman and after the debacle of Willowsweep, he liked the man even less.

"Sociable? Bradford? He is the most unsociable fellow ever breached. You were very near to them, Jenkins. I saw you playing chaperon, walking that hound about the drive while they spoke. Did you not hear a word of what they said?"

"Not a word, sir."

"Well, I do wish you had, Jenkins," sighed Spelling, knowing that the butler must have heard a bit of the conversation at least and pondering what he could say that would cause Jenkins to open his duffle. "I do wish you had, because the fellow has sent Miss Chastain running off in tears."

Jenkins' face remained perfectly passive. "Most unfortunate," he stated quietly. "Perhaps, sir, you would do best to discuss Miss Chastain's conversation with Miss Chastain."

"Yes, perhaps, though if I could get even the vaguest hint, Jenkins, of what was said, I would know how best to approach the thing without bringing more tears to my cousin's eyes."

"I do perfectly understand that you cannot wish to upset Miss Chastain more than she is at present, Mr. Spelling," Jenkins replied grimly. "But I cannot tell you one word that passed between them. I am one who has never been inclined, sir, to listen in on a private conversation. Now, if you will excuse me, I must be on about my duties."

Spelling nodded curtly. Liar, he thought. You have pressed your ear to every closed door in this establishment.

"Liar," Jenkins mumbled under his breath as he walked off through the hall, "if you care anything for Miss Chastain's welfare, it is only because you have discovered some way in which a benefit to her welfare will prove beneficial to yourself."

"Eugenia, you are not eating," the dowager countess observed.

"I am not very hungry, Aunt Diana."

"No, well, that is what happens when dinner is set back. One loses one's appetite. I do hope that Mr. Arnsworth will nibble at something on his tray," Lady Wickenshire added with a shake of her head. "After such a frightful day, he must have some sustenance."

"What is sustenance?" asked Delight, ceasing to hide her green beans beneath her potatoes and gazing curiously up at Lady Wickenshire.

"Another reason why children ought to eat in the nursery and not at the table," sighed Mr. Spelling. "I cannot think why Nicky could not have hired a governess."

"Because he did not could find one nice enough," Delight replied. "The only ladies who wished to be my governess were all grumpidy-grouchy ol' things."

"Delight," warned the dowager Lady Wickenshire softly.

"Well, Mr. Spelling asked. And they were."

"Yes, dearest, but you need not say so in just those words. You must just say that the applicants were unacceptable."

"The applicants was un'ceptable," repeated Delight, her light blue eyes fastened on Mr. Spelling. "An' I do not like to eat dinner all by myselfs."

"No, of course you do not," agreed Lady Wickenshire. "Eugenia? You are so very quiet."

"Yes, Aunt. I am sorry. I was thinking."

"You are worried about poor Mr. Arnsworth," deduced the dowager logically. "I have had a tray sent up to him, my dear, and he has sent down word that he is feeling a good deal more the thing. He shall be as good as new tomorrow."

" 'Cept for his nose," murmured Delight. "That will not never be as good as new. It got broked."

"A most unfortunate incident," Lady Wickenshire sighed.

"Probably all Bradford's fault," offered Mr. Spelling. "Cannot think how Gilly could have run straight into a fence rail without some assistance from Bradford."

"Lord Bradford was nowhere near Mr. Arnsworth when it happened," Eugenia said softly, pushing a piece of a partridge breast about on her plate with the tines of her fork. "Lord Bradford was running across his pasture at the time."

"Running? Across his pasture?" asked the dowager. "Well, of all things! What is wrong with that man?"

"Nothing!" exclaimed Eugenia, coming near to slamming her fork down on the dinner table. "There is nothing wrong with Lord Bradford! He is a perfectly wonderful gentleman!" Tears began to pour from her eyes on the instant and, thoroughly embarrassed by them, Eugenia rose and fled from the dining room.

"Oh, my goodness!" cried the dowager in a small, but amazed, little voice. "Whatever is the matter with Eugenia?"

"I have been attempting to discover just that for the best part of an hour," Spelling drawled, "but she will not answer the least of my questions, nor will Jenkins."

"Jenkins?"

"Indeed. Bradford and Eugenia had a quaint little tête-à-tête upon our very doorstep when he returned the wretched hound, and Eugenia has been near tears ever since."

"Stanley Blithe is not a wreck-ed hound," offered Delight with a pout.

"The word is wretched not wreck-ed," Spelling pointed out with some asperity, "and whether he is or is not is not the point. And I am not addressing you, in any case."

"Oh."

"Jenkins knows what is going on, Aunt Diana. He was walking that nuisance of a hound up and down the drive the entire time. I am certain he knows all, but I cannot pry a word out of him."

"Well, I should hope not," declared Lady Wickenshire. "Of all things, Neil, to attempt to pry information from my butler!"

Eugenia quite expected the knock which sounded on her chamber door a quarter hour later. "Come in," she called, dabbing at the remnants of her tears with a fine lawn handkerchief.

"Eugenia, are you better, my dear?" the dowager asked, going to sit beside her niece upon the plain little settee with the yellow tufts that stood before the empty hearth. "I would have come at once, darling, but I thought that you would like some time alone."

Eugenia nodded. "I am thankful for it, Aunt Diana. But I am thankful that you came as well, because I have been thinking and thinking and I cannot for the life of me think what it is that I can do to help him."

"To help whom, my dear?"

"Lord Bradford."

"Lord Bradford. Eugenia, you have not developed a tendre for Lord Bradford?"

"N-no. It has naught to do with love, Aunt."

"And yet he has caused you to cry!" The dowager count-

ess placed an arm about Eugenia's shoulders and drew her
tenderly against her, brushing stray wisps of hair from the
young woman's hot cheeks with oh so gentle fingers. "Tell
me, Eugenia, what did Lord Bradford say to make you cry?
He did not insult you?"

Eugenia shook her head slowly from side to side. "He
is so sad, Aunt Diana. If I could have done, I would have
taken him into my arms and held him and kissed him and
told him that all would be better soon. But I could not, you
know. He would never have stood for such a thing. He pretends to be so very strong and he would have the entire
world believe that his heart is made of rock and his soul
of salt, but it is not true."

"No, it is not true. I thought it might be so at one time,
but of late I come to think myself that he is not the ogre
he pretends to be."

"Not anywhere near. You ought to have seen him this
very afternoon. He was so sweet and gentle with Delight.
And funny, too. And though he was not exceedingly careful
with Mr. Arnsworth when he carried him to the house, still,
he did tend to the man, and he did not tease him very much
for running into the fence."

"That was kind of him."

"Y-yes. And he would walk Stanley Blithe home rather
than attempt to send him in the carriage with us, because
Mr. Arnsworth was in such pain, and Stanley Blithe is such
a rambunctious puppy, you know."

"But there is nothing in any of these things to make you
cry, my dear."

"N-no. Oh, Aunt Diana, he was so very sad when he
came with Stanley Blithe that I thought my heart would
break! I ought not tell you. He was afraid, I think, that I
would tell someone and so did not wish to confide in me,
but he had to do so. He had to tell someone, and I was
right there."

"Do you know, Eugenia, I am a very old woman—"

"Not so very old," protested Eugenia, her head resting securely upon Lady Wickenshire's shoulder and her smooth young hands safe within the dowager's aging, wrinkled ones.

"Old enough, Eugenia, to have kept innumerable secrets in my life. And there is one thing I have discovered about secrets. They are generally best forgotten and never referred to again. But there are some that can be so very hurtful and so very important, that you cannot ignore them. Those secrets require one to use one's head and one's heart in deciding what is best to be done to aid both the person who has confided in you and the person whom the secret undoubtedly affects."

Bradford, his dinner long ago nibbled at and abandoned, sat at the table alone, pondering over his port. He did not feel quite so overwhelmed now. It had been a severe blow, Peter's letter, and for all the time that it had taken him to walk Stanley Blithe back to Wicken Hall, he had felt the crushing weight of it pounding his soul to pulp. But then Miss Chastain had convinced him to confide in her, and ever since, he had felt a good deal more capable of dealing with the thing.

How odd that she should give me strength, he thought, sipping at the wine. A young woman. A crippled young woman. But she is not so crippled as I, limp though she always will. No, I am the crippled one, and that's a fact. I have been crippled for years and years and never so much as realized it. Well, but I will fight against it now. I must. I must do something besides bury myself in a shell of sarcasm and ennui.

And then a light of determination sparked in his eyes and he stood up from the table and went to tug the bellpull. "Fetch Mr. Stanley," he ordered the butler who appeared in answer to his summons. "I will speak with him at once. Oh, and Wagons—it is Wagons, is it not?"

"Waggoner, my lord."

"Yes, just so. I am vile with names. Waggoner, say that he must bring with him the most recent letter from my father. He will know where it is."

"Yes, my lord."

Bradford paced the carpeting most methodically for a good three minutes, then went to the sideboard, took a crystal wineglass from it, carried it back to the dinner table and sat down. He filled his own glass to the brim and filled the second glass equally as full.

"I am sorry, my lord. I came as quickly as I could, but the letter was packed away in your portmanteau and—"

"Yes, yes, never mind, Stanley. You have it?"

"Yes, my lord."

"Give it to me."

Mr. Stanley handed the letter to the marquess and stood watching as Bradford unfolded the thing and scanned the lines.

"Sit down, Stanley," the marquess said then, looking up at the valet. "I have something I wish to say to you."

"Sit down, my lord?"

"Yes, sit down. In this chair right beside me, and take this glass into your hand and drink from it."

"No, my lord. I cannot. It is not seemly."

"Balderdash! Are you my valet or are you not?"

"Yes, my lord, which is precisely why I cannot possibly—"

"Do you wish to remain my valet or go looking for other employment?" Bradford cut him off in midsentence. "Because if you do not sit down right this moment and drink with me, Stanley, you will be seeking a position in the morning."

"But, my lord."

"Please," Bradford said, his voice lowering to such an

extent that Stanley was hard-pressed to hear him. "Please, Stanley. There is something I need to tell you and I cannot—"

Though every sensible fiber in Stanley's being protested the impropriety of it, he pulled back the chair and sat. He took the wineglass into his hand and sipped the port, then set it back upon the table. His fine gray eyes filled with worry, he stared at the marquess and saw not the tall, trim gentleman dressed in the height of fashion who sat before him, but the small, unkempt, wildly passionate little boy Lord Bradford had once been.

"Just so," Bradford nodded. "I thank you for joining me, Stanley."

"I am a deal too old to be bouncing about seeking another position," murmured Stanley. It was not at all what he wished to say, but it was all that would come from between his lips.

The marquess smiled a bit. "I am glad of it. Drink some more, Stanley. Have another sip. It is not bad port."

Stanley raised the glass again, sipped, and again set it aside. "There is something that you must tell me, my lord?"

"Yes." Bradford raised his own glass, swallowed every drop of port in it, set the glass down hard upon the table. "Yes. Something." He tipped the wine bottle over his glass until the long-stemmed crystal glowed crimson again in the lamplight all the way to the top. He set the bottle aside and stared at the wine in his glass in silence for a full minute. Then he shifted his gaze to Stanley. "My mother is dead, Stanley," he said in a low, flat tone.

"Oh, my lord!"

"Dead, dead, dead; a meal for worms these four years past."

"F-four years p-past?" Mr. Stanley did not so much as think to keep the amazement out of his voice. "Four years, my lord?"

"Just so, Stanley. And my despot of a father could not be bothered to so much as mention it to me."

Mr. Stanley reached for his wineglass, drank what was left in one swallow and allowed the marquess to refill it again.

"There is nothing you have to say, eh, Stanley? Well, how could there be? What can one say about such an— oversight?"

Lady Wickenshire stood and began to pace the chamber. "Sotherland? Sotherland? There is something I ought to remember about the Duke of Sotherland."

"Other than the fact that he is an unfeeling monster?" asked Eugenia quietly.

"Yes, other than that. Your Uncle Evelyn knew him. I am sure of it, but—oh, yes."

"Oh, yes, what, Aunt?"

"He married Isabella Winthrop and she left him."

"She left him?"

"It was an enormous scandal at the time. She departed most abruptly. Fled into the wilds of Yorkshire."

"With—with—another man?"

"No, of course not. With one of her boys. I remember hearing that—she had twin boys. Sotherland forced her to leave his heir behind but she took the other with her. She was very beautiful, the Duchess of Sotherland. At least, your Uncle Evelyn told me that she was very beautiful—I do not think that I ever saw the woman. Well, regardless, we must do something for Lord Bradford. To discover that a Mama he thought alive and well has been dead for four years, and his father never said a word to him about it!"

"There is even more than that," Eugenia whispered.

"More?"

"Lord Bradford's brother wrote that he has done something so terrible, so horrendous, that he cannot ever again face Lord Bradford or any of his family. He tells Lord Bradford to forget that he ever had a twin."

"Heavens!"

"He cannot, you know."

"Cannot what?"

"Forget that he ever had a twin. He has been searching for his brother and his mother ever since he reached the age of eighteen, he says. He has searched practically everywhere and has not had a word of them until he was given this letter."

"Who gave it to him?"

"Well, that is what I cannot quite understand, but he says that it came to him through Mary Butterberry."

Mr. Stanley raised another glass and drank it down. He stood and fetched a decanter from the sideboard and filled the marquess' glass with brandy before he refilled his own. "Port is gone. Brandy is better," he said, retaking his seat.

"I ain't about to stop looking for him," muttered Bradford. "I will find him. I vow it."

"Of course you will. What a thing, to imagine himself sunk so low that even his own brother will not have him! But Lord Peter always was the most dramatic of the two of you."

"He was?"

"Indeed, my lord. A veritable William Shakespeare from the day you both was born."

"I never thought that."

"Take my word for it, my lord. And now he has written a tale for himself in which he portrays the heinous villain. He does not write what it is he did?"

"Yes. Apparently, he killed someone."

"Killed someone? Lord Peter? Who?"

"I am not quite certain. Someone named Quinn. It ain't a perfectly understandable letter, Stanley. I mean—it rambles about and does not explain much. You think I am right to go on searching for him?"

"Indeed, my lord. He must need you now more than ever."

"I think so as well, and so does Eugenia."

"Eugenia?"

"Yes, Miss Chastain."

"Miss Chastain knows about—"

"Not everything. I could not bear to tell her every detail about myself and my family, but I did confide in her a bit. I could not help myself. I was feeling so overwhelmed, Stanley, and so alone, and then she came and took my arm and urged me to speak of my sadness to her and—and—I did."

Mr. Stanley's fine gray eyes studied his marquess from head to waist, which was all he could see of him, since the rest was hidden by the dinner table.

The marquess, having had that precise stare focused upon him as a boy, squirmed litle in his seat. "What?" he asked.

"Nothing. I was merely checking for any outward signs, my lord. But apparently there are none as yet."

"Signs? Signs of what? I ain't foxed, Stanley. Just beginning, in fact."

"No, of course you are not foxed. What is it that you propose to do with that letter from His Grace, my lord? You have not conceived the idea of throwing it back in his face?"

"No, I am not so brave as that, Stanley."

"Bah, you are as brave as you can stare."

"I do not think so. What I plan to do, Stanley. I plan to visit this woman, just as the Old Squire wishes, but not merely to hand her over the bank notes he sent. My plan is to ask her just what she knows about everything—about Mama and Papa's separation, and Mama's death and what happened to Peter. And she will answer me, too. I will see that she does."

Mr. Stanley shook his head, but that particular motion made him feel a bit ill and so he ceased to do so at once. He was not accustomed to drinking. He was less accustomed to drinking port and brandy in the same sitting. But he did not mind at all becoming ill if it served to help his lordship over the very rough news of his Mama's death and his brother's determination to hide away from him. "He means to hide away from you," Stanley mumbled incoherently.

"Who?"

"Lord Peter. If he says he cannot face you, it means he has got it in his head not to let you find him even if you do keep searching. Probably has run from you time an' again already, my lord. Just so. Prob'ly has."

Bradford thought about that and nodded. "Likely, Stanley. Will need to change m'style, eh? Looking for someone who wishes to find you, too, ain't quite the same as looking for someone who wants no part of you."

"Not the same at all. Have to go about it much more careful. Sneak up on 'im."

"Just so. Sneak up on 'im." Bradford downed the rest of his brandy and poured himself another. "Drink up, Stanley. You will be a full glass behind else."

"A full glass behind," nodded the valet, feeling his stomach surging like the ocean tide. He drank down the brandy, nevertheless, and presented his glass to be filled again. "Ought not to be drinkin' bran'y out of a wineglass," he observed to himself quite loudly. "Mos' unfashionable. Needs a blandy grass."

"Yes, but we did not bother to fetch them," the marquess responded a bit dazedly. "It don't matter, Stanley. One glass is as good as another."

"Waggonleer willn't think so. Waggonleer will think we are most unciv'lized once it comes to his attention."

"Who the devil is Waggonleer?"

"Waggonleer," Stanley stated with great precision, "is the butler, my lord."

"I thought his name was Waggoner."

"Have you ever actually looked at 'im, my lord? Truly looked at him? Permanent leer, he's got. That is why I call him that—Waggonleer!" Mr. Stanley giggled. "Not to his face, of course. Wouldn't want to—to make him feel bad."

"No. Of course not. Waggonleer! Ha! And the cook, Stanley?"

"M-Mrs. Horseby," giggled Stanley. "Mrs. Hooorsebe-hehe!"

Lord Bradford, who had just taken a sip of his brandy, burst into laughter and the brandy came spraying out all over himself and the tablecloth and Mr. Stanley. He began to cough and laugh at the same time and Stanley jumped up to pound on his back. "Spit it out, my lord," he urged. "Spit it out."

"I d-did," laughed Bradford. "All o-over everything."

The liquor in Mr. Stanley's stomach sloshed about in a most unruly manner as he pounded Lord Bradford's back and giggled and pounded some more, and giggled again, but he did not give a fig. My lad has got beyond it now, he thought to himself happily. It were dire, but he has got b'yond it for a while at least. An' he will gather hisself back together in the mornin' an' it will not seem near as ter'ble. Not now that I have got him to laughing in spite of it, it willn't.

Lord Bradford, visions of the Peabodys' butler and sounds of the Peabodys' cook cavorting about in his rapidly fuddling brain, ceased to choke, but continued to laugh heartily, and threw an arm around Mr. Stanley's shoulders. "You are the bes' friend I ever had, Stanley," he confessed with amazing vigor for one who had been so low only a short time before. "The best friend I ever had, man or boy. An' I am goin' to tell you a secret, Stanley."

"Not another, my lord."

"Yes. Yes, I am. Do you know Miss Chastain? At Wicken Hall?"

"Yes, my lord. I did meet her this af'ernoon when the gen'leman broke his nose."

"So you did. So you did. Well, the secret is about Miss Chastain, Stanley, an' you must not tell no one."

"I willn't, my lord."

Bradford fell into whoops again. "She does despise that word, willn't. Says it ain't a word at all."

"Is that the secret?"

"No. No, the secret is, Stanley, the secret is, that Miss Chastain is the most beautiful woman in all of England."

Mr. Stanley nodded—mostly to himself. I knew it were the case, he thought, though I cannot see it on the outside as yet. An' it has come jus' in time, too. One more hour without someone to love an' love him an' he would have turned right into the same kind of old piffle-paced—pickle-faced—curmudgeon as 'is father.

Eleven

Mr. Arnsworth was not looking at all well. The flesh around his eyes had grown an ugly purplish color through the night, and though his nose was not as swollen under the sticking plaster as it had been, it remained red and rather large. He stared at himself in the looking glass as his valet tied his neckcloth for him into a perfect waterfall. "Are you certain that you wish to go downstairs, Mr. Arnsworth?" Bedley queried solicitously. "There is no one will hold it against you if you do not, sir."

"I am not ill, Bedley. Merely uncomfortable. And I have been abed a deal longer than I ought. It is very late."

"Merely eleven, sir. There are any number of gentlemen do not rise until eleven."

"Yes, but I am not generally one of them. Thank you, Bedley. Looks fine. You may go about stuffing things away and whatever else it is you do. I shall be out of your way in a moment." Arnsworth stared at himself in the looking glass, took his brush from the table before it and attempted to brush his lank, blond hair into something resembling a style. It would not be brushed into a style, of course, because it never would. And so, in a moment or two he gave up and set the brush aside and made his way out into the corridor, along it to the staircase and down the stairs to the first floor. He hesitated upon the first floor landing, attempting to remember in which direction lay the morning room and breakfast. Spelling had been right about one thing,

Wicker Hall was literally a pile of stones and a regular rabbits' warren of rooms and corridors and staircases.

"Mr. Arnsworth?" Eugenia's voice from off to his left caught him quite unaware.

He turned and smiled as best he could with his aching face. "Miss Chastain. I expect I am lost," he said. "I know I am on the first floor and that the morning room is also on the first floor, but that is all I know."

"Come. I will lead the way," smiled Eugenia. "You must simply remember that your chamber is in the east wing, so you have descended the east staircase and the morning room, because it catches the rising sun, is also in the east."

"Fair enough," nodded Mr. Arnsworth. "Am I too late for breakfast, do you think?"

"Not at all. Neil rarely breaks his fast before eleven. He will be there now. How are you feeling, Mr. Arnsworth?" she added as she accompanied him down the corridor, the skirt of her morning dress rustling beside him.

"Well, I have felt better, but I shall survive, I think."

"That's the ticket. Pluck to the very core," Eugenia commended him. "But then, I knew you would be."

"You did?"

"Certainly. I have gathered, since my association with him, that anyone to whom Lord Nightingale takes a fancy is generally brave and kindhearted. He has proven to be an excellent judge of character."

"I do like Lord Nightingale," Arnsworth confessed softly.

"Well, I know you do. And once you have broken your fast, you must come into the summer parlor and play with him for a time. When I left to fetch Aunt Diana's writing paper, his lordship was rolling a large wooden bead about on the floor and had Delight, Sweetpea and Stanley Blithe all following behind him in a wavering little line. Playing at following the leader, I should think. At any rate, we are all of us in the summer parlor and would welcome your presence. Do come. Here is the morning room, Mr. Arnsworth. And there is Neil, champing at the bit, it appears, to have a gentleman with whom to speak. He grows weary of all the females in this establishment." Eugenia bestowed a wide smile on Arnsworth and continued down the corridor to the point where another corridor, leading to the west wing, intersected. There she disappeared from his view. Mr. Arnsworth did not take a step into the morning room until all sight of her was lost to him.

"Watching Eugenia, eh?" asked Spelling, when Mr. Arnsworth did enter the room and strolled to the sideboard to help himself to a boiled egg, a rasher of bacon and a piece of buttered toast. "Sit down, Arnsworth. Here, let me pour you a cup of coffee. It is coffee you prefer?"

Arnsworth nodded.

"Thought I remembered that. So, how do you feel? Silly business, what? Chasing after that wretched bird and running smack into a fence. Ought to have let the bird fly, Gilly. Fly right off into the sky and lose himself. I should have done precisely that."

"Yes," Arnsworth replied, tapping the shell of his egg to open it.

"Nose hurt?"

"Yes."

"Well, I expect it will for a time."

"Yes."

"But you will not mind. Get you a deal of sympathy from all the ladies, you know."

"Yes," murmured Arnsworth, nibbling at his toast.

"A bit of sympathy never hurt a man's chances with a woman. Perhaps you ought to go out this afternoon and fall from a horse."

"Yes."

"Yes?" asked Spelling, peering intently across the table. "I was merely jesting, Arnsworth. Gilly? You are not hearing a thing I say, are you?"

"Just so," Arnsworth replied, raising a piece of bacon to

his lips, his blackened eyes focused upon a place somewhere over Spelling's left shoulder.

"Devil a bit," grinned Spelling, "you are floating about somewhere in the clouds."

"Yes."

Spelling chuckled. "Gilly," he said more loudly, leaning toward the man across the table and waving one hand before Mr. Arnsworth's eyes. "Speak to me, Gilly. Come down out of the clouds and let us have a bit of conversation here."

"W-what?"

"There, that's better. Lost in thoughts of love, were you?"

"Yes," nodded Mr. Arnsworth. "I expect I was. Sorry."

"No, do not be. I am quite certain that with a bit more time, she will be heels over head in love with you as well."

"She—she will?"

"Indeed. What is there not to love about you? You are rich, presentable, and you attempt to rescue wretched birds at the risk of your own life. I am certain she is already captivated by you. Do you like her?"

"Indeed. She is beautiful. Absolutely beautiful."

"Is she? I have always thought her rather plain, myself, but love will change the way a gentleman looks upon a lady."

"Her hair is like fresh honey from the comb and her eyes the most glorious blue, and her voice—like the voice of angels."

"Hair like honey?" Spelling gasped. "And her eyes a most glorious blue? Her hair is brown, Arnsworth. Her eyes are brown."

"No, no, not at all. How can you be so mistaken? Her hair has twists of gold among the brown and her eyes are like the bluebells in the field."

"Deuce take it, they are brown!" Spelling exclaimed. "I have known her since she began to toddle about and her eyes were brown then and they have been brown every year since."

"Oh! You are speaking of Miss Chastain!"

"Who else would I be speaking of?"

"Miss Clara," sighed Arnsworth, taking a sip of his coffee, his gaze once again leaving Spelling to stare off into the distance. "Miss Clara Butterberry."

"Parson Butterberry's daughter?" Spelling thought he might explode on the spot—just pop off into shards of himself, destroying the morning room in the process. "By gawd, Arnsworth, I have gone and brought you all the way out here to introduce you to my cousin so that you might fulfill your mama's dream and marry into a family of ancient and honorable lineage, and you have fallen in love with one of the parson's daughters?"

Lord Nightingale had been hurriedly stuffed into his cage and Stanley Blithe expelled to the stables and Sweetpea scooted down to the kitchens and Delight placed in Bobby Tripp's charge, because that very afternoon the summer parlor of Wicken Hall began to overflow with visitors and there was no room at all for pets and children.

Well, perhaps we are not overflowing precisely, thought Eugenia, but it seems as though some of us must at least trickle out of the summer parlor and into other places or no one will have room to breathe. "Perhaps we ought to take a stroll through the rose garden," she suggested to Mary and Clara Butterberry, who had come calling with their mama to discover how Mr. Arnsworth was feeling after his mishap.

"Dare we?" asked Clara, glancing over her shoulder at her mama and Lady Wickenshire, and the very elderly Lady Vermont who had brought her granddaughter, Alice, all the way from her estate at Wilderly Crossroads because word had reached her that Mr. Spelling was visiting his aunt at Wicken Hall.

"Why not?" asked Mary.

"Well, because Lady Vermont is here, and Mama will say that we are rude not to remain and converse with her."

"Poppycock," Miss Alice Daily declared. "My grandmother only came to introduce me to Mr. Spelling in the hope that I might find him charming. And there he stands across the room with Mr. Arnsworth and here I stand with all of you, when we ought to be standing about together."

"Truly? She hopes that you will find Neil charming?" asked Eugenia, amazed that anyone—even someone as old as Lady Vermont—would imagine that Neil could possibly *be* charming.

"Indeed. She is determined to marry me off to someone this year and she thinks Mr. Spelling would be just the gentleman. Grandmama is fond of money, you know, and rumor has it that Mr. Spelling is as rich as Golden Ball."

"Oh, he is," nodded Eugenia. "Neil is extremely rich and a veritable scoundrel to boot."

"Is he?" Miss Daily's charming smile widened considerably. "I am fond of scoundrels. Do let us go for a stroll in the rose garden and petition the gentlemen to join us. That will make Grandmama exceedingly happy."

"And she will tell Mama so, too," Clara replied with enthusiasm. "And so Mama will not think it rude of us at all. I shall take Mr. Arnsworth's arm and Alice, you must take Mr. Spelling's and Eugenia and Mary, you may walk along together and say whatever you please to each other without fear that the gentlemen will overhear."

Mary bestowed upon her sister the most scathing glance.

"What?" asked Clara. "What have I said? Certainly you do not wish to stroll with either of them, Mary. You have told me time and again that your heart belongs to Peter Winthrop and that you will wait for him no matter how long it takes."

"Mr. Arnsworth," Mary stated quite plainly, "is Eugenia's guest. He did not come to Wicken Hall to see you, Clara."

"Oh? Oh! Oh, I am such a goose. Of course, Eugenia,

he is your guest. You must take Mr. Arnsworth's arm, and Mary and I—but we have nothing to say to each other, Mary, that we have not said time and time again."

Eugenia studied the sisters thoughtfully. "Clara," she asked after a moment, "do you like Mr. Arnsworth?"

"Well, I do not know. I liked him for a moment, when he stared at me so bemusedly in Lord Bradford's pasture, but then he ran into the fence rail and lost his senses."

"He what?" asked Miss Daily, giggling.

"Ran into a fence, broke his nose and had to be carried, dangling over Lord Bradford's shoulder, to the house," Miss Clara elucidated, "which is why he looks the way he does this afternoon. Yesterday was the most extraordinary day."

"Yes, it was," agreed Eugenia. "A most extraordinary day." Her thoughts went immediately to Lord Bradford, her heart increased its beat in the most annoying fashion and her cheeks flushed the prettiest pink. "I do not mind a bit if you care to stroll with Mr. Arnsworth, Clara. Honestly, I do not," she managed, turning to gaze down at the rose garden through the window, hoping that none of the young ladies would take note of her blushing. "You must have an opportunity to get to know him, and he to know you," she said in almost a whisper. Was that Lord Bradford below her in the garden? No, it could not be. Yes, it was. He was below her in the rose garden with one hand shading his eyes, staring up at her as bold as you please. Eugenia felt the most scorching heat rise at the back of her neck, over her ears and up into her cheeks, which had not so much as cooled down from her first blush.

"I cannot see a thing, Delight," Bradford replied. "The afternoon sun is glinting off the windows. Are you certain?"

"Uh-huh. She has climbed right up them roses on the trellis, an' she will not come down. Can you climb up an' get her?"

Lord Bradford looked upward again and then back at Delight. "I do not think so," he replied. "The trellis is much too light and I am much too heavy, my dear. It will break beneath my weight and send Sweetpea and me both tumbling to the ground."

"Oh." Delight bit her lower lip.

"You are not going to cry, are you?" asked Bradford, beginning to nibble at his own lip.

" 'Course not. I am brave as I can stare. Nicky says so. An' I have got bottom, too."

"You have, have you?"

" 'Strordinary bottom. I am plucked to the backbone. But we have got to get her down because she does not know how to get down by herself."

Bradford knew nothing about cats, but he was almost positive that Delight was correct because, though he could not see Sweetpea, he could hear her meowing plaintively above him. "A ladder," he mused.

"Mr. Tripp is going to bring a ladder, just as soon as he has taked Nod to the stable. He said so."

"Good. That will do the trick. Ah, here he comes, Delight. Now we will be able to fetch her down."

"What on earth?" Eugenia whispered, marveling at the sudden activity going on below her.

"What?" asked Mary Butterberry, walking to the window and looking out to see for herself. "It is Lord Bradford. A ladder? What can he possibly be doing with a ladder?"

"I cannot imagine," replied Eugenia. "That is Bobby Tripp helping him, and Delight pointing. Goodness, they are setting it up against the house right beneath us."

"Setting what up against the house?" asked Clara, as she and Alice came to peer out the window as well. "A ladder? Eugenia, why is Lord Bradford climbing a ladder up to this window?"

"He *is* climbing up to this window!" Mary exclaimed softly. "You do not think that he is coming to call and this is his way of gaining entrance?" she giggled.

"Well, of course not," Eugenia responded.

"I would not be so very certain," Clara said. "Only yesterday the man sent Mary and I out to await him in a pasture."

"Yes, but that was merely a misunderstanding. He thought that you and Mary were Delight and me."

"He did? And he thought it proper to meet with you in a pasture?"

Eugenia laughed at the look upon the other young ladies' faces. "It is a very long story."

"Yes, and this is quite likely another one," nodded Mary, somewhat bemused. "Oh, dear, the ladder is wobbling!"

"Bobby Tripp has grabbed hold at the bottom," Eugenia observed. "It will not fall."

"I certainly hope not," declared Alice. "You already have one gentleman residing in your household with a broken nose. You do not need another to take up residence with a broken arm or a broken head."

"No, we certainly do not," agreed Eugenia, her gaze fastened on the marquess as he climbed to the very top rung of the ladder and stretched an arm out to his right. Whatever it is that he is about, he ought not be balancing upon a ladder and reaching about him so, she thought. And then she gasped as Lord Bradford let go the ladder with his other hand as well. "He *will* fall!" she exclaimed, nudging the other young ladies aside, unlatching the window and swinging the casements outward.

"What the devil?" Bradford gasped, startled to hear the casements rasp open above him. He came so close to plunging back to earth that he had to grab the sides of the ladder with both hands and push himself forward to keep from falling. Sweetpea, who had managed to back herself almost into his outstretched hands, absolutely wailed when he took them away.

"What are you doing?" Eugenia whispered leaning over the sill. "Get down at once, sir! You will fall and kill yourself! Great heavens, is that Sweetpea crying so?"

"Just so, Miss Chastain," Bradford replied, leaning back a bit to peer up at her. "She is stuck up here on the rose trellis. I almost had her."

"Who is Sweetpea?" asked Mary Butterberry, leaning out over the sill beside Eugenia.

"Delight's kitten," Eugenia explained. "Well, she is almost a cat, but not quite."

"Oh, the poor thing," sighed Mary. "Just listen to her. She is frightened beyond anything."

"Yes, well, I shall have her in a moment," Bradford responded, checking his balance and then loosing his grip upon the sides of the ladder and reaching to his right with both hands one more time.

"Knollsmarmer," muttered Lord Nightingale inside his cage as he recognized Lord Bradford's voice. "Yo ho ho. Knollsmarmer," and he began to pick at the latch of his cage door.

"Come here, cat," Bradford mumbled, his thumb and index finger now close enough to give a gentle tug upon Sweetpea's tail. "Back down just an inch, willn't you?"

"Oh, yes, do," urged Miss Alice Daily softly, peeking over Eugenia's shoulder. "Go to the nice gentleman, kitten."

"Mrrrrrrph," Sweetpea replied to them both, no longer wailing, but studying over her shoulder how near she was to Lord Bradford's hands. With a shake of one back foot and then the other, and a waggle of her rear end, she searched for footing amongst the climbing rose vines and then backed as neatly as you please into Lord Bradford's grasp.

"Got her," he said, relieved, and hurriedly tucked the cat against his chest with one arm. "Safe and sound now, Miss

Chastain," he added, looking up and giving Eugenia the most victorious grin. "Nothing to it."

And that was precisely when all the young ladies except Eugenia began to scream as Lord Nightingale, who had known precisely how to open his cage door for years on end, flapped and fluttered his way through their little gathering, sailed out the window, knocked the marquess' hat from his head, set Sweetpea to swatting at him from the safety of Bradford's arm and sent Lord Bradford and the ladder tipping awkwardly to one side, thoroughly surprising Bobby Tripp who let go the thing for an instant, but caught it up again and tugged against the marquess' weight. "Move back to yer lef'," he cried up at Bradford. "I be goin' ta lose ye! Move back to yer lef'!"

Delight put both hands over her mouth as she watched the marquess attempt to regain his balance, which he did without ever once thinking to let Sweetpea go, and she burst into a round of giggles as Nightingale landed on Bradford's shoulder and cried, "Knollsmarmer! Mrrrrrw! Rarrrffff!" all the way down the ladder.

"Here you go, my dear," Bradford said, setting the cat securely into her arms. "Do not let her climb up there again will you? You are laughing at me, you little minx. Did you enjoy the entertainment so very much?"

"You were very funny!" giggled Delight. "An' Lord Nightingale was too!"

"Anything to please, my lady," grinned Bradford, bowing neatly before her as Nightingale skittered about for a better hold. "I am always at your service."

Above them, a cheer went up from the young ladies gathered at the window, and Bradford turned and bowed to them as well. Now why did I do that? he wondered as he straightened. I have never done such a totally silly thing in all my whole life.

"What the deuce is going on?" asked Spelling, sauntering across the room to where the ladies stood and staring down into the garden. "Bradford? What the deuce is Bradford doing in the rose garden?"

Mr. Arnsworth, who had come to investigate as well, stared down at the gentleman with the parrot on his shoulder and muttered under his breath.

"What did you say, Mr. Arnsworth?" asked Clara.

"I said, he is the most unusual gentleman I have met."

"Who is unusual?" asked Lady Wickenshire from the sofa.

"Children, whatever is going on over there?" queried Mrs. Butterberry with a lift of an eyebrow. "You have thoroughly disrupted our conversation, you know."

"Lord Bradford is in the rose garden with that wretched parrot perched on his shoulder," reported Spelling.

"Lord Bradford?" Lady Vermont's glance fell immediately upon Spelling. "The Marquess of Bradford?"

"Yes, my lady," Spelling replied. "Exactly so."

"Here? He is here?"

"In our rose garden apparently," Lady Wickenshire nodded. "Do you know the gentleman, Fiona?"

"No, no, we have never met," Lady Vermont murmured, her hands clasping and unclasping in her lap. "He is Sotherland's heir. The eldest of Sotherland's twins."

"Just so. There is nothing in him to set you all a-twitter, Fiona. I assure you, he is not so spoiled and crotchety as Sotherland was at his age."

"The Marquess of Bradford?" asked Mrs. Butterberry. "Is he the gentleman who rented Squire Peabody's house for the summer?"

"Indeed," nodded Lady Wickenshire. "I did think him a spoiled dunderhead at first, Fiona," she added, studying Lady Vermont thoughtfully. "But he has since redeemed himself."

"Yes, no, yes," replied Lady Vermont, her hands fluttering to the reticule which lay at her feet, then to the bodice of her gown, then back to her lap. "He is not coming inside, is he?"

"I cannot guess. Eugenia? Come to me for a moment."

Eugenia left the congregation at the window and made her way across the carpeting to her aunt's side. "Lord Nightingale is safe, Aunt Diana. He is perched securely on Lord Bradford's shoulder, nipping at his collar. I doubt he will fly off. He is most fond of Lord Bradford."

"Yes, so I trust. He does not seem to fly off at all unless Lord Bradford is in the vicinity. Does his lordship intend to come inside, Eugenia?"

"I expect so, Aunt Diana. I expect he has come to see how Mr. Arnsworth does."

"Oh, my goodness," murmured Lady Vermont.

"Do you not wish to make the gentleman's acquaintance, my lady?" asked Mrs. Butterberry solicitously.

"No. Yes. No. I have never thought of it. Lord Bradford. Who would have thought to meet with the duke's son in such a tiny little place as Wicken? No, I do not think I wish to make his acquaintance. Not at this very moment. Perhaps—perhaps if Alice were not here— Heavens, I cannot think what to do. Can you not make him go away, Diana? Can you not send your butler to him to say that Mr. Arnsworth does well and send him off? No, of course you cannot. That would prove to be extremely rude, would it not? Oh, if only Alice were not here."

Lady Wickenshire and Eugenia and Mrs. Butterberry all glanced at each other with wonder. "I know," Eugenia proposed. "I shall go down and give Lord Nightingale into Jenkins' keeping and then take Lord Bradford for a stroll through the rose garden."

"I thought he is already in the garden," replied Lady Wickenshire. "Will he wish to stroll through it again?"

"Well," Eugenia grinned, "he was not exactly strolling through it, Aunt Diana. Apparently Sweetpea climbed the trellis and Delight pleaded with Lord Bradford to rescue her."

"Oh, what a kind gentleman!" exclaimed Mrs. Butterberry.

"Well, he may wish to stroll with you then and see the roses," Lady Wickenshire concurred. "Very well, do as you suggest. But, my dear," she added as Eugenia made her way toward the door, "do take someone with you. Mr. Arnsworth and—and—"

"Me!" exclaimed Miss Clara Butterberry, who had steadily made her way closer and closer to the conversation until she could overhear it. She cried out so eagerly that she totally embarrassed her poor mama. "May I go, Mama? Please?"

"Very well," Mrs. Butterberry acquiesced. "But you must mind your manners, Clara, and not be tugging Mr. Arnsworth every which way to look at this and look at that."

Eugenia made her way to Mr. Arnsworth, drew him aside from the others and whispered in his ear. He nodded enthusiastically. Then she drew Mr. Spelling aside, said a few words to him, and he nodded as well. "Though I do not see," he whispered back, "why we do not all just go for a stroll in the garden."

"I do not know," Eugenia responded. "There is something very odd in it, Neil, but Lady Vermont is most determined that Lord Bradford should not meet Miss Daily. So you must discover some way to entertain Miss Daily and Mary without letting on where Mr. Arnsworth and Clara and I have gone."

Why should not Miss Daily meet Bradford? Neil wondered as he turned back to the young ladies beside the window. I have heard innumerable tales about Bradford's ill temper, but not one word about his being any threat to young women. No. Ridiculous. The man detests the entire sex. He is most likely down there now ringing a peal over Delight for being such a ninnyhammer as to let that dratted cat escape her. Still, there must be some reason. Some very private reason, no doubt. "I have just had the most amusing idea," he said then, taking Miss Daily's hand and placing it on his arm. "Arnsworth and Eugenia and Miss Clara have gone off upon an errand for Lady Wickenshire, and we are left to our own resources, you and I, Miss Daily, and Mary, and I was just thinking. Have you ever seen the pouting room?"

"The pouting room?" Mary's sea-changeable eyes lit with laughter. "Do not say that Nicky has restored the place?"

"Better than that," smiled Spelling, offering her his other arm. "Nicky has improved upon it immensely—in memory of his papa, you know. Come, my dears, and I will escort you to it. It will be the very highlight of your day."

Twelve

Each step of the way from the west wing to the north-ernmost rear of Wicken Hall, down the stairs and up the stairs and down the stairs and back up them again, Mr. Spelling pondered the significance of it. Lady Vermont did not wish Miss Alice Daily and the Marquess of Bradford to meet one another. Now why was that? What possible harm could come from the sharp-tongued marquess making the gentle Miss Daily's acquaintance?

Should think the old dowager would want them to meet, he mused, glancing down at the young lady to his right. Lady Vermont is out to make a match for the gel after all. Why not Bradford? He will be a duke one day. And he ain't poor by any means. Does not make a bit of sense to hide the gel away from him. She is a charmer, he thought then, noticing, not for the first time, how very interesting the young woman actually was. With her dark hair and blue eyes, she reminded him greatly of someone, and she was quite likely one young woman to whom Bradford would be attracted. Unless they had already met and— "I say, Miss Daily," Spelling asked, as he paused before a closed door, his hand upon the latch, "have you ever had the privilege of making Lord Bradford's acquaintance?"

"Lord Bradford?"

"Yes, the gentleman who rescued the cat. Do you know him?"

"No, I do not think so. I did not get a very good look at him, but I do not recall a Lord Bradford."

"Oh."

"Likely you will meet him," offered Miss Butterberry, as she relinquished her grip on Spelling's arm. "He intends to remain in Wicken the entire summer, you know, and there will be any number of entertainments around the countryside to which you will both be invited. And of course, Papa will talk him into attending the Twilight Ball."

"I do hope so," sighed Miss Daily, gazing up at Mr. Spelling out of the corner of her eye. "Do you remain for the summer as well, Mr. Spelling?"

"I, ah, I have not as yet decided," Neil replied. By gawd but when she glanced at him in that way, it made him want to grab the gel up and kiss her. "I expect I shall s-stay a while yet. Yes, I ex-expect I shall. At least until the ball." Now why the devil has my collar grown so tight? Spelling wondered, running his index finger between the offending article and his neck. It is like to choke me to death. And it grows horrendously warm all of a sudden. "Now, ladies, this is it."

"Do cease to be intriguing, Neil," grinned Miss Butterberry, tugging at his sleeve, "and open the door. Miss Daily and I wish to *see* the pouting room, not simply stand outside the door to it. I cannot imagine why Nicky did not make it into something more acceptable, like a billiards room."

"Why is it called a pouting room?" asked Miss Daily.

"Because it is the room in which Nicky's father always came to pout," Miss Butterberry provided with a giggle.

"Came to pout?"

"Precisely," nodded Neil. "Uncle Evelyn did a good deal of pouting in his day. Came and sat and pouted for hours on end."

"Do you not mean that he pondered?" Miss Daily asked.

"No. Pouted!" exclaimed Miss Butterberry and Mr. Spelling together and then they both laughed.

"We ought not to laugh, though," Miss Butterberry managed on a lingering giggle. "It was not very funny for Nicky or Lady Wickenshire at the time."

"No, I expect not," Spelling agreed. "Do you remember, Mary, when we were children and my papa rode all the way to the parsonage to beg your papa to come and speak to Uncle Evelyn, because he took up residence in this room for an entire week and would not come out?"

"I do," nodded Miss Butterberry. "Papa brought me with him, and you and I and Nicky stood right here with our ears against the door, hoping to hear what went forward."

"Yes, and it was a terrible row."

"He was the most foul-tempered gentleman, Nicky's papa."

"Well, but that was because he could never come about. Every thing he did went wrong."

"Everything he did *was* wrong."

"No, do not say so."

"He could not so much as open his mouth without a wager falling out, and you know it, too, Neil."

"Yes, but some of them were fairly good wagers."

"Pooh! I never once heard of a wager that the man actually won. I doubt there was one.

"At any rate," Spelling said, turning his attention from Miss Butterberry to Miss Daily, "whenever Uncle Evelyn came home from London to escape the duns, he would eventually end up in this room, pouting over his ill luck and his foul treatment at the hands of innumerable tradesmen and the cent-percenters, so Nicky named it the pouting room." Neil lifted the latch, pushed the door inward and stood aside so that the young ladies might enter before him.

"Oh, my goodness," breathed Mary, looking about her, her eyes wide with wonder. "Nicky ought not to have done this."

"Yes, he ought," Neil said. "It is precisely what he ought to have done. If I had been Nicky and my papa had wagered away everything that ought to have been mine, I should have done exactly the same."

Miss Daily looked from one to the other of them and then began to walk about the room and read the walls. "They are all—all—"

"Vowels, duns, notices from the papers about his remarkable losses," Neil explained. "There is even a page that Nicky ripped right out of the Betting Book at White's. He truly ought not to have done that. Walked right in, called for the book, turned to the page and tore it right out in front of everyone. They have not let him back into White's since. Yes, here it is," he said, strolling across to stand beside Miss Daily and pointing out to her a page from a large book on which were listed the terms of a number of wagers.

"But which was—oh, here! Lord Wickenshire proposes that the ravens at the Tower will caw no less than thirty-four times before Lord Bellingham can eat one meat pie. Lord Bellingham says that they will not. On the outcome both gentlemen wager the sum of five hundred pounds," Miss Daily read aloud. "Well, of all the stupid things. And to wager five hundred pounds upon it! The man must have been mad."

"Yes, well, but Uncle Evelyn was desperate by that time. He had lost everything and all the entailed properties were falling to ruin. I expect he thought he might use the monies he won on that bet to stake himself in a game of whist and recover a bit. It was his last bet, however. He fell down the staircase at Willowsweep two days after he lost it and broke his neck."

"I do remember something about that particular wager," murmured Mary Butterberry, staring at the newsprint. "I remember that when his papa died, Nicky wished to bury thirty-four ravens in the casket with him. Papa was thoroughly appalled, but Nicky was adamant. He took his long gun in hand and went out and shot them one by one and brought them right into the church to give to Papa. I was very young at the time, but I remember it as though it were yesterday. Papa had such a time to convince him not to put those birds in that casket. They argued over it for hours. And Nicky cried."

"He did? Nicky?" asked Spelling, amazed.

"Well, he was merely thirteen at the time."

"Then you, my dear, were barely in leading strings."

"I know. But still, I remember. Is that not the most peculiar thing? Neil, can that be the legendary pouting chair?" she added, pointing to a padded red-velvet armchair made from deer antlers. "But it looks a good deal more intimidating than it was used to do."

"Because Nicky had the antlers turned around to point directly at the person who sits in it," grinned Spelling. "Take your life in your hands to sit in that chair now. Likely never get out of it alive. And that table came directly from Howard and Gibbs in London. They were the cent-percenters with whom Uncle Evelyn dealt, Miss Daily. See how scarred it is? Nicky says the scars are from his papa's nails biting into the wood with every note he signed. He went in and demanded to purchase it just last February. I had the tale from Bing."

"I do not remember this carpet," observed Miss Butterberry. "Oh, my goodness, he did not!"

Spelling nodded gleefully. "He always said he would, and deuce take it, he finally did."

"Did what?" asked Miss Daily, noticing the carpeting on which she stood for the very first time. "Why it is not carpeting at all!"

"No," laughed Spelling, "it is a great many horse blankets sewn together and stretched out and nailed into the floor."

"I cannot believe he did it," giggled Miss Butterberry. "Is there one from every horse?"

"Aunt Diana says there is—from every horse on which

Uncle Evelyn lost money. Got a list of them from Tatt's, Nicky did."

Spelling noted that Miss Daily's eyes were unaccountably filling with unshed tears. "What is it, Miss Daily?" he asked solicitously. "Is something wrong?"

"I do not see how either of you can find the least thing amusing about this room," she replied with a tiny sob. "It is the saddest thing I have ever seen. Only think all that the gentleman's family has suffered because of these— these—horrid things. I would never marry a gambler."

"Never?" asked Spelling.

"Never. Any lips that whisper wagers will never whisper sonnets in my ear," the young lady declared emphatically.

"Well, but Miss Daily," Spelling replied with the cock of an eyebrow, "then you do never intend to be courted at all."

Mr. Arnsworth trailed along the cobbled path through the roses with the beautiful Miss Clara Butterberry upon his arm and could think of not the first thing to say. Ahead of them, Miss Chastain and Lord Bradford were deep in conversation, but Mr. Arnsworth's mind was a complete muddle.

"You are from London, Mr. Arnsworth?" asked Clara softly.

"No, yes, no. That is, I c-came from London with Spelling, you know, but my h-home is in B-Bath actually."

"I have never been to Bath."

Mr. Arnsworth nodded. Say something, you fool, he told himself silently, but no further conversation occurred to him. She had the most beautiful eyes and the most beautiful hair and the most beautiful smile. Damnation, he thought, I do know other words besides beautiful. I know lots of other words, only I cannot think of a one of them at the moment.

Clara held his arm and smiled the most beguiling smile. "You are very quiet, Mr. Arnsworth. Are you thinking?"

"Yes."

"Of what?"

"I—I—of how b-beautiful—the roses are."

"Indeed, they are quite grand."

Grand! thought Arnsworth. Grand is a word! Her eyes are beautiful and her hair is grand! No, that will not do at all. She will think me addlepated.

"Only look there at that perfect red blossom about to open," murmured Miss Clara, drawing him to the side of the path and caressing the sweet velvet of the flower's slowly unfurling petals with one long, narrow finger.

Mr. Arnsworth felt his Adam's apple abruptly block the opening to his throat and gulped.

"Is it not amazing, Mr. Arnsworth, that such sweet, enticing scent and such glorious, seductive beauty are produced on such viciously thorned bushes as these?"

"A-amazing," echoed Mr. Arnsworth, fishing madly in his pocket for his handkerchief, tugging it out and mopping at his brow. Amazing is a word, his mind muttered in a whirl. And sweet and enticing and glorious and seductive and—and—vicious!

"A penny for your thoughts," said Miss Clara as they paused before the single blossom. "A penny for your thoughts," she repeated, clinging more tightly to his arm and standing on her toes so that she might whisper directly into his ear. "Or are they very secret thoughts, Mr. Arnsworth?"

"I, ah," he whispered back, hoarsely, as his neck prepared to melt into his shoulders and his collar to swallow his chin. He cleared his throat and began again, ignoring the odd rearrangement of his anatomy that he felt was coming. "Miss Clara, I—you—you are like this blossom! Your eyes are sweet and your hair is enticing and your lips are glorious."

"Mr. Arnsworth!"

"Oh, I ought not. I did not intend to say—that is, I ought not to have spoken in so bold a manner. I am—I am—be-fuddled by you, Miss Clara. I have b-been be-f-fuddled by you since first I saw you in B-Bradford's pasture."

Clara blushed most becomingly and she gazed down at the ground, then up at him from beneath dark, curling lashes. "You are a proper flirt, Mr. Arnsworth. And un-doubtedly a regular rascal with the ladies."

"M-me?"

"Yes, sir. You. Such a way with words you have. I am almost overcome to be compared so to such a wild and beautiful flower."

Mr. Arnsworth's shoulders broadened on the instant and his chest swelled and his chin rose higher than it had ever done. He tucked his handkerchief hurriedly back into his pocket and then tucked Miss Clara's hand more securely within the crook of his arm. "Well," he declared most cou-rageously. "Well, you *are* a wild and beautiful flower. In-deed, you are. Any man who does not see that must be blind, Miss Clara."

"And so, I hope that you will understand and find it in your heart to forgive me," finished Eugenia, staring up into Bradford's startled blue eyes. "You do not understand," she sighed when he did naught but stare down at her for what seemed an eternity. "You will never forgive me."

Bradford opened his mouth to speak, closed it again, cleared his throat. He pushed his hat farther back on his head, setting a number of dark curls free to cavort across his brow. He swiped at them with the back of his hand. And all the while he stared down into Eugenia's upturned and very troubled face.

"I see I was m-mistaken," whispered Eugenia, her eyes filling with sorrow. "I have overstepped the bounds of friendship, then. And I did so wish to be your very good friend—t-to be of some h-help to you."

Lord Nightingale shuffled about on Bradford's shoulder, rubbed his head against Bradford's jaw and muttered, "Tempest fugit. Yo ho ho. Knollsmarmer."

"Tempus," whispered Bradford in a low, soft voice drawn from the very pit of his stomach. "Tempus fugit, Nightingale. And—and you are quite right. Time does fly. Though we grasp and clutch at it in every way we know in order to hold onto a moment of it here and there, it is always gone before we can do so. Miss Chastain, I—there is nothing to forgive. Nothing."

"Your eyes say otherwise, my lord."

"No. No, they do not. Or if they do, they lie. It is merely that I am—amazed. I have not been amazed by anything since I was a mere babe. I thought never to be amazed by anyone or anything ever again. But now you have done this thing, Miss Chastain. Something that no one of my acquaintance—except Stanley, if he could—would ever think to do. Stanley is my valet, you know."

"Yes, we met when Mr. Arnsworth broke his nose," offered Eugenia and thought it a perfectly mindless thing to have said.

"Just so. What I mean to say, Miss Chastain," the marquess whispered hoarsely, "is that no one has ever w-wished to h-help me before, except Stanley. Not truly. Not without g-gaining something in return."

"Oh, but that cannot be. Surely you have any number of friends who—"

"No. I am too ill-tempered and too sharp-tongued to be at all likeable. I am not the sort of person who does have friends."

"Balderdash," replied Eugenia. "You have a friend in me, if you but desire it. Yes, and in Aunt Diana as well. And in my Cousin Nicky. He will be pleased to call you his friend, I think. I know he will be pleased to help you. And Delight.

Delight is your friend and will remain so, whether you wish her to be or not. Children are very stubborn about such things, you know. Once they are your friend, it is near to impossible to drive them away. Do you understand, my lord, why I shared your words with my Aunt Diana? Can you forgive me that?"

"You saw a way to help me and did so. There is not the least thing in that that requires forgiveness. I am grateful rather. But do you truly think that your cousin will know?"

"I cannot say," Eugenia replied, taking his arm with both hands and urging him to stroll onward along the cobbled walk. "But Wicken Hall is Nicky's main residence and unless your brother was here at some time when Nicky was forced to be away, it is likely that the two of them will have met once or twice. Perhaps at church, my lord. At any rate, if they have, Nicky may be able to tell us something useful about Lord Peter. And Aunt Diana is certain that Nicky and Sera will not mind to ask after him as they travel through Scotland. I know you did that, looked for him in Scotland, but he may have returned there. That is why when she offered to write to Nicky and Sera in Edinburgh, I thought it a good idea. And she wrote to Uncle Ezra as well."

"Uncle Ezra?"

"Yes. Well, he is Nicky's uncle, actually, just as Neil is his cousin. They are from his mama's side of the family and Papa and I from his papa's. But I have always thought of us as simply one big family, you know. At any rate, Uncle Ezra knows everything that can be known about the shipping industry. If your brother *has* gone to India, and if he has used either his real name or the name Peter Winthrop to do so, then Uncle Ezra will be able to discover on which ship he sailed and when."

"Even if Peter signed on as a—deck hand—or something like?"

"Indeed. And," Eugenia whispered, tugging him to a stop and glancing back over her shoulder to discover if Mr.

Arnsworth and Clara might be close enough to hear. "And if he has joined with the freebooters, Uncle Ezra can discover that as well."

"Smugglers? You think my brother would become a smuggler?"

"Yes," nodded Eugenia. "His letter to you drew a portrait of a very desperate gentleman. And desperate gentlemen do desperate things, even join in with the dark-of-the-moon lads."

"And your Uncle Ezra would know?" Bradford's eyebrows rose to a considerable height. "He could discover if Peter were—"

"We are friends, my lord? You have quite decided?"

"Yes. Though I will require a deal of practice at being a friend, Miss Chastain."

"Well, then, I shall give you this to practice upon. It is a most lowering family secret and I share it only to give you confidence in Uncle Ezra's abilities. My Uncle Ezra was, is, has been involved in the *trade* for any number of years and knows all of the captains and all of the ships by name, even down to the tiniest little dinghy. If he approaches them and asks after Peter Winthrop, or Peter Finlay, they will tell him all they know."

"Your Uncle Ezra is a smuggler?" asked Bradford in something approaching awe. "Miss Chastain, I should never have thought that you—that your family—"

I should not have told him, Eugenia thought in dismay. It is a deal too much for him. He is going to have palpitations of the heart right here and now. He will not wish to have anything more to do with any of us. How could I be such a fool as to think that the son of a duke would not find Uncle Ezra's association with smugglers appalling?

"Well, by gawd!" exclaimed Bradford softly. "I am sorry, Miss Chastain, for my language, but—by gawd! I wish I had come to know you and your family years ago. I truly do. To have an uncle in the *trade!* And to trust me with the

knowledge! And to offer me even *his services* in locating
Peter! You are more than a friend, Miss Chastain. You are
an angel sent to me by God!" And so saying, the Marquess
of Bradford leaned down and kissed the very tip of
Eugenia's nose. And then he kissed her cheek. And then his
lips came slowly toward her own. And then Mr. Arnsworth
coughed and Clara Butterberry giggled, and Lord Bradford
pulled back without actually kissing Eugenia's lips at all.

"So sorry. Did n-not intend to c-cough," stuttered Mr.
Arnsworth, his cheeks flaming. "I mean to say, it was not
a signal or—or anything. I just—something caught in my
throat."

"Quite all right, Arnsworth," Bradford sighed. "Saved
me from losing all perspective, I expect. I do apologize,
Miss Chastain for having—having—"

"Almost crossed the boundary," provided Clara suc-
cinctly. "And it is a very good thing that you did not, my
lord, for then Mr. Arnsworth and I should have been obliged
to tell Lady Wickenshire that you took advantage of
Eugenia in the rose garden, and you would certainly have
been obliged to marry the girl."

"Clara!" Eugenia exclaimed, her cheeks quite as red as
Mr. Arnsworth's. "Do not you say such things! You will
have Lord Bradford running for the hills when all he meant
to do was thank me for something as any gentleman would
thank a sister."

"Oh?"

"Do not you raise your eyebrows so, Clara Butterberry!
I know that you have always been the most dreadful tease
and that you are teasing now, but Lord Bradford does not
know any such thing and is likely frightened senseless!"

"I am not," protested Lord Bradford. "I am not frightened in the least. If I were to be married, I should think
a friend who is as dear to me as a sister would be just
the sort of person to be married to, would not you, Miss
Chastain?"

Miss Clara Butterberry laughed the most wonderful laugh, filled with the fluttering of faeries' wings and the chiming of tiny bluebells in the meadow, and Mr. Arnsworth thought that his heart would cease to beat at the sweet sound of it. Then she took both Mr. Arnsworth's hands into her own and, standing upon her tiptoes, kissed him full upon the lips. "So," she said. "Now, Lord Bradford, you must do just the same to Eugenia and then we shall all be obliged to hold our tongues when we return to the summer parlor."

Bradford chuckled. Eugenia had never actually heard him chuckle before and she found it to be the most comfortable sound. "You are a minx, Miss Clara. Best watch yourself, Arnsworth, or she will have you at her feet in the blink of an eye." And then, to Eugenia's utter astonishment, the marquess took both her hands into his own, leaned down and kissed her full on the lips as well. "There," he said, as he straightened. "Our bargain of silence is sealed. You are not angry with me, Eugenia?" he added, a scowl rising to his face. "I did not think to ask if—"

"N-no," murmured Eugenia in the oddest tone. "N-no, not at all. I—I merely think it would be best if we returned to the house now. I am not accustomed to—"

"Kissing," supplied Clara Butterberry, spinning about and strolling toward the garden gate, tugging Mr. Arnsworth with her.

"Is she actually a parson's daughter?" Bradford asked as he and Eugenia fell into step behind them. His thoughts flew immediately to Miss Mary Butterberry, who had kissed him so capably beneath the Conqueror's Tree. "What sort of parson is the Reverend Mr. Butterberry, Miss Chastain, to raise such—such—forward—young ladies?"

"A desperate one, I should think," giggled Eugenia. "The gentleman has six daughters and only enough money put by for two dowries, if Mrs. Butterberry is to be believed."

"Heythere—mister," Nightingale sang out loudly from Bradford's shoulder. "I saw—Hiiiiram—kissyersister."

"Oh, you naughty bird," Eugenia scolded. "Do not you sing that song once you are inside. Mrs. Butterberry and Lady Vermont will be thoroughly scandalized. What? What did I say?" she asked then as Lord Bradford came to an abrupt halt.

"Lady Vermont is inside?"

"Oh! I ought not to have said—" Eugenia's hand went to her mouth, then fluttered to play with the skirt of her dress.

"Lady Vermont is inside?" Bradford asked again.

"Yes but—do you know Lady Vermont?"

"No. I have not had that distinct pleasure."

"Well, she is, ah, very old and—and—boring."

"Is she?"

"Indeed. You will not wish to make her acquaintance, I am certain of it, my lord. She will try your patience no end."

"I see."

"What do you see?"

"That Lady Vermont has asked you to keep me from her."

"No. She only wished to meet you at another time when—"

"When what, Miss Chastain?"

"Well, when she did not have her granddaughter with her, though I cannot think why that should be, because Miss Daily seems a very nice sort of young lady."

"Miss Daily? Her granddaughter?" Bradford's brow wrinkled, his eyes began to squint the least bit and his eyebrows seemed to crawl slowly toward one another.

Something fluttered in Eugenia's stomach and tickled at the back of her throat as she watched.

"She has a granddaughter?" Bradford queried. "How can she have a granddaughter? Are you certain it is Lady Vermont?"

"Quite," replied Eugenia.

"Knollsmarmer," Nightingale muttered in Bradford's ear and began to peck at the marquess' collar.

"Yes, Knollsmarmer to you too, you villain," Bradford replied. "And a yo ho ho as well. I do believe that I will escort you all the way to your summer parlor, Miss Chastain."

"No, you need not."

"But I must. I feel it my duty to return you to your aunt. And it is my duty to return Lord Nightingale as well. I was the one drew him out the window after all. Yes, I cannot but return the both of you safely into Lady Wickenshire's care."

"But why?" asked Eugenia as Lord Bradford led her toward the garden gate. "She is an old lady and the very thought of you meeting her granddaughter sent her into the twitters. You will likely give her palpitations of the heart, my lord, do you go strolling into the room."

Bradford ceased to walk again and, placing one hand upon each of Eugenia's shoulders, turned her to face him directly. "Are we friends, Eugenia, as you said?"

"Indeed we are."

"And with all you and your aunt have done to help me, would you not help me in one more way?"

"Well, of course, but—"

"Hush, Eugenia. I wish to go inside and make my bow to Lady Vermont. I feel that I must. And if you will allow me the space of a moment or so to set straight in my mind the precise words to use, I shall tell you why I feel that I must. But—but—if I tell you and you still think I ought not go inside, I will give Lord Nightingale into your butler's hands and take myself off home. Only listen to me and decide."

Thirteen

Bradford deposited Lord Nightingale atop his cage, strolled across the room and, ignoring completely the dowager's scowl, he bowed before all three of the elderly ladies. "A pleasure to make your acquaintance, Mrs. Butterberry," he drawled. "And a pleasure to make yours at last, Lady Vermont. My father has spoken of you often. He has, in fact, charged me to pay a visit to Wilderly Crossroads as soon as may be convenient, to give a certain something into your hands."

"What?" asked Lady Vermont. "I cannot think what you mean. What would your father have to send me?" He would never send it by your hand, Lady Vermont thought, trembling inside, though outwardly she did not dither in the least. Why would he do such a very cruel thing? How *could* he do such a thing to his own son?

Bradford studied the lady, his cool blue eyes taking in the black ruffled cap that covered most of her silver hair, the very fashionable afternoon dress that nonetheless seemed most unfashionable because of the age of its wearer, and the ancient hands encased in black lace gloves that fidgeted in Lady Vermont's lap. Though he gave no outward sign of it, the sight of Lady Vermont was throwing Bradford's soul into raging turmoil. She must be in her seventies, he thought, appalled. Her seventies! Have I been mistaken for all these years? And yet, this *is* the woman. Lady Vermont of Wilderly Crossroads. I am not mistaken in that.

And a thousand pounds in bank notes resides in my jewelry box at Peabody House this very moment along with the letter instructing me to deliver them into her hands. But no, he thought then, with a slight shake of his head, even the Old Squire would not have taken this particular lady to be his mistress. Could not have done so. She is twenty years his senior and would not have had him, I think, even if she were not. By gawd, what is going on? First Mama, and then Peter, and now this? Is there anything at all that I may depend on to be as I assumed it to be? Bradford smiled rather shakily and commented on the delightfulness of Lady Wickenshire's rose garden. He felt rather than saw someone come up to stand beside him and glanced over to discover Eugenia supportively at his side.

"Lord Bradford cannot stay for tea," Eugenia said, "but he did so wish to meet you, Lady Vermont and Mrs. Butterberry."

"Just so," nodded Bradford. "And to tell you, my lady," he added, his glance falling on Lady Wickenshire, "how grateful I am that you have chosen to take up my cause."

Lady Wickenshire blinked in wonder at this response to her meddling in the gentleman's business without first having asked his permission. "You are most welcome, my lord," she replied, her cheeks flushing the tiniest bit. "I shall make you aware of the news I receive from all quarters."

"Thank you, madam. I must be going," he said then, his hands sweating profusely. "I do hope, Mrs. Butterberry, that we will have cause to meet again. And, Lady Vermont, I shall come to you at Wilderly Crossroad soon with a package from my father." He bowed from the waist, gave Eugenia's hand a surreptitious squeeze, and strolled toward the doorway.

"I shall just accompany Lord Bradford to the front door, and return at once, Aunt Diana," Eugenia said, giving all of the ladies a quick smile of her own and then hurrying after him.

"What a very cordial gentleman," remarked Mrs. Butterberry, watching as Bradford and Eugenia stepped out of the summer parlor. "And how very kind of him to come all the way up here simply to make our acquaintances."

"Thank you for helping me over that bit of a rough spot," Bradford said, offering Eugenia his arm as they walked toward the staircase. "I did not think at all to find Lady Vermont so very old and I could not possibly confront her. She cannot be what—what I thought her to be, can she? For a moment I felt the poltroon come over me. Cut and run, I thought. Cut and run."

"I know," Eugenia nodded. "I could tell. But you did neither cut and run nor embarrass her and I am proud of you for it."

"You could tell I wished to be out of there? Even standing five feet behind me?"

"Yes, because you suddenly stood so very stiff and straight, as if every muscle in your body had been wound to the snapping point, and then you put your hands behind your back and clasped them together so tightly that your knuckles turned white."

"Well, but her very appearance was torture to me, Eugenia. Who is she? What has she done? Why have I always known her name? Why does my father send her monies each and every quarter? She is not the person I have imagined her to be for all these years, that much I know to be true. She is a proper old lady, Eugenia. I did not expect that. I did not expect that at all." He paused as they reached the staircase, leaned for a moment against the rail, took Eugenia's hands into his own and studied her soberly. "You do not need to walk with me all the way down and into the Great Hall, my dear. I am perfectly capable of finding my own way."

"Oh."

"Well, your leg is giving you some pain, Eugenia. I can see that. You have done quite enough walking about for today. Yes, and your Jenkins will undoubtedly be pleased to hand me my hat and gloves and help me speedily out the door."

"No, that is not so. Jenkins likes you now. He said as much to me this very morning."

"He was merely being polite."

Eugenia giggled.

"You ought to do that more often," observed Bradford.

"Do what?"

"Giggle. I do not generally like to hear women giggle, but you do it so infectiously that it makes me smile. If Lady Vermont was not my father's mistress, and she cannot have been, what is she to him then, do you think?"

"I hesitate to guess."

"Yes, so do I, but I must, because the Old Squire will never tell me plain. She trembled like a blancmange when I entered the room, Eugenia, did you see? And then she became like granite."

"You persist in doing that and you ought not, you know."

"Persist in what? Making old women tremble?"

Eugenia giggled again. She could not help herself. "N-no. You persist in calling me Eugenia. You know perfectly well that you ought not. I am to be Miss Chastain to you."

"Even though we are friends?"

"Well—"

"Come, Eugenia. I have never truly had a friend. Must we be so very formal always?"

Eugenia thought most seriously for a moment. "What must I call you, if I am to be Eugenia?"

"Edward."

"Edward."

"Not Ted," Bradford grinned. "I cannot bear to be Ted or Teddy. I am not at all the type for that."

"Edward is a fine name," Eugenia informed him. "It

does not require shortening of any kind. I shall be pleased to call you Edward, and so will Aunt Diana."

"I see. It is both of you or neither?"

"Aunt Diana has chosen to be your friend as well, Edward."

"Indeed, she has. So be it then. With the ladies of this house, I am Edward. You must tell your Aunt Diana so, and Delight as well. I shall not mind particularly to have that little minx call me Edward. She calls Wickenshire Nicky, does she not?"

"Indeed, but he is her brother-in-law now."

"Just so," nodded Bradford, grinning. "She must call me Edward, I think. Goodbye, Eugenia. Return to your guests now and repair any damage I may have done, will you?" He gave both her hands a definite squeeze and then made his way down the staircase. He waved to her when he reached the first landing, then turned and continued downward until he reached the Great Hall. Eugenia heard his boot heels clacking across the stone as she turned back toward the summer parlor.

"But surely, Miss Daily, a gentleman must be expected to make a wager now and then. It is one of the most popular of London pastimes," Spelling explained as he and the two young ladies strolled back through the Great Hall toward the main staircase to the west wing. "A gentleman would be ostracized should he never make a wager at all."

"Balderdash," Miss Daily replied. "As if a gentleman's standing depended upon his ability to put his monies and his lands at risk. A true gentleman's standing amongst his friends ought to be measured by his loyalty, his honor and his forthrightness."

Mary Butterberry laughed. "She has got you there, Neil. A gentleman may see his popularity rise and fall by the nature and frequency of his wagers, but his true standing amongst his true friends must depend on something else entirely."

"No, but honorable gentlemen do place wagers all the time."

"Not all honorable gentlemen," declared Miss Daily. "And most certainly not the gentleman to whom I shall one day give my hand and my heart."

Bradford, who was just then tugging on his gloves turned at the sound of their approach and froze, staring over his shoulder with one hand gloved and the other only partially so, as Miss Daily looked up and met his cool blue gaze with one of her own.

The immediacy of his reaction and the true oddity of it forced Jenkins, who stood by with the marquess' hat in hand, to harrumph in order to recall his lordship's attention to donning the left glove. When the harrumph did not so much as cause a twitch in the marquess' entire body, Jenkins coughed significantly. When that, likewise, had no effect, Jenkins turned to see just what had so fixed the marquess' attention and drew a deep, shuddering breath. He turned his attention back to Bradford on the instant. "Your hat, my lord," he offered a bit more loudly than he had intended, but that increase in volume was all that betrayed the state into which his insides had just coiled.

"Wh-what? Oh, yes, my hat," Bradford responded at last, drawing on his glove, taking his beaver from Jenkins' hand and placing it firmly on his dark curls. "Are they coming this way still, Jenkins, or have they discovered something on one of the walls at which to stare?"

"Mr. Spelling and the young ladies continue to approach, my lord. I shall get the door for you, shall I?"

"Indeed, Jenkins."

"Bradford!" Spelling called, his instructions to keep that gentleman from Miss Daily rising into his brain and bringing a veritable ton of curiosity and temptation with it.

"Come and make Miss Daily's acquaintance before you leave."

"I did not hear, Jenkins. I have a—a—"

"You have an earache, my lord, and it makes a ringing in your head."

"Yes, that will do nicely. Thank you, Jenkins. Ah, there is Nod," he added as Bobby Tripp brought the roan around and into the drive. "I am off then." And before Spelling and the ladies drew close enough to hail him properly, the marquess was out the door, into the drive and urging Nod toward home.

"Now what the deuce was that all about?" asked Spelling as they reached the bottom of the staircase.

Jenkins stood with his back to the closed door and cocked an eyebrow. "Pardon, Mr. Spelling?"

"Bradford. Why did he run off as though a mad dog were at his heels? He did not so much as pause when I called to him."

"His ear, sir," Jenkins stated. "Earache. Ringing in his head. Likely did not even hear you."

"But you heard me, Jenkins."

"Yes, sir, but Lord Bradford could not comprehend what I was saying to him when I asked him to remain a moment. He was feeling a sight queer, Mr. Spelling."

"Yes, well, he was acting a sight queer at any rate. Comes from tugging cats out of trellises I expect."

"Is there anything else, Mr. Spelling?"

"No, nothing. Go on about your duties, Jenkins. Miss Daily and Miss Butterberry and I will find our own way back to the summer parlor."

Jenkins took himself off to the butler's pantry directly, closed the door and then turned the key on the inside. "Devil!" he muttered, sitting down upon the high stool he kept there for his convenience in stowing away the china.

"Devil! The lad knew at once, but did the young lady know?
No, no, she cannot have thought anything of it. At least,
she gave no evidence of having noticed. Mr. Spelling and
Miss Butterberry did not note it either. But why would they?
I thought nothing of it until I had them both before me at
one and the same time. But the lad knew."

Yes, and he left directly, Jenkins thought, rising from the
stool and beginning to pace. So, we are all proved correct—
Miss Delight, Miss Eugenia, Lady Wickenshire and myself.
Lord Bradford is not the ogre he makes himself out to be.
Not at all. Certainly he would not have taken leave of this
place so quickly were there the least bit of villainy in him.

"I thought I should die upon the instant," Jenkins declared, climbing on the stool and fishing about in the very
top of the cupboard. "Ah, here it is." His hand closed
around a cut-glass decanter filled with a golden liquid and
he brought it carefully down, setting it upon the counter
where he generally polished the silver. Then he fetched a
glass from behind another of the cupboard doors and poured
himself a drink. He did not bother to so much as glance at
the brandy or inhale its aroma. No. He tossed three fingers
of it straight back. He gulped. His eyes watered. His insides
burned all the way down to his stomach. He poured himself
another glassful and sat down again upon the stool. This
time he did swirl the brandy about, and stared down into
its golden depths. "Brother and sister," he murmured. "As
alike as two peas in a pod, except that one of the peas is
smaller, wears skirts and has rosebud lips."

Devil, what a shock it must have been to see his own
eyes glancing back at him for that instant! Jenkins thought
then, recalling the way Lord Bradford had turned to ice on
the spot. But the lad is as noble and as kind as our Mr.
Nicholas. He would have confronted the girl and Lady Vermont else. Would have confronted them that instant—
grabbed Miss Daily's hand and tugged her back up the stairs

and demanded to know when, where, with whom it occurred, and why he had not been told.

Lord Bradford and Nod ambled toward Peabody House amidst birdsong and bright sunlight. It was the clearest and loveliest of afternoons, but it might have been the blackest night. They would not have noted the difference. It was only when Stanley Blithe caught up with them and loped alongside that Nod began to cheer up a bit. Still, he would not prance, because his master was riding him in the most listless manner, heavy upon his back—the way he rode when he was injured or ill or very, very sad. Therefore, Nod shook his head at Stanley Blithe and stuck out his long tongue and nickered a bit, but he would not dance with him across the meadow, no matter how much he wished to do so.

"Do be quiet you worthless hound," Bradford grouched following a series of Stanley Blithe barks by which the puppy had hoped to lure Nod into a mad dash off the road and into a field spread with wildflowers. "Go home, you dastardly rascal. Go home, sir, at once."

"Grrrarf," replied Stanley Blithe and continued to lope along beside them.

"Is everyone from Wicken Hall out to plague me? Even you? What is it that I have done to deserve such a fate, eh? I have not done anything. Nothing! I simply rented a house in the county of Kent to find a bit of peace for the summer."

"Rrrrrrrowwf," Stanley Blithe agreed and Nod gave another shake of his great head and twitched his ears back to hear his master better.

"I did not come to Kent begging to have my heart torn to shreds. I did not so much as realize that I still had a heart when I came here. And yet, everywhere I turn, I am taught that not only do I still possess the thing but that it still knows how to ache as it once did."

"Grrrrooof," Stanley Blithe observed.

"Yes, just so. I am losing all my hard-earned mettle. I am coming apart bit by bit."

Stanley Blithe whined in commiseration. Nod reached around and nuzzled Bradford tenderly on the knee.

"Oh, for heaven's sake," sighed the marquess, a smile quivering at his lips. "Nod, you will force me into accepting this stupid puppy yet. How can you possibly like such an animal, eh? Look how he follows us, not caring in the least where we are bound or if he will ever get home again. By Jove, Nod, he looks like a perfect lunatic with his tongue flopping out of the side of his mouth like that."

Nod whinnied in agreement and continued to amble slowly and carefully along the road until at last Bradford steered him onto the verge beneath an enormous oak, dismounted, and sat upon the grass, resting his back against the tree trunk and tossing his hat onto the ground beside him. Nod took up a stance at his master's left and nibbled encouragingly at his master's curls. Stanley Blithe wiggled and pranced and then sat down on his haunches at Bradford's right and gave the marquess one excessively wet lick across the cheek.

"She has Papa's eyes. Papa's eyes. The very same as Peter's and mine. And Papa's nose and eyebrows and hair, just as we have. I have not one doubt. She is my sister," the marquess informed them both, one hand playing with Stanley Blithe's ears and the other rubbing Nod's velvety nose. "That is why the Old Squire sends such sums to Lady Vermont every quarter, for my sister's support. But who is the gel's mother? Certainly not Lady Vermont. Certainly not my mother. Gawd, Mama is dead now four entire years. Did she know of Papa's little by-blow from the first and never say? And Peter, who wishes that I shall never set eyes on him again, does he know there is a young woman who shares our blood so obviously? Why must I find her now, when she is practically a grown woman? Why could I not have discovered her all those years ago?"

"Mrrph," observed Stanley Blithe.

"Brrrrr," agreed Nod, blowing in Bradford's ear.

"Just so," murmured the marquess, swiping angrily at an annoying itch in his eyes. "And now what am I to do, eh? What am I to say to Lady Vermont and—the girl? What a dog my Papa is!"

"Rrarrf!" objected Stanley Blithe, pawing at Bradford's knee.

That made a weak smile quiver once again to the marquess' lips. "No, I ought not to have called him a dog, Stanley Blithe. I apologize to you, sir. It—it was a m-most unfortunate choice of w-words." Bradford gasped then at the incredible pain that shot through his stomach and up between his ribs. He gulped and coughed at the horrid lump in his throat, and though he fought against it, biting down on his lower lip so hard as to make it bleed, he could not stop himself. He began to sob.

With short, quick licks, Stanley Blithe attempted to stem the tide of tears that streamed down the marquess' cheeks, and Nod, not to be outdone, added his tongue to the task, but the tears kept falling. Bradford, thoroughly humiliated, put an arm around each of them and sobbed all the more.

The moment Lady Vermont and her granddaughter and Mrs. Butterberry and her daughters departed, Spelling literally grabbed Arnsworth by the arm and tugged him off down the corridor. "Arnsworth and I are off to play a game of billiards before dinner, Aunt Diana," he called back cheerfully over his shoulder while dragging Gilly away.

"I—I—do not play billiards," Mr. Arnsworth protested, his boots' heels and Spelling's making the most outrageous racket as Spelling propelled him along the uncarpeted corridor. "I am v-vile at it."

"We are not actually going to play billiards," hissed Spelling, turning in through an open doorway.

"We are not?"

"No. We are going to have a talk, Gilly. Just you and me, with no women around to distract us."

"Oh."

"Here, take one of these," he instructed, lifting a cue from the rack and handing it to Arnsworth, then taking one down for himself."

"All right," agreed Arnsworth hesitantly.

"We are just going to pretend to play, Arnsworth, in case Aunt Diana or Eugenia should stroll past. They will not think to disturb us as long as we appear to be playing."

"Very well," Mr. Arnsworth nodded. "What is it you wish to discuss, Spelling?"

"You."

"Me?"

"Just so. You are making a muddle of everything."

"Me?"

"Well, I certainly ain't! You said that you wished to marry into an old and respected family, one of the upper ten thousand, Gilly. You told innumerable people that such was your mama's dearest wish for you. That you had set your heart upon pleasing her in it. You came to London and were rebuffed left and right, but did you abandon the idea? No. When you discovered that the *ton* would not so much as let you set foot amongst them, did you go running back to Bath? No. And I admired you for that, Arnsworth. I truly did. I thought to myself, now there's a gentleman deserves to get exactly what he seeks. Got perseverance. Got bottom, Arnsworth does."

"You thought that?"

"I did, Gilly. That is precisely what I thought," grumbled Spelling, taking aim at the cue ball and sending it careening across the table.

I have got to do something, Spelling thought, watching

the ball ricochet from one end to the other. If I cannot turn his eyes from Clara Butterberry back to Eugenia or to some other one of the gels who came out this Season, Carey will win the damnable wager. Yes, and word of it will spread through the *ton* like wildfire, and Uncle Ezra will part my hair with a carving knife. Tivally Grange. I must have been out of mind to wager Tivally Grange on anything!

"And thinking you to be a deserving fellow, Arnsworth, what did I do, eh? What did I do?" he rasped, running his fingers through his hair.

"You—"

"I will tell you what I did, Arnsworth. I brought you here to Wicken Hall to introduce you to my Cousin Eugenia. Do you not like my Cousin Eugenia, Arnsworth? Has she been unkind to you? Do you find her lacking in some way? You despise her because she limps a bit, is that it?"

"No!" protested Mr. Arnsworth, his face growing a shade paler. "I could never despise Miss Chastain. She is a kind, gentle, pleasant young woman and she has been exceedingly congenial to me."

"So I thought, Arnsworth. Exceedingly congenial. And yet you abandon your efforts in Eugenia's direction and go trailing about after the daughter of a country parson. A mere Miss Nobody. A penniless child with not one attachment to the upper ten thousand. Your mama would be horrified, Gilly!"

"I—she—Miss Clara—"

"Miss Clara Butterberry is a brazen little milkmaid with the lineage of a mongrel and the decorum of an opera dancer."

"Do not you dare insult . . ."

"I am not insulting the gel," Spelling interrupted. "I am merely speaking the truth about her. I have known Clara Butterberry since she was in the cradle. She comes from quite the same stock as her sister, Mary, and neither of them is any better than she ought to be."

"And what does that mean?" glowered Gilly, setting his cue down with a deal of force upon the table.

"It means precisely what you think it means, Arnsworth."

"No, it cannot. Miss Butterberry and Miss Clara are the daughters of a clergyman for goodness' sake."

"And they are also the two most forward romps in all of Kent. By gawd, Gilly, take them up to London and they would both of them give Caro Lamb a run for her money. They would be wearing damped muslins and driving down St. James's of an afternoon without the least thought for their reputations. The *ton* would ostracize the both of them within a day—if they were part of the *ton*—which, I remind you, they ain't."

"Well, but—"

Mr. Spelling rested his cue across the billiard table and put both hands upon his hips. "Do you wish to heed your mama's wishes and marry into the upper ten thousand or not, Gilly?"

Say yes, Spelling thought as Mr. Arnsworth stared down at the toes of his boots in silence. Say yes, you ninnyhammer. Do not set your heart on Clara Butterberry, because I can tell already that she will have you. Yes, and once the parson learns how blasted rich you are, he will have you too. I will lose my wager. Uncle Ezra will lose Tivally Grange and be forced to discover yet a third place to store his smuggled goods. He was not at all happy when he had to give up Willowsweep to Nicky and take the Grange instead. But now, if he must make a third switch and discovers it is because of me, I will be food for worms within a se'nnight of his learning of it.

"Well, I—I—," stuttered Arnsworth.

"If you cannot like Eugenia, I shall be pleased to look around for some other young lady for you," Spelling offered solicitously. "I will, Gilly. I vow it. But Clara Butterberry will not do. She will not do at all!"

Mr. Arnsworth gave a shake of his head, causing his lank,

whitish-blond hair to flop across his brow. "I do not want you to go looking about for anyone else, Neil," he replied softly.

"You do not? You will be satisfied, then, with Eugenia?"

"N-no."

"No? What do you mean, no?"

"I mean," gasped Mr. Arnsworth somewhat frantically, "that I have fallen in love, Spelling, with Miss Clara Butterberry."

"And you do not give a fig for your mama's wishes?"

"Well, well, I do, but—"

"No, you do not," growled Spelling, picturing the deed to Tivally Grange floating softly and quietly into Lord Carey's pocket and his own head bobbing along, bodiless, with the current of the Thames. "You do not care one thing for your mama, Arnsworth, or you would not dare to fall in love with that—that—underbred hoyden! You will be sorry if you do not bring yourself to see Clara for what she is, Gilly. I promise you that. You will be the sorriest man alive."

Fourteen

Eugenia could barely keep her attention on Mr. Arnsworth's words as he attempted to hold polite conversation with her at the dinner table because Jenkins was acting so very queerly. Why, he was actually wobbling, now, from one foot to another as he stood behind Lady Wickenshire. And his eyebrows had been waggling at the footmen from the moment the soup tureen had arrived. Really, they were most distracting, those thick eyebrows above those fine gray eyes, wiggling up and down like caterpillars.

And he keeps bestowing on me the most pleading glances, Eugenia thought as she spooned the last bit of plum pudding into her mouth. Something is terribly wrong, I think. Something that he does not wish to speak of with Aunt Diana. Well, I shall find a way to be alone with him for a moment or two directly dinner is over. I cannot possibly allow him to spend the rest of the evening in such a state as he is in now. For one thing, he is much too old to remain so very uneasy for such a length of time.

It was not, however, until after the gentlemen had joined the ladies in the drawing room and Lady Wickenshire had taken up her embroidery, sending Eugenia off to tuck Delight safely into bed, that the opportunity to speak privately with Jenkins arrived.

"An' God bless Sera an' Nicky an' Lady Wickenshire, an' Genia an' Stanley Blithe an' Sweetpea an' Lord Nightingale, an' Lord Bradford an' Nod," Delight finished her prayers enthusiastically, then climbed happily between the sheets. "G'night, Genia." She grinned as Eugenia tucked the bedclothes in around her and placed a soft kiss upon her cheek.

"Goodnight, dearest. Dream splendid dreams."

"I am going to dream about riding Nod."

"You are?"

"Oh, yes. I am 'termined to. It will be the most splendidest dream. Where is Stanley Blithe?"

Eugenia looked to the window seat and saw Sweetpea stretched out on her back upon it, her little cat feet flopping in the air. She glanced down to the carpet at the foot of the bed and then to the space just beside the chest of drawers. There was no sign of the puppy. "I expect that one of the footmen has taken him out for a walk."

"Then you must leave my door open a smidgen so that Stanley Blithe can get in," Delight instructed. "He doesn't not like to sleep anywhere else."

"No, he certainly does not. Of course I will leave the door open for him, Delight. Now close your eyes, dearest, and go to sleep. You have had a very busy day."

No sooner had she left the bedchamber than Jenkins approached her in the corridor. "I must have a word with you, Miss Eugenia. I do not mean to be a bother, but—"

"No, no, it is no bother, Jenkins. I did take note that you wished a word with me at dinner, but there has not been an opportune moment since."

"Perhaps in the alcove above the gallery, Miss Eugenia. We shall not disturb Miss Delight there."

No, and we shall not be disturbed by anyone else either, thought Eugenia. It is something most private then that he wishes to say to me. She nodded and accompanied him in silence to the alcove, which lay at the very place where the corridor to the west wing intersected with the east wing. "What is it, Jenkins?" she asked, once they had reached the place. "You have had the fidgets all through dinner. Jenkins! You smell of brandy!"

"Yes, miss, I did splash a bit of it. I was that upset."

"You splashed a bit of it?"

"While I was drinking it down, Miss Eugenia."

"Jenkins!"

"Yes, miss, I know, but I required a good stiff drink. Indeed I did. I could not have gone on attending to my duties without it. It was the most startling thing."

"Startling? What was startling, Jenkins?"

"Lord Bradford and Miss Daily, miss. I ought not—It is not our business—but his lordship grew so very still, Miss Eugenia. Flabbergasted, he was. Never so much as suspected, he did not. I could see that. And—and—I cannot possibly address her ladyship upon the matter. And—you do care for the gentleman, miss. I ought not say so, but I have eyes and ears and—"

"Jenkins," hissed Eugenia in exasperation, "out with it!"

The butler heaved a great sigh, clasped his hands behind his back and stared at his shoe tops. "Miss Alice Daily and Lord Bradford are brother and sister, Miss Eugenia, and his lordship did take note of it at once and left the house as pale and frozen as though he had seen his own grave open up before him."

"Brother and sister? Miss Daily and—and— No, you must be mistaken, Jenkins. How can that be? Certainly if his lordship had a sister he would know about her." And then Eugenia's face began to color and she felt the air in the tiny alcove go rushing out, making it extremely warm and extremely hard for one to catch one's breath. "You mean Miss Daily is—is—"

"Just so, miss. I should not have known, had his lordship not been so overcome as to direct my attention to the young lady. But then he recovered himself and departed, miss."

"Well! What kind of man must the Duke of Sotherland be!" Eugenia exclaimed with righteous wrath.

"Hush, miss. Someone will hear."

"But—but—to send his wife off to Yorkshire and sepa-rate his twins, and go about bestowing babies upon women to whom he is not married—why, the man must be the Devil Incarnate!"

"But his lordship is not, Miss Eugenia, and he was dev-astated. I am that worried about the gentleman. He rode off so pale and quiet and with a most dejected slump to his shoulders. And I thought—I thought, perhaps, you might think of some way to—to—cheer him—and quickly, too."

"Jenkins, you do not think that—"

"He has had so very much bad news of late. I could not help overhearing about his mother and his brother, Miss Eugenia."

"But he would never think to do himself harm, Jenkins. He is not such a coward as to—"

"When a gentleman's mind is clouded by grief, miss," whispered Jenkins hoarsely, "the distinction between cow-ardice and nobility is not always so very clear to him."

Eugenia, finding sleep far from her, stared out into an unexpectedly stormy night and pondered what to do. She could easily escort Delight to visit Nod on the morrow. And if Edward came out into the pasture, well, Delight would be involved with the horse and Bobby Tripp would allow them a deal of privacy in which to speak.

"But I cannot simply take his arm and say, 'By the way, Edward, let us discuss your papa, The Devil Incarnate, and Miss Daily, your papa's by-blow.' Great heavens, I cannot do that!"

And what if he is in such despair that he does not come out to speak with me? No, no, he will come. He always comes whenever anyone approaches Nod. "Oh, dear God," Eugenia whispered. "Only let him make it through this one night and I will say something, do something, to help him see all clearly. He is not such a coward as to take his own life. Jenkins is quite off there. He must be!"

Yes, indeed he is, Eugenia assured herself. No matter how far into despair Edward has tumbled, it is merely from the abruptness of his discovery. He could never sink so far as to actually. . . . And if Jenkins is mistaken there, she thought, perhaps he is mistaken about Miss Daily as well. Perhaps he and Edward are both mistaken about her.

She called Miss Daily's countenance to mind and compared it most thoughtfully to the face of the gentleman she was coming fast to love. "I expect Jenkins is right," she told herself after a good five minutes. "They both have blue eyes and dark hair, but I did not look at Miss Daily very closely. Did the two of them stand before me side by side perhaps. Perhaps they are cousins!" she exclaimed suddenly. "Any number of cousins resemble one another. I know cousins who look much alike! Perhaps we need only speak to Lady Vermont to discover that Miss Daily is a cousin of Edward's once or twice or even thrice removed! Why did I not think of that at once?"

Well, she thought, because Jenkins jumped immediately to the wrong conclusion and I already believed Edward's papa to be evil, so I did not doubt him. Which is exactly what happened to Edward. He believes his papa to be evil and so when he saw Miss Daily—. Well, I will speak to him the very first thing tomorrow and ask him if he and Miss Daily could be cousins. That will bring him out of the doldrums and set him to considering the matter.

Feeling a good deal better, Eugenia took a last look out at the storm that had swept down out of the north with not the least warning. Lightning shattered across the sky, thunder rumbled and the rain poured down as if all the wells of heaven were being emptied upon the earth at the same time. Just beyond the window of her bedchamber, a bolt of lightning struck one of the elms and sent an ancient branch thwacking to the ground. Eugenia jumped at the sight and sound of it. "God bless us all this night and keep us safe," she whispered. "The wind is blowing as if it would blow the entire world away." And then, as the lightning flashed again and the thunder veritably roared in her ears, Eugenia glimpsed a shadow dashing wildly about below her window. "What in the world?" she asked, straining through the darkness to gain a second glimpse. "Stanley Blithe?"

Eugenia slipped the latch, opened the casements and stuck her head out into the rain. "Stanley Blithe?" she called as loudly as she was able.

"Rrrarf!" came the answer, blown up to her by the wind. "Rrrrarf-arf, arowowowow!"

Eugenia closed the casements and allowed the draperies to fall across the windows. She seized the paisley shawl that lay folded upon her chair, swung it about her shoulders, took up her bedside lamp and limped hurriedly from the room. She made her way down the servants' staircase to the ground floor, crossed to the side door, unlocked it and pulled it open. "Here, Stanley Blithe," she called. "Come in at once, you poor puppy!"

"What is it, miss?" asked Jenkins, his unexpected voice causing Eugenia's heart to skip a beat.

"Oh! Oh, Jenkins. It is Stanley Blithe. He is out in this storm. Come, Stanley Blithe. Come in at once, sir. However did he get out? Did not the footman close the door properly?"

"The footman?"

"Yes, whichever one it was, Jenkins, whom you sent to walk Stanley Blithe after dinner. Why does he not come in? Stanley Blithe, come out of the rain at once, sir!"

"I did not send anyone to walk Stanley Blithe, miss," Jenkins replied thoughtfully. "I have not had sight of Stanley Blithe since this afternoon when he ran off after Lord Bradford."

"Arrrowowowoow!" howled Stanley Blithe pitifully, sitting down on his haunches a good ten feet from Eugenia and the open doorway. "Arrrowowowoow!" Then he stood and pranced toward Eugenia and Jenkins. He turned and ran back a bit, then approached again. "Rrrraffff!" he demanded. "Rrrraffarf!"

Jenkins gasped as an extraordinary array of lightning split the night asunder, and then he was dashing to the tiny alcove under the servants' staircase. In a moment he was shrugging into a coat and slamming a hat upon his head. The lamp in Eugenia's hand began to tremble as she peered out, hoping to see what it was that Jenkins had seen. "What is it, Jenkins?" she asked as he rushed toward her again. "I can see nothing but Stanley Blithe."

"Beyond him, miss, beyond him and to the right. Damn this thing!" Jenkins exclaimed as he bent over a lantern, attempting to light it with shaking fingers. "Go into the armaments room, Miss Eugenia, and ring the bell until someone comes, then say that you require all three of the footmen and send them out to me at once. Ah, there. I have got it now. I am coming, Stanley Blithe. Good dog. I am coming."

And then, in the blaze of a spear of lightning, Eugenia saw them. A sob burst unbidden from her throat and she turned and stumbled toward the armaments room almost dropping her lamp, coming near to tripping on the hem of her robe. She found the door open, fumbled along the wall for the heavy satin riband and tugged it again and again and again.

Nod stood like a statue amidst the storm. He had come as far as he dared, moving like an inchworm along the flooding road, blinking against the rain that pelted his eyes, stung his ears and made his back shiver with cold—following the dog, because the dog was free to run ahead and be certain that the way was clear. It had not been clear in the direction of Peabody House. An oak had fallen across the road and water had topped the ditches. Nod could not have negotiated the tree or waded through such water or climbed the hill beyond without unbalancing his master and sending him crashing to the earth. So they had turned about, the dog and the great strawberry roan, and made their way back in the opposite direction, Stanley Blithe dashing ahead and returning, urging Nod to proceed first this way, then that. But Nod could move no farther now. The gentleman on his back had tilted into a most precarious position and he would be down at Nod's feet with one more step.

"Steady, my lad. Steady, my darling," Jenkins called, battering his way against the wind—toward the horse, toward the seemingly lifeless figure upon its back—his heart fluttering in his throat. Stanley Blithe ran and barked and charged at the butler's heels. "Yes, Stanley Blithe," Jenkins yelled over a patch of thunder. "Good dog. You are all of you safe now, my boy!"

Lord Bradford awoke to the soft brush of feathers against his cheek and the indisputable knowledge that someone's gaze was pinned fast upon him. His right shoulder throbbed, his head ached. He found it difficult to open his eyes and even more difficult to focus them.

"He is blinkin'!" cried Delight, slipping out of the big wing chair beside his bed and skipping to the open door. "Genia, Lord Bradford is blinkin'!"

I am Blinkin? Bradford thought, confused, the old rhyme abruptly becoming entangled in his brain. "Winkin and Blinkin and Nod one night," he heard a low, tender voice from long ago whisper. "Winkin and Blinkin and Nod one night, sailed off in a silver shoe." And he closed his eyes to listen.

"Knollsmarmer," interrupted another voice. "Yo ho ho. Knollsmarmer." Again the soft brush of feathers against his cheek urged him to open his eyes. He attempted to do so and saw a most beautiful but muzzy rainbow moving about before him. And then he heard the laughter of faeries and felt a pixie of one sort or another dancing a jig on his stomach.

"Nightingale, do give over," said one of the faeries. "Sweetpea, do *not* tromp about upon his stomach. You are both taking advantage just because he is feeling poorly and cannot push you away. Edward? Edward, can you look at me, dearest?"

"D-dearest?" mumbled Bradford, blinking mightily to bring the rainbow and the faeries and the pixies and Winkin and Blinkin and Nod into focus. "Eugenia!" he exclaimed in a most gravelly voice as her face appeared before him.

"That is much better, Edward. You have not recognized anyone for three whole days. Delight, run and tell Mr. Stanley that his master is awake. Oh, and remind him that he must bring some more of the powdered comfrey."

"Mus' bring some more of the pow'ered comfy," Delight sang happily. "Mus' bring some more of the pow'ered comfy."

"Powered comfy?" asked Bradford, squinting up at Eugenia.

"Powdered comfrey. You are not quite awake, are you, my lord? No, of course you are not, but you are attempting to concentrate and that is a most gratifying thing. We thought that you had bought the farm, you know."

"M-me?"

"Oh, yes," Eugenia nodded, urging Lord Nightingale from Bradford's pillow and sending him climbing up to sit upon the headboard. "You were so pale and cold and lifeless and we could barely hear you breathe. But you are a deal better now."

"Wh-what happened?"

"Well, we think that you were hit by a falling tree branch," began Eugenia, settling into the wing chair beside the bed. "Bobby Tripp found your hat squashed beneath one. The tree had been struck by lightning."

"A tree b-beside the road."

"Exactly so."

"I—I—" Visions flickered through Bradford's mind. "It was afternoon and—and—then it was n-night. My head aches something dreadful."

"I should think it might. Were you sitting beneath a tree for some reason?"

The specter of himself, his face buried between Nod and Stanley Blithe arose then, clearly and humiliatingly. "M-my sister," he said. "Eugenia, I h-have a sister."

"Perhaps and perhaps not, Edward. We shall discuss the possibilities of it, you and I, but not at this precise moment. At this precise moment, I wish you to remember how you came to be lying so precariously on Nod's back in the midst of a storm."

"On Nod's back?"

"Yes, my dear. Somehow you were felled and yet Nod brought you to us—Nod and Stanley Blithe."

"I m-must have fallen asleep. I remember w-waking. It was dark and w-wet. Very wet. And then I whistled to N-Nod and he and Stanley Blithe— I d-do not remember them coming. I r-remember them starting to come. And then I w-woke all over again!" he added amazed, "and I hurt something d-dreadful. Nod was beside me and I p-pulled myself up into the saddle."

"And Nod very kindly brought you to Wicken Hall because he could not get around a fallen oak to take you home without dropping you into a ditch filled with water—where you would have quietly drowned," declared Mr. Stanley as he strolled into the room. "I thought as much."

"Have you remembered the comfrey?" Eugenia asked.

"Indeed, and Mr. Jenkins will be along in a moment to help me cleanse his lordship's wounds again and put more of the powders upon them, miss. I am quite sorry that you were forced to look in upon him."

Eugenia could not help but grin. "You are truly the most subtle gentleman, Mr. Stanley. I do know that I ought not to be in his lordship's bedchamber, but Delight did call to say that Lord Bradford was awakening and you were otherwise occupied."

"Just so, Miss Chastain. And some adult must come, of course. I am most grateful to you."

Eugenia rose from the wing chair and looked down, smiling into Lord Bradford's pale face. "I leave you in the most capable of hands, my lord. Do be good and do as you are told." She gave his hand a supportive squeeze and departed the chamber.

"Mornin' Genia!" cried Lord Nightingale raucously after her, strutting about upon the headboard. "Mornin'. Mornin'."

Late that afternoon, Eugenia entered the stables with some trepidation. "I am not afraid of horses," she reminded herself softly. "It is merely that they make me sneeze." Throwing her shoulders back and lifting her chin, she strolled down the aisle between the several stalls to the box stall at the very rear. Quietly she opened the door and peered in. "Oh, no," she sighed.

Bobby Tripp glanced up from beside the strawberry roan who lay stretched upon the hay-littered floor, covered with horse blankets. "He will not cease shiverin', miss, an' it soun's like he 'as got the rattles."

"The rattles, Bobby?"

"Aye, miss. "When 'e breathes, ye know, 'e rattles. I do guess the old fellow ain't goin' ta make it, miss. Once a 'orse lies down like 'e has done jist this mornin', an' his lungs begin ta rattlin', it don't bode well, miss, if ye know what I mean."

"Mmmmmmm," whined Stanley Blithe, glancing worriedly up at Eugenia from where he lay near Nod's soft, velvety muzzle.

"Just so, Stanley Blithe. Your friend is not feeling at all the thing. You say you can hear these rattles, Bobby?"

"Aye, miss. Ye must only put yer ear agin 'is ribs here."

Eugenia entered the stall, pulled the door tight behind her and, with only the vaguest hesitation, knelt down beside Nod and placed her ear where Bobby Tripp pointed. Even through the horse blankets she could hear the rattling. "There must be something we can do, Bobby."

"We have done ever'thing, miss."

"Then we must do more. Lord Bradford loves this animal beyond reason. We cannot possibly allow the old fellow to die."

"No, miss, but there ain't nothin' more I know ta do an' there ain't no one in Wicken knows any better. Her ladyship did send Mr. Spellin' and Mr. Arnsworth inta the village yes'erday ta ask fer 'elp, but weren't no one knew anythin' differn' ta do."

"Mmmmmmmmm," whined Stanley Blithe again and gave Nod's nose a lick. Then he stood and walked around to curl up in the space between Nod's chin and chest.

"L'il Miss Delight will be heartbroken as well, miss," sighed Bobby Tripp. "In love with this beast, she be, jus' like his lor'ship."

"Yes, I know."

"She will likely be comin' any minit now ta see 'ow he does. There ain't no keepin' 'er away. He weren't lyin' down, miss, the last time Miss Delight came, an' I din't say to her how bad the poor fellow were feelin' then."

The door to the stall opened and Lady Wickenshire appeared, followed by a young maid carrying three large quilts. "Help me spread these over the poor animal, Bobby," she ordered, taking the first of the quilts and shaking it out. "He will be warmer under these for they will cover all of him and not just bits and pieces. Eugenia, darling, what is it?"

"I have just had a thought," declared Eugenia. "Aunt Diana, the comfrey!"

"The comfrey?"

"Yes, we can make a tea of it."

"Indeed we can, my dear, and I am certain it will do Lord Bradford quite as much good to drink some as to have the powder put upon his poor split head and torn shoulder."

"Oh, yes, that too."

"That too?"

"For Nod, Aunt Diana. I was thinking to make the comfrey into a tea for Nod."

Lady Diana shook out the next of the quilts and she and Bobby Tripp placed that over the horse as well. "My mama was accustomed to give Ezra comfrey tea," she mused as she took the last quilt in hand. "Your Uncle Ezra was prone to a congestion of the lungs when he was a fledgling, but—"

"That is exactly what is wrong with Nod, Aunt Diana. He has a congestion of the lungs."

"He does? I thought he rattled. Well, but if it is a congestion—how much comfrey tea must one give a horse? Yes, and how much of the powder must be dissolved in how much water?"

"A deal more than for people, I should think," offered Eugenia.

"Well, let me think." Lady Wickenshire leaned down before the horse and rubbed her hand up and down along his nose. "Ah, I have got it! 'One one six you quickly fix and let it steep one five. You give it four to do the trick and keep the imp alive.' Yes, I am certain that is the way it goes."

"The way what goes?" Eugenia asked, a bit bewildered.

"The recipe, my dear. The recipe for people, that is. We must expand upon it somewhat for this animal, of course."

"N-Nod?" said a soft voice, its unexpectedness startling Eugenia, Bobby Tripp and Lady Wickenshire, all.

"Nod?" Lord Bradford repeated, peering through the open door at the strawberry roan that shivered beneath the quilts. In shirtsleeves, breeches and bedroom slippers, face unshaven, hair uncombed, with bandaged brow and right arm strapped against his chest by strips of muslin, the marquess stared at Nod with eyes as full of love and pleading as any Eugenia had ever seen.

Nod raised his head a bit and nickered softly. Bradford crossed to him on the instant, knelt and rubbed the roan's ears and muzzle, rested his own cheek against Nod's, whispered words of love and encouragement and pleaded with the great beast to "hold on, my lad. Just hold on."

"Miss Delight peeped around the door of his chamber and asked if Nod was better," sighed Stanley from the doorway to the stall. "Well, I could not prevent him from coming once he heard that Nod was ill. I did not think it right to try," he added, his eyes grown most sorrowful. "Helped the old fellow into this world, his lordship did. Only right he should see him out of it."

"See him out of it?" whispered Eugenia. "Balderdash!"

"B-balderdash?" asked Bradford, his blue-eyed gaze suddenly fixed upon her. "What is balderdash?"

"That Nod is on his way out of this world, of course."

"But Stanley said that everything had been tried and all he does is grow worse."

"Not everything, my lord. Not the comfrey."

"The comfrey?"

"Comfrey tea. We are just puzzling over how to mix it properly for a—a—horse."

"Comfrey is to heal wounds," murmured Bradford with a pain-filled blink of his eyes. "It draws the parts together."

"Yes, the powder does, Edward. But the powder can be made into a tea, and the tea eases congestion of the lungs. With luck, it will drive out the congestion completely. Aunt

Diana and I are just discussing what mixture would be best
to give Nod. We will make it up for him. And you, my
dearest Edward, must see he drinks it. He will drink it if
you give it to him, will he not?"

The marquess nodded and then put a hand to his aching
head. "He will do what I ask of him," he murmured through
stiff lips. "He has always done whatever I have asked of
him."

Fifteen

Lord Bradford spent the day in the box stall beside Nod. Neither the pain of his own injuries nor a stern rebuke from Mr. Stanley, who rocked back and forth from heel to toe to heel to toe while he delivered it, had the least effect. The marquess would not leave Nod. He fastened one of his own gloves awkwardly to the wine bottle filled with comfrey tea that Eugenia brought to him and poked holes in two of the fingers with a leather punch. He sat cross-legged upon the floor and attempted to get Nod's heavy head to rest on his lap. He could not do it.

"It is because this fool arm is bound up," he muttered. "I cannot move it at all and I cannot do the thing with one hand."

"Do not you dare to tug at those straps," Eugenia ordered, standing with hands upon her hips above him. "Your shoulder, sir, was popped right out of its socket and it took Jenkins and all three of our footmen to pop it back in. Do not think for one moment, Edward, that I am going to allow you to flail that arm about and give Jenkins and the footmen all to do over again, because I am not."

"But, Eugenia, he cannot drink it lying so flat."

Lord Bradford's eyes were so filled with worry and his brow—what she could see of it beneath the bandage—so creased with frustration at his own helplessness, that Eugenia could not but offer her own services. She scooted Stanley Blithe out of the way and she and Lord Bradford maneuvered Nod's heavy head into an acceptable position. Then she sat and watched, playing with Nod's mane, as Bradford urged and pleaded and commanded the great beast to drink. Some of the liquid spilled upon the marquess' breeches, his shirt sleeves, and the floor, but he seemed not to notice. When at last the old horse had drunk all of the tea that had not spilled, Eugenia was hard put not to smile at how pleased the marquess appeared to be.

"Did you see, Eugenia? I knew he would do it. He will do anything I ask of him."

"Just so, Edward," she nodded. If only it will do the poor animal some good, she added in silence. It is all just guessing about the strength of the tea and how much to give a horse and how often. "He has ceased to shiver so," she pointed out. "That is a good sign, is it not? It was kind of Aunt Diana to bring some of her quilts."

"Most kind," Bradford agreed. "Oh, lord."

"Oh, lord, what?"

"Listen. There are tiny little footfalls running toward us. Damnation, wings flapping, too. It will be Delight and Nightingale."

"Brarwk! Mornin' Knollsmarmer," squawked Lord Nightingale, soaring into the box stall through the open door and landing upon Bradford's shoulder. Lifting his feet high, as if he were a soldier slopping through mud, the parrot sidled first toward Bradford's cheek, which he rubbed his red and white head against with great goodwill, and then sidled back across the broad shoulder, turned about, turned about again and settled down to groom his feathers.

"Is Nod better?" asked a tiny voice moments afterward as Delight came running into the stall and stopped to stare at the great horse. "H-he is not," she observed with a trembling lip. "I th-thought he would be all b-better now that Lord Bradford is with him."

"Oh, dearest, come here. Come to me," urged Eugenia, holding her arms out to the child. Delight moved quietly around Nod and sat down directly upon Eugenia's lap, reaching out to pat Nod's neck tenderly with one small hand.

"You mus' be b-better, Nod," Delight whispered with a tiny sniff. "I have b-brought Lord Nightingale to cheer you up an' I have brought you some sugar c-cubes, too," and she abruptly burst into tears and buried her face against Eugenia's shoulder.

"Dearest, do not cry. Nod is trying to be better. Truly he is. He is a very brave horse, you know. You told me so yourself."

"Y-yes. He has g-got lots of bottom."

"Just so. And he will not give up, dearest. He will fight and fight to be well again."

Delight rubbed at her eyes with tiny fists, gulped back a sob and stared at Lord Bradford. "Will Nod be well again?" she asked plaintively. "He has got to be. I love him!"

Bradford reached out to her with his one useful arm, sending Nightingale scurrying to the injured one, and she climbed from Eugenia's lap and went to stand beside him, allowing him to gather her up into a one-armed hug. Eugenia watched, her heart near to breaking, as he kissed the tiny tears away one by one. "Nod is very proud to have you love him," Bradford said at last, his voice faltering only a bit. "In all his life, he has never had such a very kind and pretty young lady to love him."

"H-he has not?"

"No. Never."

"H-have you?"

"Me?" Bradford smiled the saddest of smiles. "Had a very kind and pretty young lady to love me, do you mean?"

Delight nodded.

"No. Never. Nod and I have only always had each other."

Delight put her arms around Bradford's neck and hugged him, then she kissed his whiskery cheek and hugged him again. "I love you," she whispered loudly in his ear. "I love you an' Nod both. An' Genia loves you both, too."

"Does she?" asked Bradford softly.

"Oh, yes," Delight assured him, her blonde head nodding vigorously. "She would not be sitting here else. Genia is not fond of horses. Horses make her sneeze somethin' terrible."

Eugenia, who could not help but overhear, put one hand to her lips as Bradford pulled Delight even closer to him and glanced around the child.

"She is correct," Eugenia murmured. "I am generally not fond of horses. They have always made me sneeze. Do you know, I have not sneezed once since I stepped into this stall."

" 'Cause you love Nod an' are worried about him," Delight pointed out most innocently. "An' you love Lord Bradford too, an' are worried about him just as very much."

"Are you, Eugenia?" asked Bradford quietly.

"Well, of course I am worried about Nod. He is as fine and beautiful and brave a horse as ever lived. And we will make him well again, Edward," Eugenia declared. "We will."

Eugenia woke to find herself covered over with one of the quilts that had been covering Nod. "What?" she mumbled, fingering the quilt and wondering for a moment where she was and why she was not in her own bed.

"Hush," whispered a voice beside her. "You will wake him."

"Neil?"

"Just so. Aunt Diana was here for a while, but she could not stay. Much too cold and uncomfortable a place for a lady of her age. And too late at night for her to be out. I promised to send someone to wake her if anything at all happened."

"What t-time is it?"

"Coming up on one o'clock in the morning, I should imagine. Arnsworth was here. Attempted to get Nightingale to go back to the house with him but that damnable bird would not have a bit of it. Flew up there on that rafter and now he will not come down. Gilly left about midnight to escort Aunt Diana inside, but Jenkins and Mr. Stanley ought to have brewed more of the tea by now, so Arnsworth will be back with it soon, I should think."

Eugenia turned her head to discover Lord Bradford, Nod's head in his lap, wrapped in Jenkin's old greatcoat and sleeping soundly where he sat, his chin almost touching his chest.

"Never thought to see the day that I would feel the least bit sorry for that particular gentleman," Spelling whispered. "Sharp-tongued despot."

"He is not," Eugenia declared quietly but adamantly.

"Yes, he is—or at least, he was. He has changed considerably, Eugenia, from the gentleman I knew."

Eugenia stared up into Neil's dark, brooding eyes. "You have changed as well, Neil," she said haltingly. "You w-would not be here else."

"No, I am still the same nefarious Neil you always knew," grinned Spelling. "You are shivering, m'dear. Here, let me." And without so much as a by your leave, Mr. Spelling moved closer to his cousin, drew the quilt more tightly around her and then took her awkwardly into his arms. "There, now you will be more comfortable," he whispered.

"Neil, why are you out here? Why are you—?"

"Splendid animal, that horse," Mr. Spelling interrupted. "Always been fond of such animals as that. Would never think to let an animal like Nod die alone."

"He is not alone."

"No, he is not. Nor are you and Bradford, which is one of the things Aunt Diana cared particularly about."

"Well, of course we are not alone. Delight was here most of the time and Bobby Tripp and—"

"And Aunt Diana and Arnsworth and now me. Hush now, you will wake Bradford. He just dropped off a few minutes ago."

"He has been awake all this time?"

"Indeed. Whispering to Nod and encouraging him to drink dose after dose of the tea. Will not be able to stand without help come morning, Bradford will not. He has been sitting there with Nod's head in his lap for almost sixteen hours now."

Eugenia stared down at the strawberry roan and rubbed a hand along his side. "He is breathing easier than he was this afternoon or even earlier this evening, Neil. I think he is breathing a good deal easier."

"So it would seem. And he has been sleeping off and on ever since the sun set, from what Bobby Tripp tells me."

"Yes, he has. And poor Edward talked to him even when he knew him to be asleep. I have never seen such love as he has for this horse. He would not so much as leave Nod's side to eat."

Mr. Spelling nodded. "Which is why you did not come in to eat either, eh, cuz?"

"I could not leave them."

"No, of course you could not. You have fallen in love with that sharp-tongued ogre over there, have you?"

"In—in love? No. I—we—are friends, Neil."

"Tell me the truth, Eugenia, because it is more important than you can imagine. Have you lost your heart to Bradford?"

"Yes," she sighed. "I expect I have been in the process of losing it to him since first we met. But I am a fool. He will never love me in return."

"Say this, then. If he does not love you and will not marry you, does Mr. Arnsworth stand one chance in a million of gaining your hand in marriage?"

"Mr. Arnsworth is attracted to Clara."

"Yes, but if he were not, could you see him as a husband for yourself, Eugenia?"

Eugenia thought about it quite seriously. Her mind was a bit foggy with sleep and chill, but she did her very best to consider the thing. "Mr. Arnsworth is a very nice sort of gentleman, Neil," she said at last, "and I would consider marrying him, but it will never happen. Clara has set her cap for him and he is mad about her. They will be married to each other before the summer is out. I have not the least doubt of it. Did you come to Wicken Hall expressly to introduce me to Mr. Arnsworth, thinking to make a match of it? I could not believe it when Edward told me so. Why would you do such a thing as that?"

"Lost," groaned Mr. Spelling. "I am a dead man, Eugenia."

"What on earth do you mean?"

"He means that he has lost a wager on the thing," yawned Bradford, blinking himself awake. "Do not stare at me with such disbelief, Spelling. It is not a secret after all. It is in the Betting Book at White's. Carey's hunting lodge against your Tivally Grange that you will marry Arnsworth off to one of the gels who came out this Season."

"T-Tivally Grange?" stuttered Eugenia. "Oh, Neil, no! Will you never learn?"

"Shhhhh, Eugenia, you will wake the horse."

"Uncle Ezra will have your guts for garters, Neil!" Eugenia exclaimed, ignoring his admonition. "How could you take such a chance with Tivally Grange, and after you promised Uncle Ezra to guard the place with your life when he put it into your name! And how dare you think to marry me off to Mr. Arnsworth just to win a wager!" she added in disbelief. "I always knew that you were a scoundrel—but this—and Mr. Arnsworth is such a nice gentleman. You cannot tell me that he knows of this."

"No, he don't," sighed Neil. "Arnsworth is as innocent

as a spring lamb. And just as stupid, too, to prefer a brazen nobody like Clara Butterberry to you."

"Hear, hear," murmured Bradford.

"Yo ho ho," offered Lord Nightingale from his rafter.

"Rrrrrrrrrr," agreed Stanley Blithe, arising from a pile of straw in the corner and giving himself a good shake.

"Brrrrrrrrr," nickered Nod, his eyes blinking open to stare up at Bradford, his right ear twitching spastically.

"Nod?" Lord Bradford's whole attention was taken up upon the instant by that nicker and the twitching of that ear. "Nod, my lad, did you say something?"

"Brrrrrr," nickered the roan again and heaved his heavy head up out of Bradford's lap, his front hooves slipping and sliding on the straw-littered floor as he attempted to raise the entire front half of his body to an upright position.

"He is better!" Bradford cried softly. "Eugenia, he is better! Your tea has done him good! Help Eugenia back, Spelling," he added. "Take her back to the wall there. Nod? Come on, Nod. Come on, my lad. Stand up, old fellow."

"Why does he attempt to make him stand?" asked Eugenia as Mr. Spelling and she moved against the far wall of the stall to give the animal more space.

"Because then the congestion of the lungs will be more apt to clear, Eugenia. When a horse goes down, it means that he has lost all strength to fight and whatever congestion is in the lungs increases at a great rate. A downed horse will likely die within a day or two. But if Bradford can get Nod to stand again, well, there is hope for the beast, you see. A good deal of hope."

"Get up, Nod," whispered Eugenia, her heart pounding with hope and excitement. "Do get up, my darling. You will break your master's heart if you do not arise."

Stanley Blithe barked fitfully, dancing about and licking at Nod's nose. Bradford caught the horse's halter up in his one good hand and attempted to add some of his muscle to Nod's to help him. "Yes, Nod. Yes, my boy," he cried, his voice filled with grief and longing and tinged with hope. "I will invite Delight over every day, Nod, to bring you sugar. I vow it. Only gain your feet this one time, Nod. Just this one more time."

Lord Nightingale, excited by the words and movement below him, gave the most raucous, hair-raising screech and dove from his rafter straight at Nod. He landed, fighting for balance, right between the roan's ears.

Nod whinnied and slid and nickered and lurched, sending Lord Nightingale tipping one way and then the other, squawking and screeching and flapping. Stanley Blithe leaped and barked even more loudly. Bradford, his heart in his throat, shouted over that lump. "Up, Nod. Up, my lad!" And Nod licked at Bradford and Stanley Blithe, lurched and slid again, and then most abruptly got his back hooves beneath him and rose, front first, haunches last, stumbling into Bradford's shoulder and sending Lord Nightingale to a safer purchase upon his back along the way.

Bradford groaned and grinned at one and the same time. He placed his one useful hand beneath the roan's chin and pressed his face against the horse's own. "Thank you, God," he whispered, his lips moving against the strawberry hair, kissing it. "Thank you for giving me Nod back. Thank you for giving me Eugenia who knew how to bring Nod back. I willn't forget it. Not ever."

Eugenia and Lady Wickenshire agreed that both his lordship and his lordship's horse were impossible patients. Neither of them would take their medicine without complaint; neither wished to be planted firmly in one place for an entire day; and neither had the patience of an ant for being ill. Nod continued to be housed in the stables at Wicken Hall until the very last tiny bit of a rattle should be gone from his lungs. And though Lord Bradford was carried back to Squire Peabody's in his coach two days after Nod had regained his feet, that gentleman persisted in arriving at Wicken Hall as soon as the sun was up and could not be convinced to depart until the sun was setting again. For a full two weeks after his accident, Lord Bradford haunted Wicken Hall from dawn till dusk, with Mr. Stanley following him about like a shadow, pestering him to rest, to sit down for a moment, to take his medicine, just as Bradford pestered Nod to do what was best for him.

Eugenia would have laughed about it, if only Lord Bradford had looked happier, had laughed and smiled more readily. But apparently he could not. And it was not Nod's illness that kept him from it. She knew most certainly what did on the day he came to take Nod home. One sleeve dangling armless, the bandage around his brow almost buried beneath a riot of dark curls, he took her hand into his and informed her most seriously that he intended to drive to Wilderly Crossroads the following day and demand the truth from Lady Vermont concerning Miss Daily. Eugenia's throat closed up immediately and she only stared at him, her eyes brimming with worry.

"I must know, Eugenia," he told her, leaning against the paddock rail, a much improved Nod nibbling at the back of his hat brim. "Perhaps we do merely share a common ancestor, as you suggested, but I cannot go on without knowing the truth. Spelling has consented to accompany me. Well, not actually. He intends to go whether I do or not, and it will serve both of us to go together. I cannot drive, you know, one handed."

"You ought not go jouncing over the roads at all. You will make yourself ill again."

"I was never ill to begin with, Eugenia. Injured merely."

"Still are injured."

"Yes, well, I cannot drive, certainly, and Spelling can, so we go together in Peabody's curricle with Spelling's cattle to pull it. We have talked about it and your cousin will take the gel for a stroll while I confront the lady."

"You told Neil about—about—"

"No, only that I wished to discuss something privately with Lady Vermont and wished Miss Daily gone. But Spelling will take note of the likeness between us when he sees us side by side. I expect everyone will."

"Everyone?"

"Yes. I expect everyone of consequence will see us together at the Twilight Ball. A fortnight Friday. At the Grecian Ballroom in Wicken. Everyone will be there, including Lady Vermont and Miss Daily. The Reverend Mr. Butterberry kindly informed me of that last evening. You attend as well, do you not?"

"You know about the Twilight Ball?"

"Indeed. The Reverend Mr. Butterberry came to see how I did, you know, and invited me himself. It is for his church, I understand. A means of collecting extra funds."

"Yes. It is a sort of tradition in Wicken. Everyone who is anyone and lives within driving distance of the village subscribes. The shopkeepers generally contribute the decorations and the villagers and farmers the refreshments, and so all of the subscription funds go directly to the church."

"Just so. The orchestra donates their music, I am told."

"Well, they are not truly an orchestra."

"No?"

"They are old men and children and a young lady or two pounding and puffing and plucking upon whatever it is they know how to play."

"And the Grecian Ballroom?"

"Oh, it is a real ballroom."

"Thank goodness for that."

"But it is not very large. And the floor rises in the middle and dips on the sides. And the roof leaks."

"Let us pray it willn't rain then," smiled Bradford winningly.

Eugenia giggled.

"There, now that is a sight better. I thought never to hear you giggle again."

Wilderly Crossroads, Bradford discovered, was neither wild nor a crossroads. It was, instead, an enormous house of soft brown brick set within a park as lush as spring itself. Roses climbed around it on all sides and a long, white-graveled drive led to a double door beneath a porte cochere.

"Lovely place, no?" asked Spelling as he handed the reins to one of Lady Vermont's grooms.

"Indeed. Lord Vermont is well-invested, eh?"

"Dead. Has been for years. No heir, either. Title has gone back to the Crown along with the entailed lands. But this little place—this belongs to Lady Vermont free and clear."

"Do you know everything about everyone, Spelling?"

"Only everything about everyone's money. No, do not frown at me like that, Bradford. We have a truce, you and I."

"A most unstable one."

"Yes, well, that is because of your crotchety tendencies, not because of anything I have done. I should warn you. Unless she has altered greatly from the lady she was when Nicky and Eugenia and I were children, Lady Vermont ain't to be taken lightly no matter how frail she looks. Tough old grouse."

"I will remember."

Having doffed their hats and gloves, they followed a butler in a smart blue coat and buff breeches along a winding and startlingly bright corridor into a cozy room with one entire wall of windows. "Lord Bradford and Mr. Spelling, my lady," announced the butler, then turned and departed.

Miss Daily was nowhere about. Lady Vermont received them graciously into her solitary presence. "Alice is reading in the little gazebo in the garden and her abigail is with her, Mr. Spelling," she said with a soft smile. "It is the same gazebo in which you, Nicky and Eugenia played when you were children. If you would care to pay her your respects?"

"Indeed I would, madam," Spelling responded with a careful bow. "Oh, and madam—"

"Yes, Mr. Spelling."

"You will not be too hard upon Bradford, eh? Injured, you know," he grinned as he departed through the French doors.

"He never was the most charming of gentlemen," sighed Lady Vermont, watching as Spelling crossed to the garden. "But he is rich, and if Alice can only find him in some way attractive—"

"Alice?" interrupted Bradford. "Her name is Alice?"

"Sit down, Lord Bradford. You have had an accident?"

"A minor mishap. I have brought you the bank notes from my father," he said quietly, though his heart beat so wildly within his breast it threatened to burst forth into the room. He reached into his coat pocket and placed a fat leather case upon the long low table between them. "He wrote that you would be expecting these. He pays you such a sum every quarter, does he not?"

"Yes," Lady Vermont replied, her hands smoothing the creases from an afternoon dress of forest-green silk. "He pays me such a sum every quarter and has for the past eighteen years. There were two of you, were there not?"

"Two of me?"

"I mean to say, Her Grace had twin sons."

"Yes."

"And you are how old now? Twenty-two?"

"Just so."

"You will wonder how I know."

"I do not give a fig how you know, madam."

"Do not get on your high horse with me, boy!" Lady Vermont exclaimed, and then she lowered her eyes, bit her lip and her hands fluttered to the riband tied at her throat.

"I am sorry. I ought not have said that. I have been expecting you since the day following our meeting at Wicken Hall. It makes one a tad nervous to await someone who never comes."

"I apologize then. I could not come sooner." Bradford leaned back in the chair and crossed one long leg over the other. "My father wrote me to command me to deliver you those notes. I was inclined to ignore him, until I saw Miss Daily at Wicken Hall."

"You saw Alice? When? She was not in the summer parlor when you came to meet me."

"As I was departing the Hall. For a moment our eyes met."

Lady Vermont stared at him. Her lower lip trembled the slightest bit. The granite gray of her eyes grew darker still.

Bradford studied her in silence.

"Do not stare at me as though I am some odd species of bug!" exclaimed the lady abruptly. "Say what it is that you have come to say and then begone."

"I cannot say what I have to say to *you,* madam. It is obvious to me that it does not apply to you. Since I was a boy of eight I thought a particular Lady Vermont to be my father's mistress. I thought her to be the woman who caused my mother's angry departure, who separated me from my brother and shattered my life. But I was sorely mistaken, it appears. It was your name I heard Mama and the Old Squire speak, but you are not the woman responsible for the turn into Hades that my life took back then."

"I am the woman who forced your father to pay for his wickedness to my family," Lady Vermont declared. "And I have compelled him to keep on paying, too. And he will pay until his daughter has made an acceptable match or he will pay forever if she does not."

"She *is* my sister," hissed Bradford.

"You have laid eyes upon her, you say. Surely, you did not doubt whose eyes flashed back at you."

"My father's eyes. Miss Daily is some cousin twice or thrice removed, a very kind friend attempted to convince me last week. But my friend has never faced my father's eyes. She *is* my sister," he added more quietly. "Her name is Alice."

"And now what will you do?" Lady Vermont asked, lifting her ancient chin with a certain arrogance. "You will not ruin the child's opportunities, I warn you of that. If you so much as part your lips to denounce her to anyone, to question her mother's morals or her own lineage, I will cut out your tongue. I vow it."

Bradford's jaw slackened a bit. Ruin her opportunities? Denounce her? The words buzzed about in his brain. What was the old woman thinking to suggest that he—

"Your father dragged my daughter down into the very pits of degradation, boy, and then kindly bestowed upon her a reminder of his lust and his lies. With his eyes like ice and his frozen heart, he drove my gel to madness, and in so doing, he gave me an orphan for a granddaughter. But Alice will not suffer defeat at his hands, nor at your hands either. I am determined to protect her."

"Your daughter was my father's mistress? She is dead?"

Lady Vermont's chin rose higher, her back stiffened visibly. "By her own hand, they said. But they lied. She died by your father's hand, my gel did, just as certainly as if your father had thrust the knife home himself."

Sixteen

Bradford's boot heels cracked against the cobblestones with the force of a man wishing to run full-out, but holding himself forcibly in check—energy suppressed and exploding at one and the same time. He reached the steps of the gazebo to discover three sets of eyes staring at him. But there was only one set in which he was interested at the moment. He mounted the steps, took four long strides toward those widening eyes, grasped Miss Daily's arm and tugged her up from the little bench upon which she sat. Awkwardly, he loosed his grip on her wrist and circled her waist with that one useful arm of his and pulled her against him, kissing her soundly, first on one cheek and then the other. Miss Daily was so very shocked that she did not think to oppose him, and Mr. Spelling, mistaking the suppressed energy for rage, thought better than to so much as tap the marquess on the shoulder in protest. Only the little abigail protested, and that was but a squeal of amazement.

"I have searched for years to find my brother," whispered Bradford avidly, his breath sending wisps of Miss Daily's dark curls fluttering, his breath tickling at her ear. "I have searched *forever* for my brother and I have discovered for myself a sister instead. And by gawd, how beautiful you are, Alice!"

"Your sister?" Miss Daily gasped in shock, bringing her palms up against his chest and pushing herself away from him. "You are mistaken, sir. I have no brothers."

Bradford's blue eyes flashed and glittered down at her and she trembled at the boiling mix of emotions she saw there. "Your face is d-dearly like my own," she managed, keeping her hands up between them, as thought contemplating an attack upon his part, "but that is not—"

"Dearly like your own and dearly like our father's, Alice."

"My father is dead."

"Our father will wish he is dead when next I see him. I promise you that. You are the daughter of the Duke of Sotherland. Sotherland sired you, not some Canterbury tale of a gentleman called Daily."

"No! That is *not* so!" exclaimed Miss Daily. "I have told you that you are mistaken, sir. My papa was Mr. Albert Daily, a fine, decent gentleman who loved my mother dearly. They were devoted to each other. Let me go!" she demanded, shoving Bradford away as he reached out a second time. "You—I do not even know you and I cannot imagine what has put such a thing into your head, but you are wrong! My mama would never have so disgraced herself as to—as to—take into her bed a man who was not her husband! You are beyond anything rude to suggest it!"

"Brother and sister," murmured Spelling, staring at the pair of them. "It is not at all obvious when the two of you are apart, but together, side by side—"

"Stay out of this, Spelling," growled Bradford. "It is none of it your business."

Spelling raised his hands in surrender and backed away. "I was merely noting the resemblance, Bradford. Merely taking note. And I stand upon your side in it, you know. You do look amazingly alike."

"It is still none of it your business," Bradford snarled. "And you willn't say a word about this to anyone or I will cut off your ears and serve them to you with bread and butter!"

"Control yourself at once, my lord," demanded Lady Vermont, climbing the steps to the gazebo with one elderly hand upon the rail and the other holding her skirt. "You are quite beyond yourself and you are frightening the child."

"No, he is not," declared Alice. "But he is making me very angry, Grandmama. The man is mad, I think. To call me his sister and to suggest that—that—"

"He is not mad," Lady Vermont replied quietly, stepping between Lord Bradford and her granddaughter. "He is aggravating and arrogant and stubborn, but not mad. Ellen, cease standing there with your ears perked so and return to the house at once!"

"Y-yes, my lady," the little abigail replied, and hurried from the gazebo, almost tripping over Mr. Spelling's feet in her rush to get away.

"And you, Mr. Spelling—"

"I am going nowhere, madam. I have already heard what Bradford and Miss Daily have to say and I will tell you that I am inclined to believe Bradford, so if you have come to gainsay him, I had best hear that as well."

"Oh, devil it!"

"Grandmama!"

"Well, what *am* I to say? All this, just when you and Mr. Spelling were getting on so well together. I will tell you, Lord Bradford, that I wish your grandmama had had the good sense to drown your papa the day he was born. We should all have been better off for it."

"I should never have been conceived, madam."

"Exactly so! All of us much better off!"

"Grandmama!" Miss Daily, her cheeks rapidly turning the color of ripe tomatoes, took her grandmother firmly by the hand, led her to one of the bench seats and sat her down upon it. "You must not say such things, Grandmama, no matter how aggravating the gentleman is," she admonished, sitting beside the elderly lady. "It is quite likely that Mr. Spelling thinks we are all mad by this time and will wish nothing further to do with any of us."

"No such thing," murmured Spelling taking a seat upon the opposite side of Lady Vermont. "Nothing could keep me from wishing to know you better, Miss Daily. Madness, mayhem and Bradford notwithstanding, I fully intend to lead you out at the Twilight Ball at least twice."

"Twice?" Lady Vermont's glowering countenance brightened a bit at that. "To lead the same young woman out twice, Mr. Spelling, denotes a certain—interest."

"Who cares about the Twilight Ball!" bellowed Bradford, stuffing his one useable hand into his pocket and glaring down at the lot of them. "Who cares what dancing with a gel twice denotes! The only dancing worth discussing at the moment is my father's dancing between the sheets!"

"Oh!" cried Miss Daily, covering her face with her hands.

"Will you tell her the truth, madam, or must I?" Bradford continued, stalking across the space between them and glaring down at the old woman. And then Miss Daily uncovered her face and glared at him. "You cease to plague my grandmama right this minute," she commanded, putting an arm around the old woman's shoulders. "I will not have you calling her a liar!"

"See how they freeze, those eyes," Bradford whispered in awe. "So cold that they could burn a fellow to the bone. Exactly like m'father's."

"And like yours," murmured Lady Vermont, turning to her granddaughter with a face grown suddenly much older. "He may call me a liar, Alice. I am a liar. I have lied to you for eighteen years. There never was a Mr. Daily, my darling. I made him up. I gave you his name so that you would not be marked for all of your life as a—a—but Lord Bradford speaks the truth. You are his half-sister. I have always known it."

Miss Daily squeaked and her hand rose to cover her lips.

"I thought to bury your shame with your mama," continued Lady Vermont, haltingly, "but now—now he—"

"Bury her shame? *Her* shame?" shouted Bradford abruptly, his hand fleeing his pocket, going to seize Miss Daily's wrist and tugging her up to face him. "Do not listen to the old lady, Alice. The only shame to be had belongs to our father, not to you. It is all his and he will never feel it. He never feels shame for anything he does! And—and—" The outrage in Bradford's voice disappeared just as suddenly as it had come. "And I willn't tell anyone," he said in a hoarse whisper, as he studied the very frightened lines of her face. "I willn't, Alice, unless you say that I may. I w-will say that we are—cousins. And you need not fear Spelling letting it slip because—"

"I do not wish to eat my ears on bread and butter," offered Spelling softly, "among other things. I will not spill it, my gel, my word upon it."

"So, you see. There is nothing to fear, Alice," Bradford managed awkwardly, freeing her, his gaze abruptly fastening itself upon his boots. "If only you will be my sister when no one is about— If only you will let me come to know you and, perhaps, you could come to know me—"

"What is your name?" asked Alice, her hand going beneath his chin, urging him to look at her again.

"Edward."

"H-how do you do, Edward. I am most confused and I do not know what is best to be done, but I do believe you now, and I do believe that I am pleased to make your acquaintance after all. I have often wished for a brother."

"You have two brothers," Bradford replied, the frustration on his face easing away at last into a bewildered smile. "I have yet to discover where Peter has got to and apparently I must get him out of some particularly sticky briars, but I will, and then he will be as pleased to have you for a sister as I am."

* * *

It was an entire week later that Eugenia sat upon the sofa in the summer parlor, with Sweetpea purring in her lap and Lord Nightingale swinging upside down from the chandelier. Her gaze was fixed upon the sunset beyond the west window, but in her mind, the sun was setting not in pinks and golds on the rose garden, but in grays and blacks on her future happiness.

"And that is a perfectly absurd thing to think," she told herself quietly. "Just because he has not come to call for an entire week. . . . He was ill. He is busy. Nod requires him. Oh, if only Edward were not a marquess, Sweetpea. If only I were not such a plain Jane. If only I did not have this wretched limp!"

"Mrrrrrrrr," Sweetpea replied in total unconcern.

"Yes, well, you do not care because you are not in love with the gentleman," Eugenia sighed.

"Knollsmarmer," muttered the macaw.

"Just so. Knollsmarmer." Eugenia's lips twitched into a smile as she turned her gaze from the sunset to the living rainbow of Lord Nightingale, who had righted himself upon the chandelier and was in the process of gnawing one of its candles into tiny pieces. "I may as well admit it. I am in love with your Knollsmarmer, Nightingale, though I know nothing can come of it. He is kind enough to call me friend now, and—and he d-did kiss me, but a kiss is nothing to such a worldly gentleman as Edward. Why, a kiss is nothing to Clara for goodness' sake. I ought not even think of it. Edward might look in the very highest places for a wife. He will find someone beautiful and titled and she will h-have two legs of equal l-length. He must be a raving lunatic to ever once think to marry me."

"Lalalalala," Nightingale sang in Serendipity's voice, and Eugenia laughed the saddest laugh. "Oh, what a fool I am to even think upon it. Delight and Bobby Tripp have been to visit Nod every day, but Lord Bradford has not come to call upon me at all. And he would come, if he cared for me. Mr. Arnsworth calls upon Clara every morning. He cannot get enough of her. She is all he ever speaks of—how beautiful Clara is, and how sweet, and how charming. He is so enthralled with Clara that Mary comes here when she can to avoid the two of them and their loving glances."

The thought of Mary Butterberry saddened Eugenia even more. "Poor, dear Mary," she whispered. "Her heart given to a gentleman who thinks himself beneath even his brother's notice. What will she do if Peter never returns for her? What will she do if Edward cannot find him and Peter is lost forever?"

"YohohoKnolls—marmer!" Lord Nightingale shrieked and tossed a candle to the carpeting. "Yohoho! Knollsmarmer!"

"Peter will not be lost forever, you know. I will find him," a most familiar voice said from the doorway as Nightingale stretched to his greatest height, ruffled his feathers, spread his tail and with one flap of his wings, sailed down and landed on Lord Bradford's shoulder. "Must you forever be riding on me, you scoundrel?" growled the marquess. "Jenkins said that I might come right up, but, you are alone here, Eugenia."

"No, she is not neither," cried a tiny voice from the corridor to Bradford's right. "I am here, too!" Delight came dashing to him, took hold of his hand and led him into the room. "Mr. Jenkins said as how I was to come an' sit in the corner as quiet as a mouse until Lady Wickenshire arrives. I am to be your chaperon. What is a chaperon, Lord Bradford? An' how quiet are mouses? An' which corner am I s'posed to sit in? An' can I have a chair, do you think, or must I truly sit right in the corner upon the carpeting?"

Bradford laughed. "Minx. I would scoop you up and deposit you atop that sideboard if I had two good arms. Sit down there beside Eugenia and frown at me from time to time, and you will be as perfect a chaperon as are the grown-up ladies. Good afternoon, Eugenia," he said then, taking her hand into his own and bowing quite properly over it. "I expect you thought never to see me again, eh?"

"I was beginning to wonder where you had gone," Eugenia admitted. "You left that afternoon for Wilderly Crossroads and I have not seen so much as your shadow since, though Neil has told me that you do still exist."

"Well, I have not come until now because I had to decide what to tell you and I—I will admit it—I was sorely torn."

"Sorely torn?" Eugenia studied him quite seriously. "How so? Over what? Edward, you have not discovered yet another secret that your father kept from you?"

"Do you mean besides Alice?"

Eugenia's eyes widened considerably and she leaned toward him as he seated himself in the chair opposite her own, sending Lord Nightingale fluttering off to the top of his cage. "Edward, are you saying that Miss Daily *is* . . ." and then she glanced at Delight beside her and ceased to speak at once.

"Little pitchers have big ears, eh?" smiled Bradford. "We had a nurse, once, Peter and I, who was accustomed to say that very thing. I vowed to say to all the world that we are cousins, Eugenia, until Miss Daily accepts an offer of marriage, of course. A gentleman who is to be her husband must necessarily be made privilege to the truth."

"But if you vowed it, Edward, you ought not—"

"Yes, I ought not tell you differently. That is what I was torn about. I thought on it for days. I attempted over and over again to lump you in, so to speak, with the world at large, but I could not. You are not a part of the world of which I spoke, Eugenia. Not at all. You are—someone very special and—well, never mind that for now. Suffice to say that Alice is precisely what I imagined her to be and not a third cousin twice removed."

"What is a third cousin twice removed?" asked Delight.

"It is a cousin of mine who has displeased me, and so I have picked her up and tossed her out the window and when she came back into the room, I did the same again," Bradford replied in dire tones. "Thus I removed her from my sight twice, you see."

"Oh."

"Just so. Do not giggle, Eugenia, you are spoiling the effect."

"What effect?" asked Lady Wickenshire as she rustled into the room. "Lord Bradford, how good of you to call. Jenkins is arranging for tea as we speak."

"My lady," Bradford welcomed her, standing and bowing quite nicely in her direction. "How kind of you to join us."

"Lord Bradford threw his cousin out a window," announced Delight, her eyes as round as saucers. "Twice."

"What?"

"He was merely teasing, Aunt Diana," Eugenia offered quickly. "Delight wished to know what was a third cousin twice removed and Lord Bradford said—"

"I do not think I wish to know," interrupted Lady Wickenshire with a shake of her head. "Whatever the gentleman told you, Delight, it was not precisely the truth, darling. Run along now and see if you cannot find Cook. She has made something special for you and has been seeking you everywhere."

"I have had a letter from your brother, my lady," said Lord Bradford as Lady Wickenshire sat and he regained his chair.

"From Ezra?"

"Yes, madam, and he informs me that no one called Peter Winthrop or Peter Finlay has booked passage for India in the past two years—or hired himself onto any of the ships as a hand."

"Truly? That is excellent news, is it not?" asked Eugenia. "I am so grateful, Aunt Diana, that you wrote to Uncle Ezra."

"As am I," nodded Bradford. "I cannot thank you enough, madam."

"Piffle," murmured the dowager with a wave of her hand. "It was little enough to do when Eugenia was so very worried about you that she was in tears."

"Was she?"

"Indeed. I never thought to see my niece so very upset over a gentleman."

"Aunt Diana!"

"Well, you were, darling. I thought your heart would break for him."

Eugenia's cheeks flamed, and then she met Lord Bradford's gaze and the decided interest in his eyes made her cheeks flame all the more. But then he grinned, and though her heart stuttered at the sight of it, her embarrassment fled upon the instant and she laughed at herself. "You were correct from the first, Edward," she chuckled. "I am a peagoose of sorts."

"Never," Bradford replied. "I was sadly mistaken there. I could not tell an angel from a fowl when she stood right before my eyes. There is one thing else I have to tell you, my dear ladies. I have received a letter as well from the Earl of Wickenshire."

"From Nicky?" they asked in unison.

"Indeed, from your Nicky. He is an exceptional sort of gentleman, is he not? I look forward to making his acquaintance."

"Oh, but Nicky and Sera do not plan to return before September at the earliest, and you have leased Peabody House only for the summer," Eugenia blurted out.

"Yes, well, I shall need to rectify that situation, for I find it necessary to remain a while longer in Kent."

"You do?"

"I believe I do. Something has—arisen—that requires my attention here and I dare not leave before I have finished the business."

"What did my son have to say, Lord Bradford, about your brother? Does he remember a Peter Winthrop in Wicken?"

"No, not at all. He does remember, however, a Peter Winthrop somewhere near Exmoor."

"At Willowsweep?" gasped Eugenia.

"Just so. Willowsweep. That was the place. Wrote that he believed he had hired a fellow by that name to work on a house for him. Said it was quite likely the fellow's name would be found in his ledger along with the fellow's direction. It does not tell me where Peter is to be found now, of course, but it puts me one step closer in my search."

"But you must drive to Willowsweep as soon as possible, Edward," Eugenia declared. "Nicky only finished the work on that old house at the end of this spring. If his bailiff has your brother's direction—"

"Your cousin has written to his bailiff to send it to me," smiled Bradford. "I am to expect it within a se'nnight. And he says the man will go into the village to see if Peter is still there, though he doubts it will be so."

"Dearest Nicky," grinned Lady Wickenshire. "He is always so efficient."

"Is he? Well, for certain I should like to know him. I have written him back, thanking him for his help and—"

"And what?" Eugenia asked.

"And asking to meet him when he arrives home. I did explain to him that I could not possibly depart Kent before the middle of September at the earliest."

"Because of the thing you must attend to?" Lady Wickenshire's eyes studied Bradford most seriously.

"Just so, my lady. It will take me until then to do the thing properly. And I have every intention to do it properly."

"I fear that I misunderstand you, my lord," the dowager said with the cock of an eyebrow.

"No, madam. I think that you understand me exceeding well."

"Whatever are you speaking of?" demanded Eugenia, looking from one to the other of them. "You are both of you being most mysterious. Aunt Diana, how can you presume to know the first thing about Edward's—about Lord Bradford's—business?"

"I am an old woman," responded the dowager, turning her gaze to Eugenia. "Old women simply know things without being told."

Stanley glowered; Stanley grumbled; Stanley rocked back and forth from toe to heel and absolutely scowled, but Bradford would have none of it.

"It is of the utmost importance that I am in possession of two good arms tonight, Stanley. Why do you think I have been going about fencing with shadows, eh? To get the strength back into this one, that is why."

"But, my lord, a sling to hold it somewhat steady. I shall fashion it out of one of the black neckcloths. It will make you look dashing, adventurous."

"No, Stanley. Now will you help me to don this blasted coat, or must I send for Mr. Waggoner or Mrs. Hornby to do it?"

Stanley held the coat for him. He grumbled as he saw the marquess wince shrugging into the tight-fitting garment.

"Never mind. It merely pinched a bit. You do not understand, Stanley. Tonight I intend to offer my support to someone, and I cannot offer it if I have only one arm with which to do so."

"You are perfectly correct, my lord. I do not understand. Tonight you are attending a ball, merely."

"The Twilight Ball."

"A man may dance with an arm in a sling."

"Yes."

"There is—you are not planning to—there is not going to be a mill afterward?" asked Stanley, aghast as this sudden thought occurred to him. "Oh, my lord, do not say that you have agreed to support some scoundrel in a mill. You cannot possibly."

Bradford stared at the horror in Stanley's eyes and burst into whoops.

Mr. Arnsworth stared at his neckcloth in the looking glass, then at Mr. Spelling. "It is not quite right," he murmured.

"No, it is wretched," Spelling observed. "Give it up, Arnsworth, and settle for a Ballroom."

"I cannot," sighed Arnsworth, divesting himself of the tragedy, tossing it to the floor and taking another of the pristine neckcloths from his valet's hands. "It is a matter of utmost importance. I must wear the Sentimental tonight."

"Something to do with Miss Clara Butterberry, no doubt."

"Yes, if you must know, Spelling. It has everything to do with my Clara. I—I—intend to—I intend to discover if she—and I will not do it wearing a stupid Ballroom."

Spelling laughed. He truly did not mean to, but he could not help himself. "She will not know the difference, Gilly."

"She will. It is a signal of sorts. If she sees I have tied the Sentimental, she will begin to suspect that—that I wish to have a moment with her alone."

"Balderdash! As if that little hoyden would not give you a moment alone on any evening of the year!"

"Do not call my love a hoyden again, Spelling, or I shall be forced to call you out."

"Coming it a bit too strong, Gilly. You and I ain't near high enough on the social scale to go calling each other out."

"Any gentleman may do it."

"No, that is not precisely true. You are certain about Clara? I mean, you are not like to change your mind?"

"No, no, I am caught up by her and I will marry her if she will have me. But I told her that when the time came, I would wear the Sentimental in celebration of the feelings of my heart."

Spelling took the neckcloth which Arnsworth had been twisting about nervously in his hands and tossed it to the floor atop the five others that already lay there. He took another from Arnsworth's valet, placed it around Gilly's neck with his own hands and began to tie the thing for him. "Just hold still, Arnsworth. I have been tying the Sentimental for years. It ain't hard. Though what I ought to do is tie a regular hangman's knot and string you up from the chandelier."

Arnsworth's valet gasped, and Arnsworth himself stared up at Spelling, his eyes wider than they had ever been. "W-why would you wish to do that?"

"Because you are going to ask Clara Butterberry to marry you, you wretch. I did not bring you into Kent to marry Clara Butterberry. I brought you here to marry my cousin."

"But I *love* Clara."

"Yes, I know you do. You will disappoint your mama because of Clara and you will let me die because of her."

"D-die? You?"

"I do not expect you to understand, Arnsworth, but once you dedicate yourself to Clara, my life will be worth nothing."

Gilly gulped. "Your life? N-nothing? Are you hopelessly in love with Clara yourself?"

"Gawd no!" Spelling exclaimed, continuing to work at the knot in Arnsworth's neckcloth.

"Then what—"

"I will have lost a wager, Arnsworth. I wagered that I would see you married to one of the young ladies who came out this Season. Eugenia is one of them, but Clara ain't. And because Clara ain't, I have lost Tivally Grange to Carey and when my Uncle Ezra hears of it, he will skin me alive, roast me upon a spit and then serve me up with the boiled potatoes. There, you have a Sentimental. I hope you will wear one at my funeral."

"A wager? You did everything for me b-because of a wager?"

"Do not look at me with such disappointment, Gilly. I did not tie that knot for you just now because of a wager. Gawd, but I am growing soft—like butter melting on a muffin. There was a time I would have tricked you into marrying Eugenia."

"How would you have done that?"

"Have not a notion. Does not matter at any rate. I find I like you, Arnsworth. And if it is Clara you must have—" he shrugged his shoulders most eloquently.

"We are t-truly friends?"

"Apparently, though I cannot think where I misstepped to have it become so."

"You did not misstep."

"Yes, yes I did," mused Spelling, "and Uncle Ezra will call me to account for it shortly. But never mind, Gilly. We shall go to the Twilight Ball, you shall ask for your Clara's hand and I will have a dance or two with Miss Daily. Tomorrow I will worry about tomorrow."

Seventeen

Eugenia sat upon one of the couches at the far end of the Grecian Ballroom amongst the dowagers, the mamas and the spinsters and listened to the music, which was dreadful, and watched the dancers, who were wonderful. She smiled as she saw Mr. Arnsworth come down the line with Clara beside him.

He looks so proud, she thought. He stands so straight and smiles so confidently. Clara is just the woman to make him sure of himself. And Neil, she mused, as her cousin led Miss Daily down the line. There is something odd about Neil of late. He actually seems to be Mr. Arnsworth's friend, and he seems drawn to Miss Daily, too—Neil, who never gives a fig for anyone. "I believe the world has turned upside down," she murmured.

"So do I," offered Mary Butterberry, plumping down beside her on the couch.

"You do?"

"Yes. I have only now left Papa, who is deep in conversation with Lord Bradford in the antechamber and—"

"Lord Bradford is here?" interrupted Eugenia.

"Did you not know he intended to come?"

"Yes, but gentlemen do not always do what they intend."

"True," nodded Mary. "I have come to that conclusion myself. Lord Bradford insists upon replacing the funds that father believes Peter to have stolen. And he has replaced Papa's old stickpin with a diamond one—in reparation for the amber one which has gone missing. It is so very honorable of Lord Bradford. He does it because Peter is his twin, you know."

"Yes, I know," nodded Eugenia.

"Not that Peter did actually steal anything, because he did not. Papa and the others merely think that he did."

"Miss Butterberry?"

"Yes?" asked Mary looking up to discover Mr. Arnsworth standing before her.

"I wonder if I might have this dance?"

"Oh! Of course you may. I should be pleased. Do excuse me, Eugenia," she added, rising to join Mr. Arnsworth upon the floor.

Eugenia watched them go and wondered, with merely a bit of envy, what it would be like to do a reel.

"I expect I shall never know," she whispered, and then her thoughts turned to Lord Bradford. What can he and Mr. Butterberry be speaking of for so very long in the antechamber? she wondered. A new set has begun and still they do not appear. What can they possibly have to discuss for such a length of time?

Unless, Eugenia thought with a sudden sinking in her stomach. Unless Edward feels compelled to make other reparations upon his brother's behalf. "No," she said softly, in horrified tones. "Mary would never have allowed herself to be compromised. And even if she had, Edward would never feel duty-bound to marry her in his brother's stead."

And then she glanced up to see Lord Bradford stroll into the ballroom on Mr. Butterberry's arm and her heart slipped all the way down into the toe of her left slipper. In a coat of midnight blue, with white waistcoat and white cravat, his black satin breeches flawless, his dark curls aglow beneath the candlelight, Lord Bradford was the most alluring gentleman in the entire room.

And Mr. Butterberry was introducing him around! Eugenia watched in panic as the parson led the marquess first

to one group and then another, the most radiant of smiles
upon his very clerical face. Mary *has* been compromised,
she thought with dread, and Edward *is* offering himself up
to atone for Peter's sins!

Lord Bradford and Mr. Butterberry made their way
slowly around the room and Eugenia, her heart in her throat,
followed their every step, her eyes beginning to burn with
tears at the certainty that Mr. Butterberry was introducing
the marquess as his son-in-law-to-be. By the time the two
gentlemen had reached the place where Lady Vermont and
Miss Daily sat against the windows, Eugenia's hands had
grown quite cold and she thought she could not take another
breath without bursting into sobs. "You cannot do this to
yourself," she whispered. "Edward, you have your entire
life ahead. You cannot spend it tied to Mary Butterberry. If
she has been compromised, it is your brother's duty to wed
her, not yours."

A loud buzzing could be heard as the music ended, arising from the place where Lord Bradford stood. Eugenia's
brow furrowed. "What is it?" she asked as Mary Butterberry returned to sit beside her. "What does everyone speak
of so suddenly?"

"Lord Bradford and Miss Daily, Eugenia," Mary informed her. "Do you not see them standing there together?
Mr. Arnsworth and I strolled right by them and it is the
most amazing thing. They look very much alike. Why, Lord
Bradford and my Peter and Miss Daily might be triplets!"

"No," Eugenia replied. "They cannot look so alike as
that. He is much taller than she for one thing."

"Yes, but you must see their faces side by side, Eugenia."

"They are cousins and neither realized that the other existed," offered Mrs. Turney from behind Eugenia. "Is it not
utterly romantic that a gentleman should come here to
Wicken to discover a young woman almost identical to himself?" she asked, turning to Lady Wickenshire. "Did you
hear, my lady, that Mr. Peter Winthrop is related to Lord

Bradford as well? I have it straight from the Reverend Mr. Butterberry. How odd that all three should come—one at a time—to Wicken."

"Very odd," agreed Lady Wickenshire. "Fate, one might say."

"Fate, indeed!" a new voice began. "I cannot but think that this must be some omen. . . ."

The remainder of the conversation did not at all register with Eugenia's brain, because drawing up before her was Lord Bradford himself. He took her hand, bowed over it, raised it to his lips and pressed those lips tenderly against the inside of Eugenia's wrist. The gentle passion of it came near to set Eugenia's teeth to chattering. And when he released her hand, she had all she could do to keep from leaping out of her chair to throw her arms around his neck and plead with him not to throw his life away in reparation for his brother's mistakes, no matter how needful he thought Mary Butterberry. And then she gazed directly up into his eyes, and swallowed drily.

"Not about to burst into tears again, are you, peagoose?"

"N-no, not at all."

"Good, because there is something I mean to do and it would look most odd if you were seen to cry over it."

"Do? Something you mean to do?" Eugenia's gaze flew from Bradford to Mary Butterberry and back again. Behind the marquess, the little group of music-makers had struck up another tune, and couple after couple wandered out onto the floor to waltz.

"They are playing a waltz!" cried Miss Butterberry, truly astonished. "Oh, Papa will have their heads at services this Sunday. Indeed he will."

"No, he will not. We have discussed it, your father and I, and he has allowed that there may be one waltz this evening. A very special dance, for a very special young woman."

Eugenia studied the two of them and a tear escaped from

her eye. She managed to stop it before it got as far as her cheek by a very quick swipe of her hand.

"Come and waltz with me, Eugenia," Lord Bradford said.

"M-me? Do you not mean Mary?"

"No, I do not mean Mary. I mean to dance with you, Eugenia." He held out both his hands to her, and though she thought to protest because she limped after all, limped dreadfully, and he knew it too, and they would look like perfect fools attempting to dance in front of everyone she knew, she nevertheless allowed him to help her to her feet. He led her to the floor and took her gently and confidently into his two good arms. "Do not look quite so terrified, Eugenia. You must only lean on me, my darling girl, and I shall do the balancing for us both," he said.

And then he smiled his most winning smile just for her and Eugenia's heart soared into the heavens. He took one step and then another and another and they were dancing. Dancing! Eugenia was floating around the floor in strong, steady arms. Floating like a veritable feather. And all around her, she absolutely knew that Nicky's Cupid was tossing his arrows with abandon, piercing the most unlikely hearts. "And the wind is blowing from just the right direction," she whispered, "and the sun has tilted just so and the faeries have arisen from the rose garden. And you did not offer for Mary Butterberry because you thought that your brother had compromised her, did you?"

"Offer for Miss Butterberry? Eugenia! These faeries you speak of, have they chipped all the cups in your cupboard? I am noble, my dear, but not so noble as to face such a fate as that."

Bradford's arms held tightly to Eugenia as they swirled and turned—more slowly and not quite as gracefully as the others upon the floor—but quite as happily. "You little peagoose," Bradford whispered. "I have waited for weeks to see that particular look in your eyes, Eugenia. It is the most amazed and joyful and smug little look. Just as I thought it would be a month or so ago, when I stood on a balcony and watched you walk away and knew that I ought to ask you to dance then and there. I wish I had not been so very unsociable then."

"Edward, I am dancing," Eugenia managed on a breath. "You cannot know. You cannot possibly realize. I am living a dream."

His eyes smiled down at her as sweet and clear and blue as the summer skies, and the slightly uneven floor of the Grecian Ballroom might have been the finest floor of the finest ballroom in the finest palace in all of England. Eugenia would not have noted the difference.

When the music ended, Bradford escorted her from the floor, right past Lady Wickenshire, out into the vestibule, down one flight of stairs, across the corridor, through the front door of the establishment, and around the side of the building, where he stopped upon a grassy verge beneath a veritable star-studded quilt of a sky and laughed down at her.

"Edward," she whispered breathlessly, "what has gotten into you? We cannot be out here alone. Already Aunt Diana must be running after us and everyone in the ballroom buzzing about where we have gone and what we are doing. I will be thoroughly compromised in front of the entire population of Wicken."

"Oh?" murmured Bradford.

"Edward, I am serious."

"Yes, so am I. We are not alone, Eugenia."

"We are not?"

"No," he chuckled just as Nod snorted rather loudly and then whinnied. "Nod is just over there."

"A horse does not count, Edward."

"He thinks he does," the marquess laughed as Nod came up behind him and nudged him in the small of the back, shoving him closer to Eugenia. "And besides, there is someone else here as well. Cannot you see him?"

"Oh! However did he—? Edward, why?" asked Eugenia, holding to his arm, peeking around him at Nod and discovering Lord Nightingale perched jauntily in the saddle."

"Do not fear, Eugenia. He is not about to come flying to my shoulder. We have been working on this for an entire week, Nod and Nightingale and I. With the assistance of Delight and Bobby Tripp, my man Stanley and Mr. Jenkins, I might add."

"W-working on what?"

"You cannot imagine how nervous I was that Nightingale would do the thing at Wicken when you were present and I nowhere to be seen. Thank heaven he did not."

"Edward, you are being most incomprehensible."

"Am I? Well then. Nightingale, begin if you will," Bradford instructed over his shoulder. And then he did something Eugenia had never guessed the marquess could do. He sang a phrase in a fine baritone. "Gentle thoughts and tender heart," he sang.

"Gentle—thoughtsan'—tender heart," Lord Nightingale repeated and then continued on without anymore urging on Bradford's part. "Car-ar-aring—kind and true-ue-ue. These be love. Aye—thesebe—loooove. I vow-ow by all thestarsabove. I didnotknowwhat true love wa-a-as. Until myheartfound you."

"I did *never* know what true love was until my heart found you," whispered Bradford, taking a bemused Eugenia into his arms and kissing her gently. "I find that I love you, Miss Eugenia Chastain, with all my heart and soul. Can you learn to love me in return, do you think?"

"I have already learned to love you, Edward."

"I hoped you had. I prayed you had. And will you, Eugenia, be so very kind as to consider becoming my wife?"

"Oh, Edward, yes! But—but—"

"But what, my darling gel?"

"Your brother, Edward. You must find Peter. You cannot just forget about your brother and—"

"I am not forgetting about Peter, Eugenia. But can we not search for him together? You and I? Husband and wife as one upon that reprobate's trail? I am willing to wait until September to marry you if it should take that long to gain your father's approval and draw up the papers and all, but I willn't like to wait until I have found Peter to make you my bride."

Eugenia giggled. "No, I willn't like to do that either."

"You said it!"

"Well, if we are to live together for the rest of our days, I do expect I must say it. You have Delight saying it already. Doubtless our children will spout it out at every turning."

"Indeed," grinned Bradford. And then he kissed her again, holding her to him as though he would never let her go. Pressing his lips against hers urgently, passionately, lovingly.

"Knollsmarmer—dit com pon—themthere-ere-ere," sang Lord Nightingale abruptly.

"What the devil did he say?" asked Spelling, peering around the corner of the building.

Miss Daily, close beside him, giggled. "He said 'indeed' and kissed her again."

"No, no, not Bradford. Lord Nightingale."

"He sang, actually, Neil," offered Lady Wickenshire, her eyes alight with love and laughter, her hand and Lady Vermont's entwined. "But I did not quite understand the words."

"Knollsmarmer ditcompon themthere," Mr. Arnsworth whispered, holding fast to one of Clara's hands while her papa held the other. "Why? It cannot be important, can it?"

"My brother Ezra might think so," mused Lady Wickenshire. "He has been puzzling over Knollsmarmer for years. There is something about that word, but he cannot remember what."

"Gads, do not speak of Uncle Ezra," groaned Spelling. "Not just now."

"No, not now," Clara Butterberry sighed. "Now is a time to speak of love. Oh, Papa, how romantic you are to help his lordship arrange for all of this."

"I did not do any of the arranging, my dear," replied that cleric with a smile. "I merely brought Lady Wickenshire down here to ease her mind and all the rest of you followed us."

"Edward," Eugenia said in a hushed voice, as their lips parted, "I hear people whispering."

"Well, well, that will be Jenkins and Bobby Tripp most like."

"Jenkins and Bobby Tripp?"

"Yes, over there in the shadows near the haberdasher's. Well, someone had to bring Nod from the stable. And someone had to sneak Lord Nightingale out of Wicken Hall or none of it would have come off right at all. But they did not hear a word of what we said, Eugenia. They promised me not to listen."

Eugenia stared up into his eyes. "Do you mean to tell me that Nicky's butler and groom have been watching us kiss?"

"Well, well, I expect so."

"Oh, Edward, whoever would have thought! Are you certain you did not invite Aunt Diana and Neil and everyone else in the ballroom to bear witness to this proposal as well?" And laying her head upon his shoulder, Eugenia burst into laughter.

Bradford, his arms holding her tightly once again, squinted toward the side of the ballroom, precisely where he thought the whispering had come from, and wondered if Mr. Butterberry had indeed been able to convince Lady Wickenshire to give him these moments alone with Eugenia, or if the dowager had insisted upon—but then the sound of Eugenia's laughter teased him into laughter himself and they held each other close, and laughed and giggled and chuckled until they lost their breath. Whereupon, Bradford set about kissing the gel again, without the least care whether the whole world spied upon them or not.

"Knollsmarmer!" cried Lord Nightingale raucously, as Nod snorted and nickered and began to prance in place. "Yo ho ho! Knollsmarmer!"

Dear Reader,

What? You still don't know what "Knollsmarmer" means? Perhaps the answer lies in book three, *Lord Nightingale's Triumph*. If you've read *Lord Nightingale's Love Song* too quickly you may have to wait a few days, but I assure you *Triumph* will appear in the stores before very long.

Now that Edward and Eugenia happily anticipate their approaching nuptials, Lord Nightingale is looking ahead to a new mission. Do you suppose he might be able to reunite Edward with his long-missing brother? And what of Mary Butterberry and her quest for that same gentleman? And then there's Neil Spelling. I myself have lingering doubts as to whether or not Cousin Neil has truly reformed. He's likely to come up with another nefarious scheme, if you ask me, and it will be up to Lord Nightingale to see to it that the scheme comes to naught.

I'd love to hear what you think of *Lord Nightingale's Love Song,* and if you'd like to hazard a guess about the meaning of Knollsmarmer you're welcome to give it a try. You can e-mail me at regency@localaccess.net or write to me at 578 Camp Ney-A-Ti Road, Guntersville, Alabama, 35976-8301. I try very hard to answer all mail promptly.

Judith

ABOUT THE AUTHOR

Judith A. Lansdowne lives with her family—two-legged, four-legged, winged and finned members—on the shores of Lake Guntersville in Alabama. She loves to hear from her readers. Write her c/o Zebra Books. Do not include a stamped, self-addressed envelope—she'll answer you anyway. Or e-mail her at regency@localaccess.net. By the way, she knows what Knollsmarmer means—do you? You will, if you join in the search for Peter in the next book of this series, *Lord Nightingale's Triumph,* coming in October 2000. No one's telling anyone until then.